I0760618

LOVE IS A CHOICE

WITHER AND BLOOM

PRAISE FOR WITHER AND BLOOM

"As I've come to expect in Twenty Hills anthologies, there's a genre here for almost everyone and a theme that resonates. This book shows how love doesn't merely have stages or phases—it's a journey and it's who we are, as humans. And Wither & Bloom lives up to the name—each piece is unquestionably heartfelt and undeniably unique, yet the message is a thread through every page: love is many things but always, always, love is valuable and worth treasuring."

—Brittany Eden, Author of the *Heartbooks Series*

"It's not always pretty and romantic—it can be—but it can also be raw, sacrificial, platonic, heartbreaking, and hopeful. These stories stay with you. They fill your mind and heart, giving you something a little more fulfilling for Valentine's Day, or any other day of the year."

—Brooke J. Katz, Advanced Reader and Aspiring Author

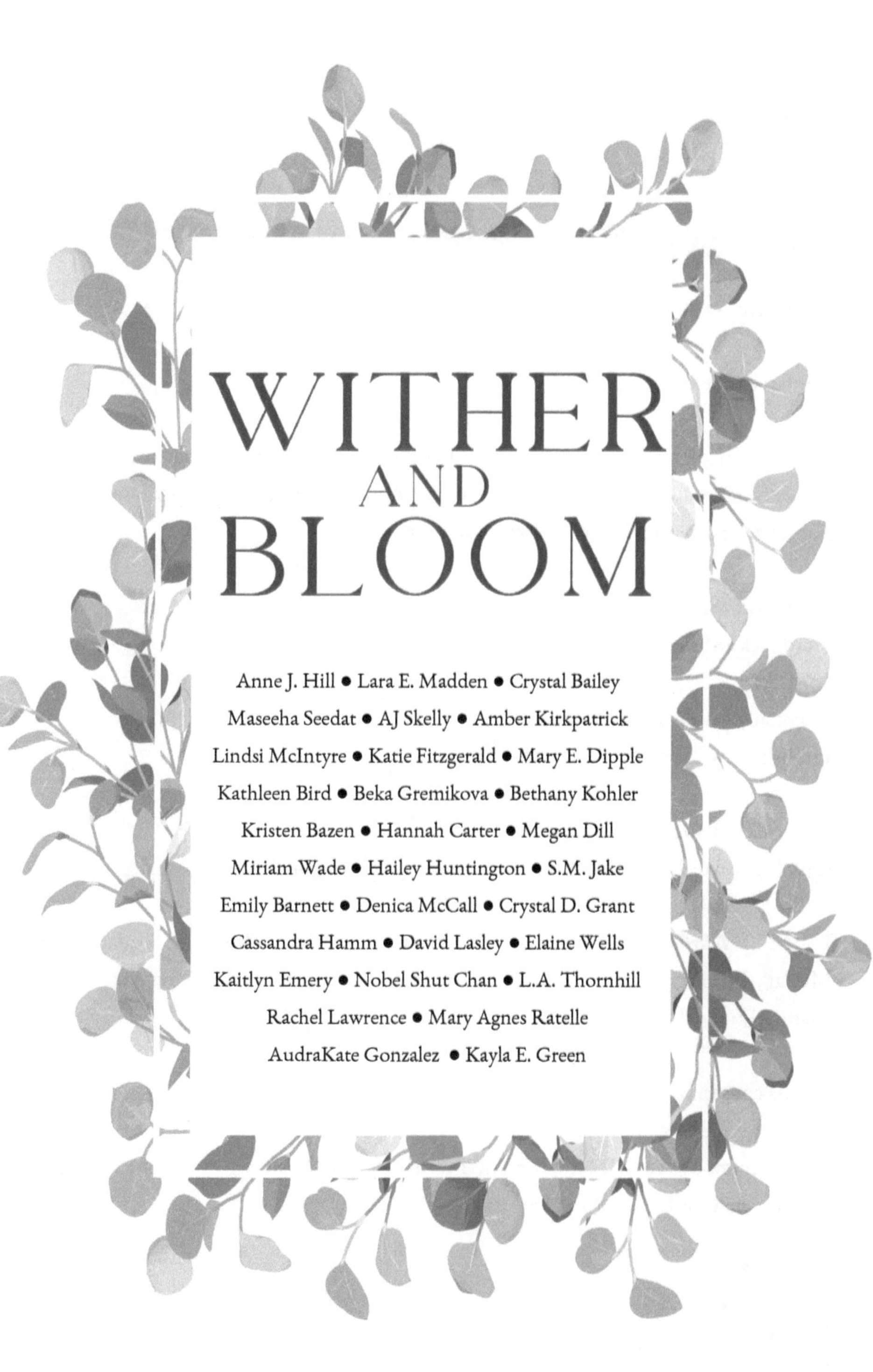

WITHER AND BLOOM

Anne J. Hill • Lara E. Madden • Crystal Bailey
Maseeha Seedat • AJ Skelly • Amber Kirkpatrick
Lindsi McIntyre • Katie Fitzgerald • Mary E. Dipple
Kathleen Bird • Beka Gremikova • Bethany Kohler
Kristen Bazen • Hannah Carter • Megan Dill
Miriam Wade • Hailey Huntington • S.M. Jake
Emily Barnett • Denica McCall • Crystal D. Grant
Cassandra Hamm • David Lasley • Elaine Wells
Kaitlyn Emery • Nobel Shut Chan • L.A. Thornhill
Rachel Lawrence • Mary Agnes Ratelle
AudraKate Gonzalez • Kayla E. Green

WITHER AND BLOOM

Printed in the United States of America

Paperback ISBN: 978-1-956499-14-8
Hardback ISBN: 978-1-956499-15-5

Originally published in January 2023
Published by Twenty Hills Publishing

Cover Art by Ophelia Illustration
Case Laminate Cover and Interior Formatting by Dragonpen Designs

Edited by Anne J. Hill, with help from Crystal D. Grant, Maseeha Seedat, Denica McCall, Brooke J. Katz, Hannah Carter, Kristen Bazen, Rachel Lawrence, Lara E. Madden and others.

Poems chosen by Elaine Wells

Book created by Anne J. Hill, head of Twenty Hills Publishing,
with the help of Lara E. Madden

Anne J. Hill:
To my sisters, Sarah, Joy, and Kerry,
for your unconditional love

Lara E. Madden:
To my parents: through all the ups and downs,
you are always my favorite love story

TABLE OF CONTENTS

PART ONE: FALLING

PART TWO: ENDURING

PART THREE: ABIDING

PART FOUR: CHERISHING

FAMILY, FRIENDS, & STRANGERS

THORN TOWER EXCERPT

INTRODUCTION

This anthology feels a bit different than the rest in our Black and Gold collection. There are still plenty of mixed genres, categories, and poetry blended in with stories. However, the theme begs for more sweet, realistic stories, and deep character dives. But don't worry! There are still plenty of fantastical tales.

We have wanted to do this anthology since the end of 2021, and it's finally here. In a world that is so heavily led by emotions and feelings, we wanted to focus on loving people even when you don't want to.

Even when doing so could cost your life. Because, after all, that's what God did and does for us.

This isn't a perfect collection of perfect people perfectly loving, but a depiction of flawed souls making mistakes or falling short in an ugly world and beginning to mend. It's raw, sometimes emotional, but always hopeful.

May you enjoy this wild ride through the different stages of love and life.

—Anne J. Hill and Lara E. Madden

PART ONE:
FALLING

THE WOLFMAN'S HEART

ANNE J. HILL

AFTER THE EVENTS IN *THE WRONG SORT OF MONSTER*, IN *SHARPER THAN THORNS*

I KILLED MY father.

And the duke.

All in one night.

Flashes of my father yelling, my teeth in his flesh, and the duke bleeding out fill my mind.

Blood. *So much blood.*

I squeeze my eyes shut like it'll help the visions go away, but all I see is my father's stained red face muttering, "I still love you, son."

And now, I'm in my white wolf form, hiding behind the bushes at the Emperor's castle. I followed the duke's ward the whole way here through the night.

Even though she saw me slaughter my father and her duke, even though I chased her, threatened to kill her for the sake of the war, she tiptoes over to me and sits beside the bush. "I forgive you. I really do." Her brown hair frames her face, and she looks about my age of eighteen.

My paws cover my nose, and my white fur bristles. She's been trying to convince me of this ever since she came back from delivering the satchel to the Emperor.

The *blood-born* Emperor who wants to protect his kind.

I can't believe my father was a Loyal just like me. *Why did my father lie to me? Why did he tell me he was a spy for the Revolters?*

The ward smiles sadly and says, "I know you must have thought I was bringing the satchel to the Revolters. Well, I wasn't. And, yes, the duke and your father are Loyals like us. I don't know why he lied to you about being a Revolter spy."

I blink at her, reminded of my sinking feeling that her blood-born powers might revolve around mind reading.

She nods. "Yes. That's it. I'm sorry. I haven't mastered my abilities."

I swallow. *So you can hear every single one of my thoughts?*

She shakes her head. "Sometimes, but not exactly. I'm still working on turning it on and off myself, but it seems to have a mind of its own."

I suddenly feel naked in front of her, even in my fur. *Oh…* I try to stop thinking about the overwhelming guilt plaguing me, or the grief over never seeing my father again, or how beautiful the ward is, or the way I feel like throwing up from the colliding emotions.

I'm sorry. I killed your duke. I'm not sure if I like or hate being able to converse to someone in my wolf form. This is usually my shield against conversation.

She smiles and shakes her head. "Oh, don't worry about Jazper."

Jazper?

"Sorry. Duke Claude. He hates when I call him Jazper, as if he's not young enough to be my brother. But anyway, he's alive and well."

I freeze. *How?* Not possible. A gunshot had torn through him.

"You know the Emperor is a blood-born, right?" She pauses, only to laugh. "Of course you do. That's the whole reason the Revolters are trying to dethrone him." She brushes her brown hair behind her ear. "He's a healer. Dorian—one of our friends—found them when he returned to Brimwood. He's a teleporter, and he brought the duke and your father to the Emperor in seconds. Jaz—I mean, Duke Claude, is already prancing around the castle, planning havoc for the Revolters."

My heart races. *Does that mean my…* I don't dare finish.

Her face falls, and she shakes her head. "No, I'm sorry. The Emperor healed his wounds, but it wasn't enough. We're not sure why."

I wince and nod. *Right.*

The ward pulls the red ribbon from her hair and brushes it between her fingers. She hesitates and then holds her hand out, palm up. "May I?"

My eyes narrow, and I show my teeth briefly. But I'm ashamed of my instinctive habit and clamp my mouth shut. I lay my clawed paw in her hand. She runs her thumb over my fur and ties the ribbon around my foot.

I sniff the ribbon, perplexed, then look at her and tilt my head in question.

"To help you remember that I forgive you." She smiles.

This ward is like no one I've met before. She saw me kill my own father and attack her guardian only hours earlier, and yet, she's treating me like a friend. *Why?*

I look down at her red ribbon on my front paw. It reminds me of the one my little sister wears to church.

My stomach churns.

Now I must return home and tell Mother and Cali that Father is gone. They'll turn me out of the house for sure. Father was the one who wanted to adopt me the most. Surely they'll hate me for what I've done. I huff out a deep breath and the ribbon quivers. I cannot go home. It'll be better to run than face my mother and sister.

The ward reaches out a brave hand and runs it through the fur on my head.

I tense, suddenly ashamed to be a beast in front of her. I duck my head and feel nauseous looking at the blood that stains my claws and white fur. I hate the claws and teeth that tore flesh, so I shift my fur into skin, returning to my human body.

Our eyes are now level, and she studies me. She's sitting directly across from me, and I'm beyond thankful that Father had found a way for my clothes to shift with me.

I swallow. As a wolf, I don't have to talk verbally because I can't. But now, I have no excuse.

She reaches out and secures the ribbon on my wrist. "I know you won't hurt me. Not now that you understand."

The duke's ward studies me, and I swallow, replaying my crimes in my head. I thought my father, the Pirate King, was a traitor in this war, a spy for our enemies, the Revolters—those who hate blood-borns like me and the magical powers that surge through my veins. So I killed him—and the duke, I thought—before they could deliver the satchel to the Revolters. I still don't know what was in the satchel, but my father had left to deliver it with such earnestness that I imagine it's highly important for the war.

"My name is Lily. What's yours?" she asks, forcing me back to the present.

I blink and run a shaky hand through my white hair. "Vivace." I glance at the horizon. "I need to...go." *Tell my family...*

She smiles softly. "Would you like company? There isn't much more for me to do now that the satchel is safely delivered."

Lily's hair dances across her cheeks in the breeze, and I stifle a yawn. It's still the middle of the night, and she looks as tired as I feel. But I'm sure I look worse off than she does, her brown eyes dazzling.

"That won't be necessary. You should rest. Someone's been making your night difficult." I strain a smile because *I'm* the one who spent the night chasing her to the castle.

She chuckles softly, and it's the most beautiful sound I've ever heard. *Shut up, Vivace. She just saw you murder your own father, and you terrified her in the forest.* I clear my throat. "How can you forgive me?"

Lily picks at the grass beside her. "Well, hearing some of your thoughts certainly helps. I can't say I wouldn't have done something similar if I thought it would protect the Emperor and this war."

I pick at the ribbon on my wrist. "I really should go." *Or run away.*

I'm beyond tired and don't want someone witnessing my thoughts right now.

"Right, yeah. Of course. Stay safe out there, Vivace. And don't forget I forgive you." She smiles again and turns back to the castle. But then she pauses and says, "I'll see you again?"

Heat rises on my cheeks. *She wants to see* me *again?* "I suppose so." I watch her go briefly before I shift back to fur and take off through the woods.

"Lily!" I'm writing a letter to Vivace in my room at Brimwood Manner when Jazper calls for me. He has been running around like a small child. He says being on the move helps him think up ideas on how to win the war. I can't blame him. If it weren't for thoughts of Vivace consuming most of my brain space, I would be going mad with ideas of my own.

"Coming!" I call back and quickly fold the letter. Vivace and I have been writing letters to each other for a few weeks, and when we meet in the forest, we deliver them. I've only seen him twice since that brutal night, even though he's only an hour's ride away when we meet in the middle.

The first time was rather awkward. We sat in the grass, picking at fallen leaves. But the second time was better. I brought a book, and we took turns reading until he told me about how detached he felt from his family after he told them about his father. And—

"Lily!" Jazper calls again, yanking me from my daydreams.

I push my chair back, the feet shriek on the floor, and I dart downstairs to his office. "I'm here!"

Jazper's hair is in a wild mess. His eyes are wide, and his shirt is untucked. Sometimes I forget he's twelve years *older* than me and not younger.

"What took you so long?" He peered at me and then waved his hand. "No matter. I need you to take over things for a time. I'm going away."

I nod. This is fairly normal, though sometimes I join him on the *Novaturient*—a privateer ship that fights for the Emperor. "To sea again?" I grip the letter behind me, rocking back and forth. Jazper better not delay my meeting with Vivace.

"No, to the circus," he teases as if that can't be true. "Yes, the sea." *Though I'd rather be at the circus right now,* his thoughts say.

I chuckle. "Once the war ends, you could open your own circus."

Jazper eyes me and then nods. "Perhaps. Here." He picks up a pile of financial books from his desk and plops them in my arms. "The books need to be done. Harper should be by to help run things if she can. If not, get Demi or Allegra or Dorian, or anyone, really, to come help."

"I can handle it, Jazper."

He pauses and squints his eyes at me. "That's *Mr. Claude* to you, tiny child ward." His lips slip up into a playful grin, and he ruffles my hair.

I slap his hand away, glare at him, and hope my hair isn't ruined for Vivace. "I haven't been a child in a year, *Jazper.*"

He spins towards the door. "Oh yes, you're so old and wise now. I forgot. A full eighteen years." He grabs his tailcoat with a playful smirk. "Don't let the manor burn down while I'm away," he calls over his shoulder.

And then he is out the door, leaving me to manage an estate full of misfit blood-borns. But right now, I have one thing on my mind. *Vivace.*

Lily should be here any moment. We said we'd meet under the old oak tree at 2 p.m. today. I pull out my pocket watch. It's half past two. If something happened to her on her way to meet me, I don't know what I'll do. I can't lose anyone else.

I'm just about to shift to my fur and sniff around for her when I hear tumbling through the trees. "I'm here!" Lily calls from horseback, and I can't help the smile that tugs at my lips.

She has been the only bright spot in an otherwise dark world.

Her hair is neatly pinned back, but a few pieces have come loose during her ride. She slows her horse and climbs off with ease. "Sorry. I had a few unexpected things to manage at the manor."

"That's all right." My hands tremble behind me. We've only known each other for a few weeks, but I know she must be expecting a formal offer of courtship. Many start courting before they've even met. And now I'm hoping she didn't just hear those thoughts.

Thankfully, she chuckles and says, "No, I didn't hear."

You'd still make one hell of a spy. You know that?

She shakes her head with a giggle.

I reach for the letters in my breast pocket. Sometimes I have a hard time thinking about what to write, but it was Lily's idea, and the way her eyes light up when I hand her the small stack makes it all worth it.

Lily hands me a bundle twice the size of mine. They're tied together with a flower sticking out of the top. I take the flower off and stuff the letters in my pocket. "So..." I twirl the flower in my fingers.

She's standing a safe distance away from me. "How are things with your family?" Lily asks.

"Not much different."

Lily nods. She pulls a blanket off her horse and lays it on the forest floor. Lifting her dress, she sits down and looks up at me. She pats the empty space beside her. "Sit?"

I still can't fathom why Lily would be interested in someone like me, especially after *that* night. But I sit and silently play with the flower. I've never been too great with words, but with Lily, my throat closes up. So instead, I think. *How have you been doing?*

"Mr. Claude just left, so I have to run Brimwood while he's away. Which is always a bit stressful, but I'll manage." She makes busy work tucking her loose hair back into her updo.

If you need any help... It would get me out of the house.

She smiles, little dimples forming on her cheeks. "I would appreciate that."

I nod and swallow. My palms sweat, and I don't know what else to say. I feel like I'm supposed to be doing something, or saying something to keep the conversations flowing, but I can't think of anything. I'm no good at this. It isn't Lily. It's me. I don't deserve love, especially not after what I've done.

Lily glances at me, then reaches over and plays with the red ribbon still on my wrist. Her fingertips graze over my skin, sending chills up my arm. "Vivace. What does this ribbon mean?"

I clear my throat as if to speak, but then, *You forgave me.*

She nods and moves her hand to my chest, nearly stealing my breath. "And now you need to forgive yourself."

A squirrel races across the branches, missteps, and slips off but grabs onto another limb at the last second and pulls himself up. He's got a big acorn in his mouth and his poofy tail twitches.

I can't look at Lily. Time has done little to soften the guilt and grief. And sometimes, when I look at her, all I see is the fear in her eyes from that night, soon followed by the blood, the screaming, the flesh tearing under my teeth and claws. My throat fills with bile, and I swallow it down. *I'm trying.*

Lily leans over and kisses my cheek. My heart races, and now I do glance at her, afraid my burning cheeks are turning my pale skin bright red. I so badly want to be whatever person Lily thinks I am, but I'm only *me*. Impulsive, assumption-led, nervous, angry, bitter, *me*. A literal monster. And I won't have Lily wasting her time trying to fix me. That's not fair to her.

So I pull away and stand up, hoping she's already read all my thoughts on the matter.

"Vivace..." Lily stands and grips my hand before I can leave.

I pause and study her. I can't deny how right her hand feels in mine.

"I don't want to fix you," she says. "I'm not a god. Nor am I perfect by any means."

My jaw clenches. "You've never killed anyone."

She raises her eyebrow. "What makes you so sure of that? Just because I wear a dress and live in a fancy manor, you don't think I've done things that haunt me in this war too?"

The thought had never crossed my mind. "I just assumed..."

"Well, I have. I've sailed on the *Novaturient* with the duke before. We all have played our part." Her grip on my hand tightens. "And what you did was no different. You fought for our blood-born kind just like I have."

My face twists. "But it was my *father.*"

"You didn't know he was on our side. I'm not saying it was good. I'm just saying, please don't condemn yourself forever. Don't let it keep you from living."

I let go of her hand. "I'm not ready to marry *anyone.*"

She blinks several times. "No one was asking you to?" She looks as perplexed as I feel. "Is that what's bothering you?"

I run a hand through my hair. "I thought that's what you'd be expecting. Courtship and then...that."

Lily's face breaks into a smile. "Vivace. Of course, I want that someday, but not right now. Just because some people our age are already wed doesn't mean we have to go fast. I personally happen to think these things take more time."

A wave of relief gushes through me, and I grin. "Oh."

Lily laughs and grabs my hand, pulling me back down beside her. She lays her head on my shoulder, and I wrap my arm around her waist, the weight of expectations gone.

"You need time to heal, and I'd like to get to know you better," she says softly.

I watch the squirrel race down the side of the tree and take off through the woods. "Then let's do it properly. When the duke returns, I'll ask him if I can court you."

Lily grins and wiggles closer to me. "And I'll make sure he doesn't push us too fast."

My chin rests on the top of her head, and I close my eyes, enjoying her company and the slowing of my anxious heart. The thought of being in love with her creeps up my spine, but I quickly replace it with, *I like you, Lily.*

She gives me a knowing look and whispers, "I like you, too, my wolfman."

THE EDGE

RACHEL LAWRENCE

They call it
Falling
As if it were some
Passive
Unconscious
Accidental thing
A meaningless slip
A careless mistake
But I know better
Because I stood there
On the edge with you
Heart pounding
In my ears
Fears welling up
In my eyes
When I stared down
Into a cloudy future
And asked you questions

Neither of us could answer
For certain
And counted
The cost
And counted
You worth it
And counted
To three
Before I decided
To jump

ELIZA

CASSANDRA HAMM

THIS DECADE, MY name is Eliza.

Last decade it was Beth, the previous one Elisabeth, Betty before that. I reuse the names over the years; one can only acclimate to so many variations.

But today, walking through the art museum, draped in violet silk, I feel like Lisbeth, the girl who loved beautiful dresses and couldn't bear the thought of settling down. The elegant golden archways and ceiling murals transport me to a time when servants came at my call.

My heels click against the tile as I make my way down the ornate hallways. I stop to study a painting that so clearly resembles our long-ago summer estate. I can almost feel the sea against my toes, the salty air against my skin, can almost hear Mother telling us to slow down and be good girls.

Shoving the ache deep inside, I stroll into the new exhibit on lesser-known painters of the nineteenth century. A museum aide walks by, and I stiffen, but it's not him. I know it's not—this man is much too broad to be Norm.

Maybe he's not working today. Even if he *is,* there's no guarantee I'll see him. He might've finally tired of my evasion and decided never to speak to me again.

A dress in a painting draws my eye. It is pale pink chiffon, cinched at the waist, with lace draping the neck and silver threads glittering throughout.

It's so vivid, so lifelike, so...*familiar.*

My feet stop of their own accord, and I turn my full attention to the new addition. *The Adoration of Lisbeth* by Claude Heron.

The girl depicted is pretty, late twenties—an old maid—dark hair caught up in tight coils. Her smile is mischievous, her gaze playful, even transmitted through brushstrokes.

Her smile is mine.

Limbs suddenly weak, I tear my gaze away from the painting. Mother hired an artist to paint our portraits, hoping they would incite marital interest from eligible young men. She often told me this portrait was the only way I would ever get married since my youth was fading. In my mind, I see Claude's powdered wig, his angular nose, his intense blue gaze.

He told me he loved me. I laughed and said life was too short for me to waste it on him.

My scorn sealed my fate.

"Wow!" A fellow patron leaves the painting she was admiring to stare up at me. She's young and blonde, her cheeks perpetually flushed. "You look just like her."

My blood runs cold. "Like who?" I adjust my skirt so it reaches my knees. Fashion nowadays can be so irksome, but I must say that I do not miss corsets one bit.

"The girl in the painting." The patron's red-haired friend rolls her eyes. "Didn't you notice? She's, like, your doppelgänger or something."

"Oh." I stare at the painted girl who knew nothing about life, who threw away every opportunity in her naïveté. The girl who insulted a sorcerer and was paying for it with every long year that passed.

"That's so cool." The first girl yanks her phone from her pocket. "Can I take a picture of you?"

I back away, hands outstretched. "No, please. I don't like—"

"Cheese!" says the red-cheeked girl.

My stomach flips, and I reach for the phone. "Please, no pictures. I don't like pictures"—and not just the one hanging on the museum wall. The internet immortalizes even those who will eventually perish. If this picture enters its archives, will people discover who I am?

The blonde jerks her phone out of reach. "Chill out! It's not like I'm going to post these or whatever."

The redhead gives an exaggerated nod and another eye roll.

Times were simpler before technology entered the world; people looked at each other instead of their devices. I know *how* to use technology, at least to an extent—I patronize the library computer from time to time, and my cell phone sits in my purse. But the more I use these seemingly-innocuous devices, the more likely it is that someone will notice my ever-present youth. I prefer to forgo them entirely.

The blonde huffs at my pained silence. "I deleted it. See?" She shows me her phone, which holds her camera roll.

Sure enough, all evidence of me has been erased. If only I could destroy the cursed painting as easily as she deleted the digital picture. But I can't exactly deface museum property.

"Seriously, you need to get a life," the redhead says.

Casting me dark looks, the girls walk through the archway into a different section of the museum. I pinch the bridge of my nose and try to keep my breathing steady.

What if they figured out my secret? What then? I know what happens to anomalies in this world—I've seen it time and time again. The strange and unfamiliar are either worshiped, studied, or destroyed. I have no desire to end up in a laboratory, and I don't want people holding me to standards I can't fulfill. As for being destroyed...well, I'm not sure they could, but I don't particularly want to find out.

What if oblivion would be better than this cursed life?

"Eliza?"

I jump at Norm's voice, honeyed-sweet and slow. He limps into view, wearing the same gray polo and slacks, one leg just shorter than the other. He pauses in front of an ocean landscape. The white-capped waves seem to crash over his shoulders, as though about to sweep him away from me.

His grin morphs into a puzzled frown as his eyes roam over my face. "Are you okay?"

"I'm fine." The words come out too clipped, and I soften them with, "It's good to see you, Norm. I thought maybe today would be your day off—but I'm glad it's not," I hurriedly add.

"Oh, I never have a day off," he says with a laugh.

Freckles dance across his nose and cheeks, and graying red hair curls over his ears. Oh, dear, I've been staring at him much too long. Cheeks burning, I clear my throat. "Well. It's a lovely new exhibit."

He beams. "You think so? What's your favorite?"

"Ah, yes." I swallow, looking around at the selection I've barely perused. "I haven't had much of a chance to look at them, actually. I got...distracted."

"By this one?" He looks at *The Adoration of Lisbeth,* then at me. His brow furrows.

Oh no. I step away from the portrait. The longer I stand there, the more people will notice my uncanny resemblance to a girl from 1880.

"That's right," Norm says. "I remember thinking that she looked a lot like you."

He thought about me? My breath catches, even though I *should* be concerned about the fact that he noticed the painting at all.

"Funny, isn't it? Maybe she's one of your ancestors."

I give him a strained smile. "Perhaps." Now, how do I redirect this conversation?

"Not much is known about her," Norm says.

I stiffen.

"Judging by her style of dress, I'd guess she was a young girl from a wealthy family in the late nineteen hundreds. But there's no record of such a girl existing. Heron—the painter—never spoke of her."

I choke on my own saliva and cough violently. My eyes water. Norm's low voice reaches my ears, but I can't understand what he's saying. Memories of Claude Heron flood my mind—of how I flirted and laughed and kissed him in a moonlit garden. He was brilliant and handsome and forbidden, and I drank in his attention like a thirsty rosebud.

I should've seen the darkness in him. Should've realized there was more to his art than sheer talent—there was *magic.* Should've realized that my actions would affect more than just me.

"Eliza? Are you—? Can I—?"

I look up to see Norm's pale, freckled hand pulling away. Was he reaching for me?

"I'm all right," I rasp.

Green eyes framed by enviably long lashes stare at me. "You sure?"

If I say no, will he try to touch me again?

"Do you need some water?" he asks. "Or maybe you need to sit down. I can find—"

"I'm *fine,* Norm."

He takes a step back, and I immediately regret my harshness. But maybe it's for the best. It'll only be a matter of time before he puts the pieces together. Maybe I should've chosen a name that couldn't be tied to Lisbeth.

"That's good." He dips his head and starts limping toward the exhibit's exit.

"Wait, Norm." I grab his arm without thinking.

He inhales sharply. I yank my hand back, but my fingers remember the heat of his freckled skin.

"I'm sorry," I say. "I'm a bit...on edge today. I didn't mean to take it out on you."

He offers me a quick smile—just a flash of white teeth, a little bit crooked, and I feel my walls slowly crumbling.

I can't do this. I can't flirt and smile and—well, maybe even *kiss*—him, knowing in a few years, I'll have to leave before he gets suspicious of why I never age. I can't tell him of my immortality and watch him walk away, and if he decided to share it with the cruel, unforgiving world... I don't want to think about that.

"I don't think we should be friends anymore." The words burst out of me, jagged and heavy.

"What?" He flinches like I've just slapped him the way Claude slapped me when I laughed at his proposal. *"Why?"*

"I just don't think it's a good idea." Tears burn my eyes, but I blink them away, focusing on a stormy painting to distract myself from the pain. "I'll be moving soon anyway. I've been here too long."

I'll miss this museum. I tell myself it's just for the paintings, the archways, the stained glass, but I know better.

"I don't understand," Norm says. "I thought...maybe..."

In his eyes, I find the same longing that courses through me. My breath catches. I take an involuntary step forward. "Norm..."

"Yeah?" he breathes.

It's just the two of us in this exhibit, and it seems a sacred space, a pocket out of time. Like maybe impossible things could happen and curses could be broken.

"I wish it could be." I bite the inside of my cheek. "But I'll hurt you."

"Everyone hurts each other," he says. "That doesn't stop me from caring."

I gaze at Norm's earnest face, so different from the blind obsession Claude once treated me with. I may have been cruel to Claude, but his actions were wrong as well—I know that now. I didn't owe him anything just because he cared for me.

Norm doesn't expect anything from me. He just *hopes*. And that same hope builds in my chest, at first small and fragile but then blooming at the idea of loving this man.

"I care too," I say before I can lose my nerve.

He moves even closer. His voice is high and breathy. "You do?"

"I want..." My hand, seemingly of its own accord, reaches toward his face. He doesn't move away. My fingers brush the reddish stubble on his jaw. It is somehow more intimate than stolen kisses in a garden.

"I want to try," I say. "But I'm not very good at staying."

His lips brush my palm. I shiver and draw back, but he takes my hands in his, gently, almost hesitantly. I squeeze his warm, solid fingers. The ghost of his kiss lingers on my skin.

"Then we'll try together," Norm says.

It may end far too quickly. But if Norm is truly as good as he seems to be, I may just have to tell him the full story of Lisbeth, the girl cursed with immortality.

And maybe, just for his brief lifetime, he will stay.

A LITTLE DITTY

S.M. JAKE

THEY HAD NEARLY died this morning. Twice. And now, here they sat. Cheap stew and warm bread in their bellies, halfway dry, ignoring their own stink.

Pretending the soldiers outside wouldn't slit their throats for the letter hidden in his boot.

He held back a yawn, glancing at Mara across the empty dishes. Her fingers tapped lightly against the sticky table as she hummed with the tiny band in the corner.

"They're pretty good," she said. Rosy undertones were finally back in her brown face, a wisp of a smile at the corner of her mouth. A *real* smile.

"Aye." A tug pulled at his heart.

He couldn't remember the last time she'd smiled for real—not since they'd begun this wretched journey, maybe longer.

"Have you ever noticed . . ." She leaned back, arms settling across her middle. ". . . how, when war breaks out, it's not the nation's anthem or the queen's song that inspires people? It's always the little ditties sung in places like this. Ballads 'bout going home, 'bout true love, 'bout ships and shores and family. Those light hope . . . lend strength."

Her dark eyes turned to him, catching gold in the light.

One or both of them could die before this was over. He'd been commanded that the letter was to trump everything. *Everything*. Yet he smiled at Mara.

"I know I shouldn't love you," he sang softly, heart settling comfortably in his resolve, the ballad becoming his own. "I know I shouldn't love you, but I will."

HOME

MARY E. DIPPLE

THE LIGHT FROM her lantern played over the scraps of paper, news articles and magazine clippings. Nails, tacks, pins, and even what looked to be an old letter opener, held each piece of her life from the last twenty years to the old barn wall. She couldn't understand why he'd kept them, let alone put them where he'd see them every day.

She'd hated this town. Hated how everyone expected her to follow tradition, marry a good man, keep a home, raise babies. It was suffocating! She had been made for more. She'd longed for adventure, excitement, to see the world, and do things that had never been done.

Liam had always fought with her. He'd not understood why she would want to leave. The old ladies had whispered that they'd make an excellent match, and it had made her hate him even more.

She was such a fool.

She'd run away and had her adventures. But at night . . . when she was alone . . . when her heart ached for the simple life she'd left behind, it was Liam's face she'd seen. When life became too much. When her adventure's soured into heartache and pain, she longed for home. For him.

"Katie, lass."

She sucked in a breath at the sound of his deep voice. She should have known he'd come to investigate her light. She lowered the lantern to the workbench and turned to see his broad figure in the doorway to the barn. A toothy smile peeked out from his red beard.

"I've been keeping an eye on you." He nodded to the board. "Been praying for you too. Praying God would bring you home safe after you'd had your adventures."

Tears came unrestrained, and she ran to him. She threw her arms around him and buried her face in his shoulder. "I missed you."

His strong arms enveloped her. "I missed you too, Katie. Welcome home."

She breathed in the sweet scent of earth and hay that was him and knew it to be true. Knew that she was finally home, and she would never leave again.

WE'VE BEEN FOUND

DENICA MCCALL

You found me
In the broken down, in the
Brambles on the road that marked my life
With
Beauty and pain, merged
Into this new smile today,
We can walk together now
Ever new, stone upon stone
Remembering when we were alone
But looking to the dawn of communion
And the day when home is
More than wood and clay and the work and play
That dances through halls which
Fill with dust, which
Floats in the rays of sun on a summer day,
Reminding us that night never lasts very long
And here, in each other's arms
We'll keep the cold at bay

You found me
Planted in this dirt which
Mars my hands, my face, and
Together
We'll dig and find the roots, we'll love
This beat up earth and
Take heart for the grace that snakes like gold,
Glittering through this soil
We'll remove our shoes now, for
Everything we build upon from this day is
Holy ground
Ever held in timeless love, we
Have been found

CHANCES AND CHOICES

AJ SKELLY

COME ON, TEAGAN Jane. Let's go." Jarrett pulled me to my feet.

"Where are we going?" It was the last Saturday night of the summer. Senior year started next week.

"Let's just go. I can't be still anymore."

I let him haul me from the fuzzy beige carpet where I'd been leaning against the couch in my white tank and cut-offs. We were at his house, polishing off a pizza, planning to do our regular weekend movie marathon.

"No movie tonight then?" I slid my feet into my flip-flops as he grabbed his keys and scribbled a note for his parents. Mine were normally next door, but tonight they were with Jarrett's parents at a fundraiser for the hospital where both our dads worked.

He finished his note and clipped it to the refrigerator, his free fingers tapping against his leg, antsy and unable to keep still. "There are only a handful of nights like this left. This year is the last. The last of a lot of stuff." He bit his lip as he glanced back at me.

Jarrett was like that sometimes. We'd been friends since we were babies. I'd known him plenty long to know his moods. Tonight, he was pensive. Uptight. Thoughtful. Restless. He was a dreamer and a thinker. He was my best friend. I was happy he included me for the ride. I'd follow him to the moon. Jarrett in the captain's seat, me the first officer. He held the door for me as we exited the house.

The heat was like a slap in the face after the cool air-conditioned living room. Humidity kinked my hair into little curls around my face, and I tossed my long blonde waves up to feel any sort of breeze on the back of my neck.

Jarrett paused and patted the side of his old beat-up Ford before he opened my door. It was half decrepit and ugly as sin, but he and his dad had lovingly restored it together. Sometimes I thought he held his truck in higher esteem than me.

"Up you go." He offered me a hand in lieu of the missing running board. He held on a second longer than necessary, and I glanced at his cloudy eyes. Normally blue like the ocean, tonight they were a stormy grey.

"Jarrett?"

His eyes snapped up to mine before he briefly shook his head. He was still thinking. Processing. He'd tell me when he was ready.

"So where to tonight, Captain?" I asked as he brought the beast rumbling to life.

"I want to see stars."

"Well, drive on then, Kirk."

A smile ghosted over his face. We were closet Trekkie nerds.

"Engage." He pointed two fingers like Picard.

I kicked my feet up on the dash as he drove past the end of our subdivision and out onto the backroads where gravel, grass, and mosquitos waited for us.

He drove for miles, saying nothing. His eyebrows were low over his eyes, his fingers drumming on the steering wheel.

"What's one thing you're afraid of? What's something that will be the last this year?" I ventured.

He startled and glanced over at me. Chewing at the inside of his lip, he turned off the gravel road and into a field. We were out by WindFall Orchards. It was a beautiful spot in an open meadow, the orchards farther back.

"Grab the blanket?"

I nodded and snagged the old quilt he always kept behind the seats. He came around and opened the door for me.

I squeaked when he reached in and grabbed me around the waist. It sent a hot rush to my face and butterflies massing in my belly. He laughed and poked me once in the ribs, earning him a swat across his stomach.

"Wanna boost?" he offered as he put the tailgate down. My cheeks were still red, but I couldn't resist the offer. It hadn't been all that long ago that I realized I liked it more than I should when Jarrett touched me. I craved it. Needed his friendship. But found it still left me feeling empty. Because I wanted *more* from him. And that could never be. I refused to be in love with my best friend. He was my *best friend.*

Still, if I could have chosen anyone, it would have been him. I memorized the way his hands felt as he scooped me up and tossed me into the truck bed.

We spread the quilt, stretched out on our backs, and looked up.

"You wanted stars," I whispered.

"Yeah. It's supposed to rain tomorrow. I wasn't sure if there'd be clouds tonight."

"Not a one." I was quiet. Waiting for him to answer my question from the truck. I knew he hadn't forgotten. He was simply biding his time.

"I'm afraid of change, Teagan." His voice was low and gravelly. I rolled to my side to look at him.

"Not all change is bad."

"No." He shook his head. "Some change would be good. Very good. But change hurts, too."

"Are you worrying about college stuff?"

"Some." He swallowed, and that told me it was something more immediate.

"Classes? Basketball?"

"Nah. Not when I have your notes to go over."

He cracked a smile, and I did, too. We always studied together because my notes were more thorough than his. Although his memory was sharper.

We were quiet for another few minutes.

"I'm afraid of missing you, Teagan."

I faced him again and blinked. He was afraid of *missing me*?

"Why would you miss me? We'll be together all the time, just like we always have been."

His stormy eyes pinned me in the dark, moonlight washing over us.

"For this year. And then we'll go to college. Meet people. Fall in love. Forget each other."

My heart hammered.

"Jarrett, I will *never* forget you. You're as much a part of me as my arms and legs."

I heard him swallow.

"Senior year feels like the beginning of the end. And I'm afraid I won't have another chance. If I don't, we'll both make different choices, and I'll always regret not taking this chance while I could." He gusted a sigh through his teeth.

"Another chance for what?"

"This."

His hand slid over my jaw, cupping my face. His face hovered over mine as his thumb brushed over my cheek.

"Teage," he rasped as heat exploded inside my chest.

All his pensiveness, all his angst. It was because of me. Because he liked me as much as I liked him. I saw it clearly in the stormy depths of his eyes, felt it in the rough brush of his thumb against my bottom lip.

"Shut up and kiss me, Jarrett."

His lips closed over mine, setting my soul on fire and pulse hammering.

Maybe this was a first last.

Because Jarrett was in every part of my past. And I wanted him in every part of my future.

DRIVE ME HOME

KATIE FITZGERALD

I'D HAVE PREFERRED working on a car, but there I sat on campus, itchy in dress clothes borrowed from my brother, drinking fancy coffee with Winnie and her brainiac friends. Devon and Asher were discussing Flannery O'Connor. Wanting to show interest, I asked, "Who's he?" I couldn't even look at Winnie when they laughed and informed me she's a woman.

"Hang in there, Grayson," Winnie whispered, squeezing my shoulder as she went to the microphone to read. I'd never understood poetry, and as metaphors and whatnot rolled off her tongue, I felt like the world's biggest idiot.

Next to me, Devon leaned in and said, "If you need to go, I can let her know. Obviously, this isn't your thing."

For a minute, I tugged at my over-starched collar and considered the road ahead. I'd always imagined I'd end up with someone who worked with her hands: a baker, maybe, or a hairdresser. This world of thinking and writing, and debating was exhausting. It'd be hard, probably, for me to do this all the time. But looking up there at Winnie as she confidently spoke the beautiful words she'd written, it was so obvious to me. She loved this stuff.

And . . . I loved her. The realization was like starting an engine. One minute there was nothing, and the next there was this hum at the center of everything, and all systems came to life. I couldn't see all the obstacles ahead, but if we were doing the journey together, we'd find a way to swerve around every last one.

"Nah, I gotta stay, man," I said. "She's my ride."

POMEGRANATE EYES

BEKA GREMIKOVA

Fresh-cut hay, upturned soil—signs of
harvest and hope to end the hunger.
But the earth's stomach still rumbles,
while Kore, with bright pomegranate eyes,
lies
in a field of wildflowers. Nymphs pilfer sweet hay
strands from her mother's cupboards.
Demeter works in far-off fields,
cleaving, tying, tossing, forgetting
that all seeds sown grow into harvest—
and there are Seeds planted in her own child.
Kore blinks back tears—

her eyes plucked from the Underworld pomegranate
by the mysterious shaper of lives and cosmos
unbeknownst to the roaming, restless gods
while Persephone slept alone in Demeter's womb,

her life slowly, surely, threading
into the very claws of death—

Red juice flows from those eyes, the seeds yearning
to return to Hades, to the Underworld, to their roots.
So when the rumbling earth finally erupts,
a jagged seam splitting the harvest fields,
and a strong hand grasps Kore's ankle—
she does not scream.
Her pomegranate eyes return the rich-brown
gaze of the under-earth king they remember
so well, so dearly.
Her soul snags with their same soft
yearning—
she must follow her eyes, those masters
of the heart. So with a dreamy sigh,
she slides her arms
around the neck of Hades and
returns
to
the
dark

STORM OF BETRAYAL

CRYSTAL D. GRANT

A ROCK FLIES through the single window, knocking the shutters open. I jump from my seat, nearly dumping my cat from my lap. The torches and loud voices outside do nothing to calm my racing pulse.

"Go away!"

"We don't want you here, girl!"

Misha gives a concerned meow, but I hardly notice. Dread and despair grip me, numbing me to all other emotions. A faint rumble in the sky reaches my ears.

Oh no. It's happening just as I feared. A storm is brewing. One that I may not be able to control.

How could Jochim do this to me?

The fire in the hearth crackles and hisses, oblivious to the impending disaster. If only I could sit in my usual spot on the floor, swapping stories with Jochim, with Misha curled up between us.

If only I hadn't told him my secret. He was always trying to impress everyone, desperate to step out of the shadows of his older brothers. I never thought he would betray me, though.

The shouts grow louder, despite the rain that begins to fall. In fact, it makes them madder.

"You don't belong here, freak!"

"Find another town to torment!"

I stumble to the table and brace my palms against it. "Please, please, leave," I whisper through stiff lips.

Stay calm. Don't give them a reason to hate you even more.

Boom!

My lungs empty in a rush at the sound of thunder, leaving my fingertips tingling. It's here. Misha darts beneath the cot in the corner, the gray fur on her tail sticking straight out in every direction.

I can't lose my head now, but my pounding heart makes it hard to breathe, much less maintain control. Another rock flies through the tiny window. Multiple fists pound on the door and wall, adding to the noise. I wrap my arms around my trembling form and try not to think about what will happen if the townsmen break through. I've seen it happen before. I blink the images away. Images of whips and chains. If I'm lucky, they'll put me on the back of my donkey and send me on my way.

One thing is for sure: I will not be living in the village any longer.

My throat dries at the thought. Where will I go? Who can I trust? Will I ever trust anyone again?

The rain gets heavier, pouring in from the tiny window. I creep nearer to close the shutters, flinching when the night sky lights up like noon. My stomach goes into spasms at the line of silhouettes in my front yard. The outside din amplifies, and wind slams against the cottage. I return to the table, gripping it with white fingers.

My single-room cabin shudders as the wind roars and thunder deafens me. Silence is forgotten in the fury of the storm.

My skin tingles while my mind goes numb. Misha shrieks from her spot underneath the cot, but I'm too swept up in my emotions to be of any comfort to her.

The voices change pitch, and I listen. It sounds as if they're fighting amongst themselves now. At least they're not screaming at me anymore.

But this is not what I want. This is why I always kept my secret to myself, so no one would ever have reason to distrust me. Or worse, fear me.

The only one I ever shared it with was Jochim. And look at where that left me. Tears blur my eyes, and a deep ache settles in my spirit.

I am alone. Again.

Something pounds on my door again, and I flinch, expecting it to break into bits, ushering in the brutal winds that will destroy my home. And take me with it.

It pounds again. Reality breaks through my daze. This isn't the sound of destruction. Someone's calling my name.

"Taya, it's me!"

The world tips. What is Jochim doing here?

"Please, Taya!"

The desperation in his voice tears at me, but I stand rooted to the spot. I can't let him in—not after what he did to me.

A bolt of lightning strikes something with a loud *pop*, and Jochim cries out. I jerk at how close it is, bracing myself for the ear-splitting crash to follow.

"Taya, you're safe! They're gone!"

It hits me that I no longer hear the angry shouts. Just the rage of the storm. It must have scared them away. But I will never be safe again. Not anymore.

A loud cracking sound rips through the air, and then a large limb crashes through the window. Wooden planks give way to a tree's crashing weight against the outside wall. I gasp. Jochim!

I rush to the door and fling the brace off. He's still standing there, safe and drenched, clutching his father's worn sword in one hand.

"What are you doing here?" I ask, retreating further into the house. I don't want him there, but I cannot let him bear the brunt of the storm.

He steps in and sets the sword in a corner, flinching at another loud roll from the sky. "I had to make sure you were safe."

I cross my arms. "I'm not, Jochim. They're ready to destroy me."

"I won't let them, Taya."

"It's because of you that they're after me!" The words rasp past my tight throat.

He drops his head. Dark, dripping hair hangs over his face. "I know, Taya. For that, I apologize."

Misha darts back out, meowing loudly and rubbing against Jochim's legs. Storms never did bother her as much as other cats. Maybe that was one reason she worked so well as my cat. Jochim reaches down and pats her head.

"It's not enough." Tears sting my eyes, and a gust blows through the door, almost knocking Jochim over. He spins around and pushes the door closed. Then he turns to me.

"Taya, I know this is all my fault." His wide hazel eyes beseech me as he raises his voice above the storm. "I never meant to hurt you; I really didn't. I—I just got caught up in the moment. And I said too much. I never expected them to react the way they did."

I press my trembling lips together. He has no idea what his actions have done. My panic has made things worse. And now I am a danger to the town, just as they feared.

Jochim steps closer. "I am sorry, Taya. I never would have uttered a word had I known it would come to this. Had I known that I would lose your trust... " His voice cracks.

I shake my head. "It's too late. There's no stopping them." I fling my hand at the damaged wall. "There's no stopping *me*."

He draws in a deep breath, the image of calmness and strength, despite the gale tearing at my cabin, piece by piece. "I believe in you, Taya."

"No! I can't!" Tears stream down my face as the door flies open again, and with it, the wind comes, battering Jochim so that he stumbles forward. Closer to me. "Stay away!"

But he takes my cold, clasped hands in his own, his eyes drilling into mine. He yells to be heard. "You are stronger than the storm within you, Taya. You can overcome this."

"You need to leave." I sob the words out as a piece of the roof peels away. Misha hides under the cot again. "I don't want you hurt." All I ever bring is hurt to the ones I care about.

He has betrayed my trust, but still, this is the man who holds my heart. I can't bear to stand by and watch the storm destroy him. "Please, leave. And take Misha with you."

Jochim shakes his head. "I'm not going anywhere, Taya. I'm staying by your side."

"I can't make it stop!" Fear and anger tangle in my head, making it hard for me to think clearly. I am helpless to do anything about it. It was always like this. This was why I had to leave my hometown, orphaned by a freak squall that killed my family. This was why I kept my secret to myself, so it would never happen again.

Jochim puts a hand on my cheek, completely disregarding the wind that buffets him from behind. "Look at me, Taya. I love you. I have for a long time. And I'm not leaving you. We'll get through this."

"But I can't stay here."

His jaw clenches in resolution. "Then we go together."

A chilly airstream rotates around us like a cyclone, closing us within it. Jochim's hair whips into his eyes, but his gaze remains steady.

My heart pinches. "I'm a freak, Jochim. Everywhere I go, they come after me."

"Then I will protect you with everything in me. Until the end of my days, I will stand between you and anyone who would harm you."

My eyes dart to the sword he brought with him. "You could have been killed."

"But I wasn't."

My chest tightens. "*I* could have killed you."

"But you didn't." He frames my face in his hands. "And you won't. You can control this."

I shake my head. "No, Jochim, you don't understand. It's too much for me."

"Alone, maybe." His gaze intensifies. "But you have me. And together, we'll get through this."

Misha meows at us from under the bed as if asking us to hurry.

I shouldn't believe him. This is the man who had revealed my secret, turned the town against me and put me in this position of vulnerability. But as he stares deep into my eyes, all I can see is the boy who befriended the lonely girl from out of town, encouraging me to step outside of my little cabin. The boy who faced the storm and angry townsmen to be with me tonight.

"But what if you're wrong?" I whisper.

A smile breaks through the serious lines on his face. "Taya. Listen."

I pause. Silence. "The storm."

He nods. "It's over. You stopped it."

My breath hitches as I stare over his shoulder through the open door. All is calm and still. A sliver of moonlight breaks through the thick clouds. Not even a breeze disturbs the leaves of the trees still standing. I can see the wreckage left behind, but for the moment, there is no danger.

"I couldn't do it alone." It was Jochim's steadiness, his belief in me, that made it happen.

Jochim pulls me in for a quick hug. "Are you all right now?"

"I-I think so." It's hard to think with his arms around me.

He sighes and steps back. "Taya, I truly am sorry. I will never forgive myself for the pain I put you through."

I press my lips together. "Why did you?"

His head lowers, and shame colors his cheeks a dusky red. "My whole life, I've been scoffed. Being the useless younger brother, no one has ever taken me seriously."

"You're not useless." My defense of him comes naturally, in spite of myself. Jochim had always seen himself as less than his four older brothers.

He shrugs. "It's no excuse for what I did. I let the scoffers and naysayers get to me. And I let slip the biggest secret anyone has ever trusted me with."

I shudder, and Jochim steps closer. "Please, help me make this right?" he whispers.

"Why, because you feel guilty?"

"Because I do love you. I truly do." He reaches for my hands, and his eyes light with fervor. "And I want to spend the rest of my days with you. A-as your husband, if you will allow it."

Then his face sags, and he releases his hold. "But even if you cannot love me, I hope you will permit me to go with you as your guide and protector." He bows his head and turns for the door. "I'll give you time to decide."

My breath lodges in my throat at the impact of his words. Rationale tells me to reject him. He had no right to ruin my life.

But the skin beneath my tunic is chilled at the absence of his touch. And my mind is conflicted.

The choices hang before me. The choice to reject him. Or to forgive him but walk away. And the third choice—to accept his offer of love. But how could I possibly?

Then again, can I reject the man who still holds my heart?

"Jochim."

He pauses at the door and looks back, his eyes lit with hope.

I straighten my shoulders. "I forgive you." My throat clogs, and I swallow, unable to speak.

The light dims from his gaze when I say nothing more, and he gives a single, resigned nod. When I step closer, hope glimmers.

"And if you'll have me, storms and all, I choose you." My voice catches. "For now and forever."

His hands return to their place, sending warmth down my arms. "Are you sure, Taya?"

And I am. Yes, he hurt me, and there will be storms—both literal and figurative—to face. But I do not want to lose the best thing that has ever happened to me because of a mistake. I open my mouth to say so when Misha interrupts with a loud, approving, "Meow!"

Our laughter blends as Jochim draws me into his arms. The last thing I see before his lips claim my own is the moon shining through the clouds outside.

IN OVER MY HEAD

BETHANY KOHLER

THE CURRENT PUSHED against my thighs as I stared intently into the stream.

"Any luck?"

I looked back over my shoulder to where Jaz was watching me from a camp chair. Her legs were crossed and she had an open book in her hand.

"Who brings a book camping?" I asked, diverting the conversation away from the fact that I hadn't caught a single fish.

She smiled. "Who tries fishing using his t-shirt as a dragnet?"

Project Diversion was clearly a failure. Our first vacation together was not going according to plan. Her words drove home the insecurities that already plagued me. I grew a bit defensive and overcompensated with a rash challenge. "You're welcome to come try if you think you can do better."

She sat looking at me for a moment. Then, to my surprise, she very deliberately marked her book with a leaf, left it on the camp chair, and waded into the stream.

A part of me was afraid she'd catch a fish right away, and prove that I was a complete failure. But I tried not to let any of that show on my face.

"Oop. Some of these rocks are very slippery," she remarked as she came up beside me.

I stood awkwardly, unsure what exactly she planned to do, and not willing to just hand over my makeshift net. That would be to admit defeat.

Jaz looked upstream, and then downstream, and then turned to me. I wondered fleetingly if she ever got tired of craning her neck to see my face. Her features and tone were serious, but her eyes gave her away. "I think the fish must have issued a bulletin about the menacing giant lurking in their waters, and no trout are traveling today."

"Or," I replied, "the ranger was mistaken and there are no trout in this stream at all."

"In that case." Before I knew what was happening, Jaz had swept her leg under the water, knocking me off balance. I fell into the stream with a splash, pulling her in after me.

We sat there in the middle of the stream, laughing. Jaz had her arms around my neck. Her eyes were sparkling with mirth. "I guess I'll cook up the hotdogs," she said.

As I looked into her eyes, I thought about what a stupid phrase "falling in love" was, as if it were beyond our control. It wasn't like falling into a stream. Jaz made it an easy choice, but it was still a choice.

I kissed her.

"I wonder what the fish will put in their bulletin now."

BUT, OUR END

ANNE J. HILL

A NATHAL POEM

I thought I knew what falling in love would feel like
A rush of emotions and instant attraction, butterflies
You'd sweep me off my feet, and we'd know right away
That we were made to be, forever and always

But that's not my story

It was slow; I didn't even like you at first
Annoying is too soft a word for what you were
To me and to other women alike, but I'll spare you
You were nothing that I expected, and for that, I'm glad

But time forced us together

I saw the way you acted and hated it, not knowing
Why you'd do what you'd do, but still, no excuses
The amazing part was when I confronted you
I expected more fighting, blaming, pointing fingers

But that's not the truth

You listened. Maybe for the first time in your life
But you did, and so did I. Because I found,
Thanks to you, that I was a fool too, imperfect
Both of us struggling through life, one day at a time

But listening is not enough

You did. You took action. You changed. So did I.
Through tears and blood and sweat and wars
I watched you hunt down your demons and slay them
And lend me a hand with my own, changing

But that was not the end

Transformation bred affection, and affection, love
I don't know the end of our story; I haven't lived it
But I know, my dear, that if we keep choosing
To fight together and not against, then one day

Our end will be in glory

SHEEP, SHOES, AND SHREWS

HANNAH CARTER AND ANNE J. HILL

WHAT DO YOU mean you betrothed me to some stuffy human prince?" Lia rounded the corner of the kitchen, armed with a frying pan.

Her father sat on their plush couch, ale in his hand. He took a swig. "I mean just that. He's dying, and marrying a fae will save him." Father downed another gulp of his drink. "Besides, the fae would like a treaty with the humans. This will be good for both our realms."

"I am not some *thing* to just be *bartered* off—" Lia swung her frying pan around in a large gesture of disapproval, only to accidentally shatter a vase. She gasped, her eyes wide.

"That..." her father said, pausing only to take another drink. "...was a priceless sea glass vase made by the mer."

"Well..." she spluttered and adjusted her corset. "Maybe you ought to show as much concern for your daughter as you do your precious *vase*!"

"The vase didn't break my daughter." Grumbling under his breath, Father pushed himself upright and shuffled over to her. His white beard swayed back and forth, and the stars on his robe seemed to sparkle with the magic that coursed through his veins. "Listen, Cerelia."

"*Lia*," she snapped.

Her father sighed. "Listen, *Lia*. You are getting married to Prince Asher, and that's that. No amount of tantrums will get you out of this one." He brushed aside a lock from his powered white wig and tucked it under his wizard's hood.

"Tantrums?" Lia gaped at him. "*Tantrums*? Is that what you call them? I'm so sorry that I won't willingly be your little prized *pig*, but—"

"But I don't want to marry a stranger. I don't want to get married at all." Asher fumbled with the end of his shirt, anxiety running wild.

His mother, the Queen, raised her eyebrow at him. "Of course you want to get married. Everyone wants to get married."

"Your mother is right," the king added. "Besides, it doesn't mean you have to even like her. Her magic will keep you alive. Don't you want to live, my boy?"

Asher looked between his two parents, shocked that they didn't see the absurdity. "I do want to live, but not like this. Can't I just visit her enough to stay alive? You can't force some poor girl into—"

His mother held her hand up. "No one is forcing anyone, Asher. She wants to. And it doesn't work that way; her magic will only heal you in wedlock." The queen's face beamed like this was the best thing since freshly-laced shoes. "It'd be an honor for her to marry the future king and save his life. To bind her people to us for years to come. This is good for everyone."

He swallowed and nodded. Asher looked down at his scuffed shoes. His manservant would have a fit when he saw them. Asher could picture his servant tossing his tall leather boots at him and begging him to use the proper footwear for outdoor activities. Princes weren't supposed to do things that scuffed dress shoes.

Asher had been sitting in a tree reading when he was summoned. The fresh air did his struggling lungs good—but the climbing did his soul even more good.

"I'll do it," he whispered. *Don't cry. Princes don't cry... or stare at their shoes.* He looked up, straightened his shoulders and repeated firmly, "I'll do it."

His father clasped his shoulder too hard, and Asher stifled a wince. "That's my boy. Now make sure you speak up when you meet her. Like you've been practicing."

Asher shoved away an eye roll. He wasn't a teen anymore. He knew how to address people and put on his fake authoritative royal voice, but he just didn't like to. "Yes, Your Highness." Asher dug his nails into the palms of his hands. This was not how he imagined spending the rest of his life.

When Lia imagined the rest of her life, standing at an altar while entering holy matrimony with a human had never been part of the fantasy.

She hardly even *had* fantasies about marriage. She was happy with her travels through the fae realm, painting and collecting trinkets. Lia reveled in mountain climbs and, sometimes, late at night, she imagined what it might be like to be a shepherd and sleep with sheep.

Sleeping with a prince instead felt, quite frankly, like a prison sentence with no foreseeable end.

"Dearly beloved, we are gathered here today..." the priest intoned.

She glanced at her soon-to-be cellmate. Everything about him seemed mousy and awkward. His brown hair was a little too unkempt to be princely, and he kept fiddling with the white cravat around his neck. He held a handkerchief in his hand and repeatedly coughed into it. Not to mention his hazel eyes were fixated on his shoes, of all things.

"...Prince Asher Whitlocke and Cerelia de Teg together in holy matrimony..."

For the love of sheep, if she didn't say something soon, her suffocating white dress might kill her. Which wasn't too terrible a fate, honestly.

She shifted and tried to subtly scratch her legs underneath the itchy dress. "I don't blame you," she whispered. When the boy—her future husband—lifted his eyes in confusion, she went on. "For staring at your shoes instead of me. They're far less intimidating and much more attractive."

Asher nodded. "Yes, they are."

Lia's back stiffened at his cruel words, and her voice turned frosty. "Well. I'm surprised you've lived this long with such a silver tongue. You must have left many heartbroken maidens in your wake, plotting their revenge with their angry spinster aunts."

Asher's eyes widened. "I didn't mean—"

"If you would now repeat your vows after me," the priest said, interrupting Asher's bumbling.

Lia spat out her vows through gritted teeth. She cursed the magic inside of her, the fae blood that she so often treasured. But thanks to it, here she stood, nothing more than a magic buffet to stop a prince's death sentence.

Unfortunately, as soon as the priest announced them husband and wife, freeing Prince Asher from his prison, the cell doors slammed shut on hers.

Asher closed the royal cottage door and locked it, the subtle click as final and condemning as a prison cell. He glanced at his new wife. She tapped her foot, arms crossed, and eyes burrowed into him. Asher swallowed. She looked like she might run him through if he even dared address her.

Asher walked across the sitting room and pushed open the bedroom door, eyeing the large bed where newlyweds were expected to spend the night consummating their marriage. Some believed them unwed until they did. But how could anyone do *that* with a complete stranger?

He cleared his throat. "If you'd prefer separate rooms, I'm sure I can arrange that." Asher had a hard time looking directly at her. She was far more beautiful than he'd anticipated, except for the scowl that ruined her copper-colored, freckled face.

"I'm sure it would be preferable to waking up next to me. Maybe you could kiss your shoes good morning, since they're more beautiful than me." She undid the white ribbon that tried to restrain her unruly black curls and shook her head until her hair stuck out in every direction like sprigs.

"That's not what I meant. I just thought you might be more comfortable that way." Asher untied his cravat and breathed deeply. He'd felt like he was being choked to death for the last several hours. He watched his wife from the corner of his eye, his palms slick with sweat. Asher had no idea what he was meant to do with a stranger for a wife.

"I'd be more comfortable far away from here, but yet—here we are." She dipped into a deep curtsey that oozed just as much sarcasm as her tone. "I suppose I should introduce myself more properly. My father often calls me his great disappointment. The neighbors call me 'that wicked girl,' and I'm sure you'll pick one of those as an *endearing* nickname soon enough." She rose back up and straightened her hair. "But my mother named me Cerelia, though I prefer Lia."

Asher shifted. "I wouldn't call you any of those horrible things."

Lia narrowed her eyes. "My name is horrible?"

Asher coughed in surprise. "No, I meant the nicknames." He shook his head. "Pardon me." He ducked into another room to change. As he undressed and put on his nightwear, he took deep breaths. He could only hope her bluntness and tendency to assume the worst of him were because of nerves. When Asher returned, he lifted the corner of the blanket and climbed in. "I just want you to know, I—" He froze. What *was* he trying to tell her? "Um..."

Lia snorted. "Don't worry, *Your Highness*. I understand. I'm good enough to save your life but not share your bed." She snatched a spare pillow and stormed back toward the door. "I'll sleep on the couch. Wouldn't want you to get a crick in that precious royal neck of yours."

He sat up fast. "Lia, no. That's not at all what I was going to say. Please. Don't go."

"Well, if you meant to imply that you *want* me to share your bed..." Her face turned a bright red, and she scowled even deeper. "Then I *also* refuse."

Asher's jaw clenched, and he spat out, "Would you stop telling me what I'm trying to say and actually let me talk for two seconds? I was trying to tell you I'm sorry you got forced into this, and I want to make you happy. But whatever. Just keep assuming the absolute worst of me." He laid back down and turned away from her, pulling the blanket over his head. He blinked away tears. Asher didn't want to be a part of this any more than the brash, heartless fae.

Maybe she had been entirely too brash.

Oh, her *mouth*! Would she ever learn to control that unruly weapon? Her face flushed as she stormed back into the living room. Tears threatened to fall, but she swiped them away in bold, angry strikes.

She threw the pillow down and thumped her fists against it a few times before she collapsed onto the couch.

She felt like nothing more than a magic heifer in all this. Something to milk when needed and butcher when it stopped being useful.

Lia sniffled. Her eyes burned from trying to control so many emotions. And on top of that, her stomach hurt since she hadn't eaten more than a few nibbles at the wedding banquet. She'd chosen to glare daggers at her father the whole time as he alternated between imbibing and drunkenly trying to assure the queen and king that this arrangement was best for their son and country. But every time he would lock eyes with his daughter, he'd take a drink and turn away.

What a wonderful father she had. Truly an exemplary man above all men.

Hot tears finally cascaded down her cheeks. She turned and tried to smother them on the back of the couch, all while her shoulders trembled, and the ache in the pit of her stomach grew deeper...and not just from lack of food.

The floor creaked.

She gasped and flipped over. A shadow waited there, just out of view, and she held up a hand as sparks jumped between her fingers. "Who...Asher?" For a blessed moment, the shock had made her forget she had a new husband sharing this cottage with her.

"You're crying...." Asher spoke softly. "I'm sorry."

She let her hand drop. "Don't apologize. It's nothing."

And everything.

Asher shifted on his feet, then slowly walked toward her. He paused for a moment before he sat down on the edge of the couch. "My parents...told me you *wanted* this. I'm realizing perhaps they were mistaken?"

"Wanted?" Lia barked out a laugh. "I didn't *want* this. I don't care about some crown or marrying. My father *made* me. He'd sold me to your family before he even informed me of my fate."

Asher winced and played with the hem of his shirt. "I see." He ran a shaky hand over his face, his skin paler than just hours before. "I didn't realize that. I never would have agreed had I known." He wrung his fingers together. "I... Lia...you don't have to do this. You can go home, and I'll handle ending the marriage. We haven't...finalized it yet, so it won't be too hard." He cleared his throat, which erupted into a fit of coughs. "I don't want you to be unhappy just for me."

He'd given her a door out, thrown it wide open, and yet...

Lia smoothed her unruly curls away from her face.

Except...the door might be open, but there were still bars and thorns right outside the opening. The path might have been passable, but it wasn't clear.

"No person in a good conscience could ever leave another person to die." She let out a puff of air.

Asher shook his head. "I appreciate it, but I'm not your responsibility."

She slumped back against the couch. “I think it’s everyone’s responsibility to try and do what they can. Even if it means giving up a lifelong dream of running away with a flock of sheep and living in the mountains next to a crystal clear lake.”

His expression softened, and he nodded slowly. "Would it help if I told you I know a spot with a beautiful clear lake? There aren't sheep, but there are the most breathtaking trees to climb. I can take you tomorrow?"

Lia wiped away the last few tears that remained on her cheeks, drying in the cool air. “I suppose it would give us something to do other than stare at one another.” Plus, out in the cool air, surrounded by nature, she could almost imagine herself as a bird, free to take flight whenever she dreamed of it. Not some pitiful creature with their wings clipped and chained, bound forever to the ground.

A lump formed in her throat.

Yes, perhaps she needed those trees after all.

The next morning, Asher woke before Lia and stumbled out to the trees so his coughing wouldn't wake her. He leaned his back against the cottage, taking in deep breaths. The sad part was, this *was* him feeling better. At least he hadn't woken up with his dinner spewing.

He ran a shaky hand through his hair and spotted a beautiful lavender wildflower. Crouching down beside it, he picked it before slipping back inside.

Asher had his own plans.

The cottage had a small kitchen in the back. There was a certain joy that came from making his own tea and breakfast, and usually, he didn't wake soon enough to do so before food was brought to his room.

Asher put the wildflower behind his ear so he wouldn't lose it. He started the fire and tossed bacon and eggs in a pan. Boiled water for tea and sliced the freshly made bread.

The bacon sizzled and cracked and filled the cottage with a glorious smell.

Situating all the food onto a tray, he placed the wildflower in a spare cup and carried it out to the sitting room. Asher set it on a small table beside Lia.

Her unruly curls stuck up in odd angles, and her mouth hung wide open. But as he crept out, she muttered something incomprehensible. He turned and caught one dark eye staring at him. "What was that?"

She yawned and tried again, her words only slightly less slurred than the first time. “I said, what time is it?”

Asher paused in the doorway. "Early morning."

Lia grunted. “If you tell me that you are a morning person, I will consider you even more insufferable than I did last night.” But she sat up and yawned once more. The neckline of her nightgown slipped down, showing just a sliver of her shoulder, and she hastily slid it into place. “What’s all this?”

"Breakfast. And a flower, for...color." He scratched the back of his head, unsure if he should leave her to wake up and eat in peace or join her.

“Hmm.” Lia reached out and took one bite of the bacon. Her eyebrows raised as she reached for another one. “Perhaps I’ll amend my opinion of morning people if I continue to get food like this.”

Asher smiled softly. "Unfortunately, they don't let me make breakfast often. But this is a special occasion."

Lia smirked. "I'm a special occasion?"

"I...yes?" Asher shifted on his feet. Lia was incredibly hard for him to figure out.

"Calm down, shoe boy. I'm teasing." She dug into the eggs. "Aren't you going to eat?"

Asher nodded toward the kitchen. "I have to go make it."

Her face softened ever so slightly, and she nodded. He offered a smile and went back to the kitchen. Tucked away where she couldn't see him, he listened to her hum as she ate.

Asher grinned to himself. Lia might not have said it, but he could tell his food made her happy to some degree, and the thought of making her happy again filled him with hope. And he knew the perfect place to do just that.

Somehow, Asher had reached into Lia’s mind and plucked a place straight from her imagination to bring to life. He called it Crescent Moon Lake, and she couldn’t think of a better way to describe it. Not only did the lake itself somewhat resemble a crescent moon, but on the far side, it was hemmed in by a half-circle of mountains. Snow dotted the tops of the crests, but down below, Lia remained comfortable in her shawl.

Evergreen trees reached for the sky, like they wanted to rival the mountains, and swayed ever so slightly in the wind. Purple, white, and gray flowers bloomed by her feet, and she took special care not to tramp on them and ruin the beauty.

"Give me a lamb or two, and I'd never leave this place," Lia breathed.

Asher coughed, which might have been his attempt to hide a laugh. "I'm very confused by your obsession with sheep."

"Oh." Lia felt a bit of heat creep up her neck and cheeks. A balmy breeze ruffled some curls that had already escaped her ribbon, and she tried her best to tuck the scraggly locks behind her ear. "I suppose it's rather silly." She glanced at him out of the corner of her eye, and when he didn't look away or laugh, she pressed on quietly. "When I was little, my mother gave me a storybook. One of my favorite stories was about a little lamb, and there was a beautiful painting. It showed a place not unlike this, with a shepherd and a little sheep. And I just thought it was so beautiful...I wanted to crawl inside it and build myself a cottage there and never leave."

"It sounds beautiful."

Her brows furrowed, and she stole one more glance just to make sure he wasn't teasing her. But he seemed earnest, and his hazel eyes weren't fixed on his shoes for once.

She tugged the neck of her shawl closer and shifted her vision back to the scenery. "I thought so. Mother always said she'd take me there, but then...she got sick and passed away soon after." Lia's voice trailed off. She crouched and gently brushed her fingers over some droopy gray petals. "I think that's why my father turned so eagerly to the drink, you know. " Lia swallowed.

"I'm very sorry." Asher knelt beside her. His fingers trembled for a moment before he picked a purple flower and tucked it behind her ear.

Lia cleared her throat, her cheeks growing even hotter. "It isn't your fault."

"No...but I'm sure it's not easy. I'm...I'm really sorry."

"Would you quit apologizing?" Lia stretched out on the ground so she could look up at the clouds as they rolled by.

"Sorry. I mean...I'm not sorry?" Asher blushed and followed suit, and soon they lay next to each other, their heads and shoulders almost touching.

They waited in silence for a few minutes until Lia pointed up at the blue sky. "Look. That cloud looks like a bunny."

Hardly a moment passed before Asher blurted out, "I thought you would say a sheep."

The comment seemed so unexpected that a laugh exploded from Lia. She quickly tried to smother it behind her hands, but the faint echo rolled throughout their small valley.

Near the tail end of her outburst, Asher also started to chuckle: a quiet, unsure thing, and she wasn't sure if his uncertainty meant he didn't often laugh, or if it meant he wasn't sure if he was supposed to laugh *with* her.

Her stomach ached from the force of the laughter. She wiped away the tears from her eyes.

"I like your laugh," Asher whispered.

"I'm sure it's much better than me arguing and snapping at you, isn't it?" Lia said dryly.

"I—I didn't mean it like that."

Lia reached out and touched his shoulder to silence him. "I know you didn't mean it like that. I'm..." She almost choked on the word, but when she remembered the delicious bacon he made for her, his laughter, the beauty of the place he'd brought her to, and the tender look he'd given her when she'd talked about the illustrated book, it strengthened her resolve. "I'm...sorry."

"For what?"

"For the way I acted yesterday. I know we got off on the wrong foot, with...nerves and tensions and whatnot." Lia gave his shoulder a squeeze before she withdrew her hand. "I really am not that sweet of a person. I'm prickly and sarcastic and much more like a porcupine than any lamb." Her mouth twitched upward on that last word.

"Well, luckily for you, lambs aren't *my* obsession." Asher blushed.

A bit of color looked good on those too-pale cheeks.

"Regardless, my mouth runs quite often, and I can't guarantee it'll stop. But while it's on a good track at the moment, I want to say thank you." Lia gestured to the world around them. "For bringing me here. It feels like I've finally found that storybook and crawled in."

"Minus the sheep, of course," he said.

"Of course. Minus the sheep."

Her eyes met his for a brief second, and suddenly, she wished he'd look at his shoes again.

"You could stay here," Asher said. His voice felt as soft as the breeze that caressed her cheeks. "If you want to stay at the cottage, you could buy a lamb and settle in to live your dreams. I won't tell anyone. If you stay on our property, we could still be considered married, which will keep me alive. You'd have enough power and funds to live here as long as you wanted."

Just like last night, Asher had opened the door for her to walk straight out, but...

Lia's heart—the one thing the people around her had long considered cold—seemed to thaw ever so slightly. She held the shawl tighter to her body. "You know...the funny thing is...had someone asked me, I might have saved you of my own free will."

Asher swiveled his head back to look at her, his brows drawn together. He very much resembled a lamb in that moment, just as innocent and curious in his mannerisms and expressions. "What do you mean?"

"I mean just that. If my father had bothered to ask my opinion instead of roping me in against my will, he might have found me more agreeable from the start. Perhaps he would not have endured so many threats from a frying pan."

Asher studied her, eyebrows furrowing. Lia wasn't quite sure if it was because he was incredulous that she'd dared to wield a frying pan or because of her sappier sentiments. "But...why?"

"Because I have the power to stop your pain, and I believe if I have the means to help someone, I should." Lia reached up and touched the flower, still tucked behind her ear. Suddenly, she wanted to get to know this shy young man better. But she wouldn't be able to do that living tucked away here, apart from him. "I think you are a person worth helping, Asher Whitlocke. Even with your silver tongue."

Birds chirped in the arms of the evergreens. The wind rushed by and rattled the grass, whistling a cheery tune. And, though she might have imagined it, Lia could have sworn she heard a sheep bleat from somewhere up in the mountains.

THE TRUTH ABOUT LOVE

KAYLA E. GREEN

Love is a lie
And you will never hear me say
It is worth fighting for
Because when you truly let your heart fall
You'll only regret it
Let the delusion shatter that
With love
All is possible
I'm sure you will agree, too, that
We can achieve
Happily ever after
Only in fantasy
When you think
It's what we deserve
Remember
Forever can be realized
Only in dreams

And no one can persuade me that
Soulmates exist
Besides
Happiness is fleeting
And it's useless to conclude
Love is true and unconditional

Now read in reverse

STONE SOUL

CASSANDRA HAMM

GEMMA'S FEET POUNDED against the ground, crunching fallen leaves. Terror lent speed to her burning leg muscles.

Horan wouldn't follow her this deep into the forest…would he?

Her lungs finally gave out, and she doubled over, hands on her knees, sucking in breaths. Gemma listened for sounds of pursuit, but all she heard was the wind whistling through the trees and her own ragged gasps.

Horan wasn't a man of the forest. He paid men to kill the deer for the venison he sold. Still, she listened for any sign of pursuit. Silence.

She was safe, for now.

Gemma slumped against a tree trunk, her dress puddling around her. Sweat soaked her back and neck. She examined the coarse linen hem and flinched when she spotted a rip. Maybe she could sew it before Uncle Roan noticed.

But the rip was nothing. Not when she still felt the press of Horan's grasping fingers on her waist.

She glanced around at the trees with their spindly branches, most of which had already shed their leaves. Shadows danced and quivered around her. Normally, she'd find the chittering birds and humming bugs a balm to her nerves, but even their steadiness couldn't calm her breathing.

If she hadn't run…if he'd let his hands slip lower…

Tears mingled with the sweat on her cheeks, and she wiped them away, even though no one was here to judge.

"Excuse me, miss."

Gemma scrambled backward, her hands slipping on damp, rotting leaves. Maybe if she ignored the low, gravelly voice, the person would go away. But it was a *male* voice, and males didn't go away until they got what they wanted.

"I didn't mean to startle you." The man's voice sounded odd, almost accented, with an emphasis on the consonants. "I was simply wondering where the nearest village is."

"Where are you?" She whipped her head around, trying to spot the man through the partially-bare branches.

A shadow detached from the trees with a tremendous *thump*. Gemma screamed. She tried to push herself to her feet, but her trembling legs gave out. She stared in horror at a mound of gray stone, almost twice her size and as thick as a tree trunk.

The stone shifted. Thick legs made of interconnected boulders scraped against each other as the mound advanced. The creature lifted blocky arms in a placating gesture.

"Please, I'm not here to harm you." The creature's mouth barely moved, if it could even be called a mouth—more like a dark hole among the gray, ridged lines of his face. "Truly."

Gemma got to her knees and edged closer to the creature, though she knew she should run away. *Those must be its eyes*—more holes on his face, situated over a tiny rock nose. A face. A stone face.

"I will move on if you don't want me to stay," the creature said. "Just, if you would be so kind as to direct me to the nearest—"

"What *are* you?" The question slipped from Gemma's lips before she could bite it back.

His arms lowered with a creak. "I am a stone golem."

Gemma inhaled sharply. She'd heard of golems, creatures made of natural elements brought to life by a wizard's hand, but those were just stories.

This stone man before her was not a story. He was *real.*

"You may call me Wynnstan."

She smiled. Such an unexpected name. A sophisticated name.

Maybe it was the kindness with which he spoke. Maybe it was the fact that he'd offered to leave out of respect for her comfort. Whatever the case, she found herself saying, "I'm Gemma."

"Gemma." Wynnstan bowed his head with a scrape.

No one ever bowed to her. A flutter built in her chest, like a trapped butterfly.

"You asked about the nearest village." She gestured back the way she'd come. "Folstad's back there, but I don't think you'd like it much." *I don't think they'd like you,* is what she wanted to say, but she couldn't bring herself to do it.

"I'm sorry to have bothered your solitude for an unfruitful pursuit." Wynnstan's mouth shifted downward, mimicking a frown. It was strangely endearing to see him react that way. Like he was *concerned* for her. But how could an inhuman creature feel concern?

Maybe he's not so different from me.

"I will leave you but always remember your kindness," Wynnstan said.

"But I didn't do anything." Gemma gazed up into the golem's black eye voids and, somehow, saw something there. Earnestness. Maybe even pain.

"You spoke to me," he said. "And you gave me your name."

That was kindness? Why, it was barely even worth mentioning. Gemma stood on wobbly legs. She barely came up to Wynnstan's chest. "Of course. Why wouldn't I?"

"Not many humans do. They are more apt to shoot first and ask questions later." Wynnstan gestured to his leg.

Now she noticed a deep fracture in his thigh. It looked like a cruel, jagged smile.

"Someone did that to you?" she gasped, inching forward to get a better look. The gash was deep. She suspected she might be able to stick her whole finger in it.

"A crossbow bolt." Wynnstan patted his leg with a *thunk.*

"Did it hurt?"

He cocked his head. She wondered suddenly how big golem's brains were or if they even *had* brains, which was, of course, a ridiculous thought. The creature in front of her was far too intelligent to be brainless.

"I can't feel the impact, but I know when it happens. And if someone knocks off my entire leg, I won't regenerate quickly enough to escape."

"Your limbs regenerate?" Uncle Roan would've slapped her upside the head for all her questions, but she couldn't help herself. Then she realized she was focusing on the wrong thing, as usual. "I mean, that sounds awful," she said quickly. "I don't know what I'd do without my legs."

A strange sound came from Wynnstan—a deep, rumbling bark. No, a *laugh.* And it made her laugh too.

"To answer your question, my limbs do indeed regenerate," Wynnstan said after he'd collected himself.

"But *how?*"

"One of my creator's secrets," he said.

"Maybe he'll tell you."

"He can't tell anyone now." Wynnstan's voice went low and soft. "He's gone."

Gemma heard the raw pain in his voice—the same kind of pain that flared whenever she thought too hard about her mother's casket. She recalled red stains around her mother's lips; the dark funeral shroud and redwood coffin; Roan's fingers digging into her arm, dragging her away from her beloved house.

This golem knows what it is to lose everything.

Maybe it was that shared pain that led her to keep talking to Wynnstan long after the sun had started its descent behind the mountains. Or maybe it was the way he looked at her as a person, not something to be claimed or devoured. Or maybe it was simply the fact that he wasn't a human man but was something entirely different, something *good.*

"Can I see you again?" she asked when the sky marked his skin a dusky purple.

His mouth shifted into a smile that glowed as brightly as the dying leaves. When he said yes, her soul lifted from its fog and dared to hope.

"Where you been goin', girl?" Uncle Roan asked.

Gemma nearly dropped Roan's discarded plate. She'd kept her daily forest visits as secretive as possible, leaving the house when Roan was at the tavern and returning long before he stumbled home. She'd kept up on her chores and given Roan no reason to suspect her of impropriety.

How did he find out?

"Gemma?" Roan said, more loudly this time.

She dunked her rag in the soapy bucket and continued scrubbing Roan's plate. There was a stubborn bit of rice that refused to budge. "What do you mean?" she asked carefully.

Roan slapped his tobacco-stained hands on the counter. Gemma flinched.

"You been disappearin' all the time," he rasped.

The stench of liquor hit her full force as he spoke, and she fought the urge to gag.

"The house ain't gonna clean itself, ya know."

Then why don't you *clean it? You live here too.* She bit back the remark and kept her features as neutral as possible, though her face was far too expressive to hide much. "The village girls have asked me to...shop with them."

Instead of placating him, the statement seemed to make Roan angrier. His cheeks splotched scarlet. "You been wastin' money?"

"No, Uncle. Just looking." She hid her trembling hands by scrubbing ever harder.

"You better be."

If he found out where she'd been going...who she'd been seeing...

Seeing Wynnstan every day was the only thing that kept her from collapsing. His gentle manner, his patient understanding, the way he listened without judging—they filled her soul, healing the tiny wounds her uncle inflicted daily.

Roan's hand descended suddenly, fiercely, like a swooping bird of prey. The slap connected with her cheek. She gasped, holding a soapy hand to her stinging face.

The door shut behind Roan. She heaved in a shuddering breath and tried to keep the tears inside, but they spilled down her cheeks.

She couldn't see Wynnstan like this. But she'd promised to meet him at midday, and she couldn't bear the thought of him waiting for someone who'd never come. Not her sweet Wynnstan.

Not that he was *hers.*

Gemma wiped her eyes and finished cleaning. Throwing on a sun hat for propriety's sake, she hurried out into the street. Her body stiffened automatically at the sight of the other Folstad villagers, and she ducked her head, trying to avoid eye contact. A low whistle split the air, and she stiffened but kept moving.

She found Wynnstan in the clearing where they'd first met. He was so still, he almost seemed to be a boulder leaning against a tree trunk.

"Wynnstan," she said.

The boulder shifted. Wynnstan's craggy features broke into what she now knew was a smile. "Gemma! I'm glad to see you."

She couldn't resist the grin overtaking her face. She removed her sun hat and pulled the tie from her hair, letting her curls spill onto her shoulders in a tangle of red.

"Your hair is beautiful, like fire," Wynnstan said.

Her cheeks warmed. Roan had compared her to fire for most of her life, but it had always been negative. "Thank you," she said.

They stared at each other for a moment. Gemma moved close enough that she could touch him if she wanted to.

"What's it like?" she asked. "Being a golem."

Stones shifted as Wynnstan cocked his head. "Much like being a human, I expect. But as you know, I can't feel."

"At all?"

"On the inside, I do feel things, certainly. But the outside..." He lifted his stony shoulders in an awkward, endearing shrug.

"I think feeling on the inside is what matters," Gemma said.

He gazed down at her with what she thought might be hope. The same tendril of hope grew in her own chest, wondering, wishing, desperate to hold onto this moment just a bit longer. She wondered how his hand would feel if she took it.

"A village man saw me," Wynnstan said, startling out of her fantasies.

"What?" Her throat worked up and down. She'd known it couldn't last. She just hadn't thought it'd be so soon. "What did he do?"

Wynnstan didn't answer for so long she thought maybe he hadn't heard her. "He called me a monster."

Gemma's jaw tightened. "How *dare* he! He doesn't know you at all. *He's* the real monster."

Wynnstan turned his head away. A chill ran across her skin, and she fought to think of *something* to fix things, to delay their inevitable parting, but he spoke before she could.

"I should leave Folstad," he said.

Her heart ruptured inside her chest.

"I've already put you in danger by being around you," Wynnstan said. "If one of your villagers saw us together—"

"Please don't go, Wynn." Her hand closed around his. He didn't react, and she realized with a pang that he probably couldn't feel it. Feeling ridiculous, she started to pull away, but his hand lightly tightened on hers.

"It's just one man and his prejudices," she hurried on. "Maybe you can go into the village, show the people who you really are, change their minds about golems—"

"I've tried before." Wynnstan's voice was low and soft. "I barely escaped with my limbs intact."

She blinked hard, his hand in hers the only thing keeping her from falling apart.

"I could try again." He reached with his other hand, slowly, tentatively, for her face. Her breath caught as his fingers hovered in the air in front of her mouth. "For you, Gemma, I would."

She leaned forward, letting her lips brush his fingers. They were cool and surprisingly smooth against her mouth, and she lingered there. His hand shifted to cup her jaw, and she rested her head against his palm.

"Wynn," she whispered.

"Get away from my niece!" came a horribly familiar roar.

Gemma jerked away from Wynnstan. She looked over just as Roan aimed his crossbow at Wynnstan and launched a bolt. It whistled through the chilly air and thudded against Wynnstan's chest, cracking the stone. Wynnstan collapsed.

"Wynn!" she screamed.

Roan pulled another bolt from his satchel with a predatory grin. "I heard about you, golem," he said. "The villagers are loadin' their crossbows right now. I expect they'll be comin' this way to finish you off if I don't get you first."

Panic seized her chest as she stared at the unmoving Wynnstan. *Help him,* she told herself, and her limbs unfroze, letting her rush to his side.

She couldn't fix stone injuries. All she knew was how to hide her bruises and cuts.

"Wynnstan?" She touched his side, almost forgetting that it wouldn't give any signs of life. All she could do was wait to see if he'd move again.

"You get away from that golem right now, Gemma," Roan snarled.

"Wynn!" Gemma shook him. Though the fractured boulder didn't seem life-threatening, the impact could've damaged his heart. How did his heart even work? She should've asked him more about the magic behind his body, but it'd felt too intimate.

Groaning, Wynnstan pushed himself to his feet.

"Wynn," she breathed.

"Gemma, you need to run." Wynnstan turned toward Roan, who aimed his crossbow. "I'll hold this man off."

"That's my uncle," she blurted.

Wynnstan whipped his head back around to stare at her. She hadn't told him much about Roan, not really. She hadn't wanted to ruin their happy times with talk of Roan.

A crossbow bolt slammed into Wynnstan's knee. He crumpled. Gemma shrieked, reaching for him, but Roan's hand clamped around her arm. She yelped, thrashing, but he whacked her shoulder with his crossbow. She flinched.

"I can't believe it," Roan said. "My own niece out in the woods, all improper-like!"

Wynnstan lay motionless on the blood-red leaves. Her heartbeat thudded against her throat. *What if…?*

"I always knew you were trouble," Roan said, "but not the kind to be messin' with unnatural folk!"

"Wynnstan isn't unnatural!" Gemma strained against Roan's vise-like grip.

"Look at it!" Roan gestured to Wynnstan with his unloaded crossbow. "Stones movin' and darin' to call themselves alive."

Gemma clenched her fists. "Wynn might be man-made, but he makes me feel alive. That counts for something."

"Now you're just talkin' nonsense."

She glanced back at Wynnstan. His knee seemed to be...*moving.* Slowly, almost imperceptibly, the stones expanded and shifted to fill the gap the bolt had left.

"We're goin' back to Folstad. *Now.*" Roan squeezed Gemma's elbow hard, bringing her attention back to him. "Horan wants you. Can't imagine why. But he's offerin' a good price for you."

A…price? The breath left her lungs. *A bride price?*

"You can't!" Not to the butcher who watched her like she was a piece of meat.

"I do what I want, girl." Roan spat on the ground. Bits of spittle landed on Gemma's face.

"I'm not marrying him."

"You'll marry him if I tell you to."

"I'm not marrying him!" Gemma finally let her anger show—a simmering flame beneath her skin that grew with every cruel word and every touch she didn't ask for. It glowed in her eyes, sparked in her words, and she relished it—*no more hiding,* she told herself.

Roan's eyes widened just for a moment, but then his mouth curled into a sneer. "You don't know what you're sayin'."

"I know perfectly well." Gemma lifted her chin and glared at her uncle. "Let me go now, and you'll never see me again. You won't have to take care of me anymore. Just let me take care of Wynnstan."

"You mean that thing over there?" Roan pointed at Wynnstan. Rocks scraped unpleasantly against one another as Wynnstan regenerated, though not quickly enough. "That *thing* is named Wynnstan," she said icily.

"Oh, come on, Gemma. Don't go feelin' bad for somethin' that ain't your own kind."

Her own kind had been nothing but cruel. She felt every barbed comment, every disgusting leer, every tiny aggression that made her feel so...so...*small.* So insignificant.

Wynnstan staggered to his feet, bleeding bits of rock. His body was crumbling but still intact, his legs barely supporting him, his chest falling to pieces. But he was still broad and beautiful and terrifying, and when he stepped toward Roan with a growl, Roan dropped his crossbow.

Gemma wrenched away from Roan's grip and ran toward Wynnstan, crunching dead leaves with each step. *Freedom,* her heart sang. *Freedom.*

"Gemma!" Roan hollered. "Look at that thing! That monster! You're taking its side over mine? I raised you!"

Bursts of memory seared her consciousness—red welts on her pale skin, jagged words that made her soul bleed. *Predators feed on fear,* she thought.

She turned to face Roan. He stood alone in the trees, his crossbow still on the ground. His face contorted in a snarl that would sear itself into her nightmares.

Wynnstan's crumbling hand touched her shoulder, and she drew strength from it.

"You're the monster here, Uncle," she said. "Not him."

She grabbed Wynnstan's hand and pulled him into a thundering sprint. Branches crashed against their faces, and Roan's yells faded into blissful nothingness as they ran toward freedom.

Gemma's stone heart cracked as hope pierced through her pain and finally reached her soul.

PART TWO: ENDURING

STONE SKIN

CASSANDRA HAMM

"YOU'RE HURTING ME, Wynn."

Wynnstan released Gemma's hand. "Sorry." He glared at his stone fingers, wishing for the hundredth—perhaps thousandth—time that his hands could be soft and delicate, able to hold Gemma like she deserved to be held.

She rubbed her palms together. The creek's low rumble filled the silence as they navigated the rocky path to the water's edge. "It's all right."

The words were a never-ending echoed refrain after every failed solution, every false hope. *"It's all right, Wynn. We'll figure this out."* But the trace of sadness never left her smile.

Gemma kicked off her sandals and sat on the rocky shore, submerging her feet in the slow-moving, murky water. One of the more pleasant spots of their latest home, Traustad, a town that seemed to accept the two of them being together. But for how long?

Wynnstan joined her. The creek meandered around his legs. Its splashes should've been accompanied by wetness, whatever that meant, and the absence gnawed at his mind.

He gazed into the water. His massive figure dwarfed Gemma's. Chipped boulders, connected at the joints, formed a monstrous body that creaked with every movement. Tiny rock nose, gaping holes for eyes and a mouth.

Could Gemma really love someone who wasn't truly alive?

"I was looking through a spell book yesterday." Faint white scars marked her freckled skin. He wished he could pound her uncle into a pulp for each one. "I found something that might change you—"

"It won't work." His rocky shoulders sagged. "Like the pig-snout potion, or the dragon breath brew—which almost killed me, as you may have forgotten."

"Really, Wynn." Gemma grabbed his hand, rubbing his unfeeling fingers. Her red hair glinted golden in the midday sunlight. The one time he'd stroked her hair, the delicate strands snagged on his hands and nearly pulled from her head entirely. "One scholar said that frog's blood mixed with human hair—"

"Stop. I don't want to hear any more."

No more vile potions forced down his throat. No more disappointment when the same stone face stared back at him. No more dreams of having a normal, human relationship with Gemma.

"I just wanted to help." She pulled her hand away.

Would my hand feel cold now without hers in it if I had skin?

He sighed. "I know, Gem."

But some things couldn't be helped. The dream of becoming a human should've died when Wynnstan's creator shriveled away under the plague's cruel grip.

He turned his eyes to the brown water meandering down the creek. "What if I stay a golem forever?"

"Then I will love you as a golem forever."

How could she? He'd never even kissed her, too afraid his stone lips would bruise hers. She'd already endured enough at the hands of her uncle. How could he inflict more pain on her?

But he was hurting her anyway—he saw it in her listless eyes, her drooping shoulders. *She isn't happy with me. Not anymore. And how could she be?*

They had been naive to think two beings from such different worlds could be together.

"Don't you... Wouldn't you rather...?" Wynnstan looked away, unable to continue.

"Would I rather what?"

"Don't you want a human?" he blurted. "Someone who can hold you? Who can love you the way you deserve to be loved?"

"I want *you*, Wynn." Gemma took his face in her hands—how he longed to feel them—and kissed him.

Nothing. He felt nothing—

Wait. There, a flicker—a soothing pressure against his mouth, his cheeks. A tingling in his chest.

Gemma jerked away and pressed a hand to her mouth. "Wynnstan, you're...*changing!*"

His body softened and drooped, almost unable to hold itself up. He gazed at his hands, gray darkening to brown, gaining shape. He bent his fingers. They flexed, silent and smooth.

The creek reflected a human—rich brown skin, hairless head, broad shoulders. He gaped.

"How...?" Gemma's eyes sparkled with tears. "All the magic we tried didn't work, yet a simple kiss..."

"I'm human." His voice was no longer gravelly, just deep and smooth. His tongue wandered around the squishiness of his mouth, the hardness of his teeth.

Now the tears streamed down Gemma's face. "You're human."

He reached out and touched one of the tears. It was the same texture as the creek on his legs—water. And her skin... His fingers roamed the blush of her cheeks, moving to the curve of her jaw. This must be what softness felt like.

"Oh, Wynn!"

She touched the hand cupping her face. Wynnstan grasped it, tracing the lines on her warm palm. She shivered. His other hand caressed her fiery hair, so delicate and intricate and perfect.

"How do you feel?" she whispered.

He took her face in his hands. His flesh throbbed with awareness and heat. "I feel...*you.*"

Her eyes brightened with the sky. "I love you, Wynn," she said. "I loved you as a golem, and I love you as a man."

He kissed her. Her lips moved against his, firm and soft at the same time, intoxicating his senses, so all he knew was *Gemma, Gemma, Gemma*. Her arms slipped around him. *This* was what being alive felt like.

She pulled back, her breath fanning against his lips. "I'm glad my kiss didn't change you back to a golem."

"Me, too." He blinked, his eyelashes resting briefly against his cheek like an embrace. "I can see why you humans like kissing so much."

Gemma entwined their fingers, milk-white against earth-brown. His newly awakened skin sang at the touch.

"Not 'you humans' anymore," she said. "Now you're one of us."

THE IMPACT

RACHEL LAWRENCE

Reality hit
Sooner than
I'd expected
And the impact
Took my breath away
But we survived
When the dust settled
It looked a lot like
Crumbs on the kitchen floor
Broken crayons
And hearts
Stray legos
Dog hair
Confetti
From a dozen celebrations
The dirt we tracked in
After burying a dream or two

Salt fallen from
Late night snacks
And my tired eyes
All the messy pieces
Of a life
Together
And so
Some days
We weep
Some days
We sweep
Some days
We shed our shoes
And dance
With dirty feet
On holy ground
We found beneath
After we leaped

WOE TO THE DREAMER

LARA E. MADDEN

I SAT IN the plush chair, twisting strands of hair through my fingers and staring at the wall so I didn't have to make eye contact with the therapist. She was studying me, scratching some notes onto a page, glancing back again with her icy stare. It was easier to look away.

"So, Miss—"

"Mrs." I reminded her, wincing at the word.

"Mrs. Bailey."

"Maybe you can just call me Alison?"

"Alison, why do you say you think that you're *going crazy*?" she asked, reading from her notes. Probably so that I wouldn't think she was calling me crazy. Because she wasn't. Although she probably thought it, or would in five minutes.

I hesitated, taking off my glasses to clean a smudge that wasn't there. "I'm falling in love, I think." I closed my eyes, took a deep breath, and got the words out. "I'm in love with someone who isn't my husband."

I knew she was shifting in her chair and looking at me sideways, but her voice remained even and unemotional as she asked, "Why do you think that makes you crazy?"

"Because," I said, staring hard at the wall. I tried to think of a way to make the situation sound less strange than it was. "The person I'm in love with isn't. . . well, he doesn't exactly exist in the *conventional* sense."

"So you are in love with a fictional person?"

"That does sound crazy." I laughed and glanced at the therapist to try and read her expression. No luck.

"Go on," she nodded.

"It started a few months ago when I was writing, really making headway with my novel. And then I just got blocked. It lasted for weeks. I would sit down at my laptop. Nothing. Go for a walk, read a good book, try to generate some inspiration. Still nothing. I tried whatever I could think of. But then I heard of this concept—lucid dreaming—which basically allows you to control your own dreams, talk to dream characters, do things you can't do in real life. I thought, yes! This is great! I can just *dream* the story and talk to my characters and write everything down when I wake up in the morning. It was perfect."

"And did this solve your problem? The dreaming?"

"It did. So well, in fact, that I was through the first few drafts of my novel within a month."

"Impressive," she said, though she didn't sound impressed. "I take it you've been spending a lot of time writing, then."

"I guess, yeah. Most of my day is spent on my novel, and most of my nights are spent dreaming about it. It's all I've thought about lately."

"And your husband? What does he think of all the time you spend writing?"

I shifted in the seat. My marriage wasn't my favorite thing to discuss with strangers.

"Carson? He's brought it up now and then." Almost every day. "When we fight, he says I don't have time for him or whatever. But that's completely unfair because he works constantly, so if he wants to be with me, maybe *he* should come home a little earlier. But he's a lawyer, so he wins all the arguments." It felt like I was ranting, so I reined it in and tried to get back on the topic of the dreams. I hadn't come to talk about Carson and me. It didn't take hiring a shrink to know that we had problems. The dreams, on the other hand, had been pricking some small part of my conscience for a while. I just wanted someone to sympathize with me, to take my side. And maybe to confirm that I wasn't actually delusional.

Before I could continue, she shot out another question. "Alison, how would you rate your relationship with your husband if you were being honest?"

"Uh, I don't know. Don't you think this is a little off-topic? I actually came here to talk about my dreams." I was beginning to feel uncomfortable, especially when she scratched more notes on her legal pad with that fancy pen of hers.

"No, Mrs. Bailey." She looked at me over her glasses. "I believe this is exactly the topic we should be exploring."

"Alrighty then. Carson and I haven't really been talking. He leaves for work before I wake up, and he doesn't get home until later in the evening." The therapist's ice gaze ebbed me on. I could have sworn that woman was reading my mind. "Okay, if I'm being honest, we have been avoiding each other. We've had some fights. Sometimes it's just easier not to talk at all." She finally seems satisfied, and I begin to hope that she'll let it go.

"And when did these disagreements between you and Mr. Bailey begin, Mrs. Bailey?"

"Alison. And I don't know if you're very good at this therapeutic communication thing."

"Answer the question, Alison," she urged calmly.

"Uh, I guess if I had to pin down a time, I would say it started . . . six months ago? I had published a short story—a mystery—and may have unintentionally, or not-so-unintentionally, included some aspects of a court case he was involved in as a defendant. They were technically supposed to be confidential, but the story was just so good I couldn't resist. Later, when he read the story, he recognized the case and got really upset. And yeah, I guess it was wrong of me to broadcast something he'd trusted me to keep secret, but the details of the case were public soon after that and I was careful to change the names and be discreet. It was *fiction*. No harm, no foul."

"And was this breach of his trust the source of the fights you mentioned?"

"I don't know, maybe? I mean, we fought about it one time and then Carson never brought it up again, so I figured it was behind us. No, the other fights started a few weeks later. He was staying at the office really late most nights, working on a new case he couldn't tell me about, and I was just starting to work on my novel. I began to get focused on it, let housework slip, and since I didn't know when he would be home, I just didn't really cook. We fought about things like that—him working too much, me not 'fulfilling my wifely duties.' Do you know that he hasn't even taken the time to read my novel yet? How about his duties? What about being a supportive husband?"

I shook my head. I was ranting again. "Now, we can hardly be in the same room without arguing about something."

"Tell me how the lucid dreaming has played into all this."

"The dreaming has sort of become a form of escapism. Some nights I go to bed early because I can't wait to tell Jay about my day or vent about something Carson said."

"Who is Jay?"

"Oh, um, Jay is the main character in my novel."

"He's the one you say you've fallen in love with?" she asked.

I took a deep breath. "Yes." I was certain that despite her impartial expression, she was judging me. "He's the one."

"And why would you say you're in love with him?"

"Well, how do you know you're in love with anyone? I mean, Jay and I talk about everything. I know him, and he knows me. He's always there for me. He comforts me when I'm upset. He listens when I need to talk. We agree on most things, but then, he sometimes offers perspectives I haven't consciously thought of yet. And he's so handsome. Honestly, he's everything I've ever wanted in a man. He's sort of perfect. We work well together, communicate, we trust each other. Isn't that what love is?"

"Do you think that this character in your dreams fulfills something you don't have with your husband? Perhaps you feel rejected and hurt, so you are seeking love elsewhere? Or you're projecting your frustration with your husband's imperfections onto this imaginary character."

"He's real!" I said defensively but immediately felt ridiculous for it. "I mean, he's real to me."

"Clearly, he's real to you, but you must understand that he does not exist in the true sense."

"Of course, I understand that."

"And he is the product of your imagination."

"Yes?"

"So Jay is not an ideal man. You simply consider him that way because your imagination created the man you wanted. He cannot know you. He cannot care for you. He cannot love or trust you because he only exists as part of your consciousness." Her tone was too calculated.

"Okay."

"Wouldn't it be more beneficial, then, to work toward fixing your relationship with your husband rather than focusing on an imaginary love interest?"

"But what if having my relationship with Jay actually makes my marriage better? You know, like, I could get what I need from Jay and then I don't have to rely on Carson to be perfect. Right?"

"How is that working so far?"

I looked at the clock. "I think our time's up."

"Yes, it seems it is." Before I left, the therapist handed me a business card along with a brochure for couples therapy. "I hope to see you again soon," she said.

I would not be seeing her again. As much as I paid for that session, I didn't feel better at all afterward.

By the time I got home, I couldn't wait to change into my comfy sweatpants and get back to writing. The novel was the therapy I used to recover from my actual therapy session. I worked for hours before the sound of the door swinging open pulled me out of my trance.

"Alison?" Carson called from downstairs. "Is dinner ready?"

Ugh. This again.

"Was it supposed to be?" I grumbled as I met him in the kitchen.

"Well, I told you this morning what time I'd be home, and I got home by that time, so, yeah, I was expecting dinner."

"I'm sorry. I guess I overestimated your ability to feed yourself. Are you such a child that you need your wife to do it for you?"

"*Seriously,* Alison?" He put down his briefcase and pulled off his tie. "I work all day, every day so that you can stay home and run the house. That's what we *agreed* to."

"Hey, I work full-time too!"

"Babe, work that doesn't pay any bills is called a hobby. You have a full-time hobby, not a full-time job."

"It's an investment. I can't sell a book until I've written it."

"Yeah, well, we can't eat an *investment* novel, can we? Look, you're home all day. I just don't think it's too much to ask—" He stopped short and sighed, rubbing his forehead like he did whenever he had a migraine. "Forget it."

I was confused. It wasn't like Carson to forfeit an argument, but I took my victory without question and turned to go back upstairs.

"Alison?" I was startled by his wounded tone. I turned back to see that his face looked tired, depressed, and almost empty.

"What?"

"Let's go out for dinner tonight, okay? You and me."

I wasn't sure how to respond, so I just said, "Sure, okay."

"And Alison?"

"Yeah?"

"I don't want to fight anymore tonight."

"Yeah. Neither do I," I said quietly.

I went to our bedroom to change. I couldn't remember the last time we'd gone out together. It had been months, at least. Sometime before we'd started fighting.

We drove to a restaurant in nearly unbroken silence. It was a beautiful French place with amazing food and even better wine. Still, the food seemed almost bland in the wake of the awkwardness between us, which lasted all through dinner. We picked at little topics, like what to order, how his work was going, how soon my novel would be finished, and how the rain was unusually heavy this spring. It was a dance on eggshells, but now and then, I looked up into his eyes. They were pleading with me to keep trying to make this work and fix what was broken between us. This had all been so easy once. Back when he was my favorite person to talk to, and every interaction we had was as natural as breathing.

"We should do this more often," I said, trying to sound casual against the sadness that was closing up my throat. I glanced down at my plate so he wouldn't see the tears starting to well in my eyes.

"Yeah, we should." He hesitated, and I thought he was done talking, but then he opened his mouth as though he needed to say something that he just couldn't quite find the words for.

"Alison," he finally said. "I need you to know that I'm trying. And I know this is so hard, and we are always fighting, and it's like we don't even know each other anymore. It's going to be hard to make this work, but we used to be so in love with each other. I know we were. And I want that back." He reached for my hand. My first reaction was to flinch away, but then I let my hand rest in his. It was such a little thing, but it was something.

"We'll make it work." I sniffed and discreetly wiped a tear away with the back of my hand. "For better or worse, right?" The words felt right to say in the moment, but even as I heard them coming from my mouth, I wondered whether they were true or just wishful thinking.

Later that night, we lay in bed. Me at my end, Carson far away from me on the opposite side, as though there was an invisible and unsurpassable wall between us. He had long since fallen asleep, and meanwhile, I'd hardly been able to close my eyes with all the thoughts branding themselves on my mind. I tried to weigh everything the therapist had said to me earlier with the promise I made to Carson that we would make things work. I held it up against everything I had with Jay, but comparing perfect Jay and difficult Carson was impossible. It felt like choosing between struggle and happiness.

Around midnight, I gave up fighting my thoughts and took a sleeping pill. My well-trained subconscious took me directly to the dream world, where I woke up with Jay by my side. We were hiking a mountain trail, one that was a favorite place of mine in the real world.

"What's wrong?" he asked when we were sitting at the summit. He put his arm around my shoulders, and I leaned into his embrace. "Bad day?"

I hesitated and tried to gather my thoughts. "Not a bad day. Just different."

"Different how?"

"I went to a therapist today."

He waited for me to say more. It was something I loved about Jay. Carson was constantly interrupting and never noticed when I had more on my mind. "I told her about us. She told me that I should invest more in my relationship with Carson. And she didn't say it directly, but she strongly implied that I should stop dreaming about you."

"What?! But didn't you tell her that we're in love? I make you happy, and I can be there for you in ways your husband can't be. Did you tell her all that?"

"Yes."

"Well, then, forget her. We're better together, and Alison, you *deserve* happiness. Don't let anyone tell you otherwise." He was so sincere, so trustworthy, that I wanted to take every word Jay said as absolute truth. I tried to push the therapist and all of her words out of my mind.

"How are things with Carson?"

"I don't really know. We had some kind of argument when he got home this evening, but then we went on a date."

"Like a normal date? No strings attached or faking it for a family reunion or anything?"

I shrugged. "We just went out to dinner like a normal couple. Does that bother you?"

"No."

"Really?"

"I don't care. As long as he's not jealous, I'm not. I don't see why you can't love us both."

I smiled and nodded. Carson never needed to know about Jay, and Jay was fine with Carson, so why not have the best of both worlds? I woke up the next morning feeling entirely optimistic.

Over the following weeks, Carson and I made a point of not fighting. Still, we were awkward around each other, clumsily acting our way through the motions. We had more dinners out. I got on top of things at home and was putting the finishing touches on the novel before submitting the draft to my editor. Carson was even reading it, finally. It all seemed to be going well.

Except for one thing that I couldn't get out of my head. With Carson and I trying to be more honest with one another, I felt like I was hiding something by not telling him about Jay. It felt like cheating, even though, technically, I wasn't.

But one Saturday night, while we were talking late, I let it slip.

"I just finished reading the last chapter of your book. It was good."

I laughed. "Did you actually like it, or are you saying that because your wife wrote it?"

"No, I really did enjoy it. The plot was solid." He paused for a moment, then made a face. "I mean, the main detective dude was a bit . . ."

My blood froze. He was talking about Jay. "A bit what?"

"I don't know. He sort of annoyed me. He was a little too . . . perfect." Carson shrugged. "I don't know much about writing stories; that's your field. You wrote him really well. I sometimes even felt like he was a real person. He just has the type of personality that would irk me in real life."

"Oh."

A silence ensued, and Carson filled it by reaching across the counter to spread cheese dip on a few crackers. Breaks in our conversations were still uncomfortable, but we'd started relearning how to sit in the awkwardness without rushing out of it. I grabbed a handful of crackers too, while nervously considering whether I should bring up the lucid dreaming while I had a good segue.

"I can't even imagine how you go about coming up with all the details for a book. Everything seems so *vivid*."

I took a deep breath. He was probably going to laugh. I chuckled, nodded, and put a cracker in my mouth to give myself more time to think of a response. As I ate it, I realized that my mouth was completely dry. Okay, if I was this nervous about telling him, that meant it was probably important.

"Actually," I said, taking a sip of water. "I tried something different this time when I was developing the story. Do you know what lucid dreaming is?"

Carson listened with curiosity as I explained how I had used the dreams to get past writer's block earlier in the year. I told him how I'd watched the events of the story unfold in my mind every night and took note of the settings and the people in them. I'd spent time with every character, learning each side of the story's events from every possible angle. They had begun to feel real to me, like close friends even.

It felt so good to finally share this world with Carson that I'd spent so much time in over the past year. He seemed surprised and amused and asked a lot of questions as I told him about the adventures I'd had in my sleep. Before I knew it, I was telling him about Jay.

"You know, it's actually hilarious. I spent so much time with him that I sort of started to have feelings for him. Isn't that weird? A guy in my head." I laughed it off, hoping he would too. Carson stayed very quiet, so I filled the silence.

"I mean, it might have actually been good for *our* relationship, you know? Because I could go talk to this fake boyfriend when I was upset at you so we didn't have to fight about things as much."

Carson's expression turned dark at the word *boyfriend.* I kept trying to explain more, to make the situation sound better, but the more I talked about Jay, the more Carson's features hardened.

"What's wrong?" I asked.

He exploded. "What's wrong? What do you mean, 'what's wrong?' How could you possibly not know this would hurt me?! You're telling me that you've been having an affair this whole time—not even with a real person, but with some fantasy man? How am I supposed to compete with *that*? What do you want me to do, congratulate you?"

"I never meant to fall in love with him, Carson."

"Well," he said, with eyes shooting arrows and an angry bite to his voice. "Far be it from your *husband* to get between you and true love." He stormed off, and everything we'd been building over the last weeks, everything we'd struggled for, crumbled into dust.

The divorce papers showed up a few days later. In one devastating, ground-breaking moment, it all began to feel so terribly real. Those papers staring up at me said all I needed to hear: my marriage, the one thing in my life that was supposed to be true and lasting, was about to be gone, and I was going to lose my husband if I didn't do something drastic.

It broke me.

With tears streaming down my face, I made an impulsive decision. A difficult decision, but one I didn't think I would ever regret. I opened the laptop I'd been writing my book on, day after day, for eight months solid and deleted every folder, document and file. One after the next, every reminder of Jay, everything that made him real, was erased.

When Carson got home late, I was inside the front door waiting for him. I shoved a heavy stack of papers in his arms the moment he came through the door. He held every printed draft of my beloved novel. Every piece of evidence that it ever existed in the first place.

"Burn them," I said. I watched his face as he looked at the pages and realized what it was I'd given to him. "I'm sorry I let them become more important than our marriage."

Carson just stood there, stunned to an almost emotionless expression, and for a moment, I was sure he'd give the stack back to me and leave me there, alone.

"What about Jay?" he asks coldly.

"Jay's gone." I stepped close enough to him that a few tears landed on the manuscripts in his arms. "The book is deleted. I'm done living some made-up perfect life with someone who isn't real. I can write something else, and next time, I promise not to use my writing to push you away." I wiped my eyes and took a breath, hoping with everything in me that he could somehow forgive my stupidity and selfishness. "I love you."

Carson stared at the reams of paper between us, then looked at me. It seemed as if he was trying to decide what to say, but instead, he tossed the papers aside and pulled me close to him. Pages flew into the air and fluttered around our feet. We clung to each other, simultaneously breaking and mending, and when he kissed me, it was everything I had been missing.

Carson and I had never been perfect and never would be. But what we had was *real.*

A love that is real, imperfect, messy, beautiful . . .

That's all I could ever ask.

THE COLOR OF LIFE

KAITLYN EMERY

GREEN WAS HER favorite color. Linzi used to call it the color of life. My wife always said Linzi could convince me to do anything from the moment she was born. So naturally, when she batted those long eyelashes at me and asked Daddy to paint the house shutters 'Island Palm Green', I did.

Now when I see green, it just reminds me of her death.

I sit next to the rain-splattered window, catching a glimpse of the dark circles marring my features in the reflection. The liquid in my mug burns, the heat tethering my mind to reality.

Barely.

I contemplate calling my doctor for another round of Prozac as memories crowd my brain again, threatening my mental blocks.

They call me a hero.

The sight outside my window is bleak—toxic trees and crumbling buildings in a grassless wasteland. Still, lights twinkle through the dreary fog that engulfs my city, a reminder of the living. Those houses hold parents and their children—children I helped protect from issue 564.

I barely remember life before the Malvada slashed open our sky, battering the clouds and reigning down bullets, terror, and poisonous gases. They brought with them death and months of chaos. What I do remember is watching the ships leave and longing for them to take my emptiness with them.

Hero. A preserver of humanity's future. But how can I be a hero when the one person I wanted to save didn't survive?

Some preservation. The sickly green haze hanging in the mist doesn't look like salvation to me.

The phone rings, startling me.

I want to ignore it, but I know if I don't answer, someone will come to make sure I'm still alive. I hate seeing people these days. "Hello?"

"Jarak?"

My heart lurches like a hummingbird beating its torn, fragile wings against my ribcage. I clear my throat. "Elora." A long, silent pause.

"How are you?" She sounds like she's been crying.

"Why are you calling me?" The words cut like razors as they come out of my mouth, but I must ask. I'm no good to her.

"The doctor says you aren't improving. Maybe it's time to come home?"

"It's true. I'm not."

When my doctors first suggested the Restoration and Rehabilitation Program, Elora resisted the idea. She thought I would do better at home. But I couldn't stand the sight of myself, let alone have her look at me, so I'd convinced her the relocation would help. Everything was kept private and out of the media, and the government was paying for my stay.

I knew all along it wouldn't change anything. I'm broken.

"Jarak, please come home. I spoke to the General. He said—"

"I can't. Not after what I've done."

"Love, you don't have to do this alone. I know you're hurting, but please come home to me. We can try to heal together."

"You can't fix this, hun." The term of endearment slips from my lips before I can catch it.

I lean heavily against the doorframe, my gaze shifting to the medals decorating the wall and then the distant lights through trailing raindrops on my windowpanes. Each light represents a child I helped save, but so many lights went out after the invasion, including the one light I most wanted to keep ablaze.

Linzi looked up to me and called me her hero long before my country burdened me with the title. She's the one who would always greet me at the door when I returned from duty. The one who called me Daddy...

I clench my fist, trying to contain my raging emotions. "Take care of yourself, Elora."

"Wait! Please, don't go yet!" Her desperation mirrors my own. I hesitate for a moment. When she speaks again, her voice is soft, dripping with need and pain. "I know you're hurting, but so am I. We lost Linzi that day, but I lost *both* of you... Please, come home. Please be *my* hero this time, Jarak."

The distant pattering of rain is the only sound between us.

She must realize I'm not going to answer. "I love you," Elora whispers, close to tears. "Remember that."

The click of the phone is one of the weightiest sounds I've ever heard.

I pick up my mug and raise it to my lips, the liquid cold.

They say we won because we survived. My superiors still herald proclamations of victory, saying that though the Malvada tried to take everything, we remain strong. They could not take our memories from us, or the will to live. Perhaps they're right, but sometimes I wish they had taken the memories.

I remember the cost of being a hero—the burn of gas on the back of my tongue despite the mask I wore as I manned the surface-to-air platform. The gas was bioengineered to target children, to take away humanity's hope. The taste was as bitter as my desperation, praying it hadn't reached my home.

Please be my *hero this time, Jarak.*

How could Elora say that after what happened?

I lost both of you.

Her words haunt me.

I try to shut out the green fog permeating my thoughts. What was it the doctor told me again? Focus on something else? Something calming? But all I can think of is green.

Gas.

Death.

As I close my eyes, trying to control my breathing, Linzi's face floods my vision. Her glowing smile. Her sparkling gaze, so open and hopeful.

Green! Her eyes were green. Beautiful and full of life, like her mother's. How had I forgotten?

I focus my thoughts like the doctor said and calm myself with memories of my daughter's green eyes. A tear slides past my defenses, breaking open the soul I thought died with my child.

She loved green...

The shutters!

I snatch up the phone and call the number burned into my brain.

“Hello?” This time I know Elora has been crying.

“Are the shutters on the house still green?”

“Y-yes. I was going to paint over them before you came home.”

I breathe a shallow sigh of relief. “I’ll…I’ll come home, but don’t paint over the shutters. Linzi loved those green shutters….”

UNTIL WE MEET AGAIN

ELAINE WELLS

Until we meet again,
I will look for you in everything,
for the parts of you that I loved the most,
I will search for your smile in every pair of lips,
for that color of blue in every eye,
for your laugh,
and your love of stones,
I will fall in love with your favorite things,
and read books that remind me of you,
you will have a piece of every poem I write,
like all the people I've missed in life,
all the great loves,
and you are one of them,
I can tell you now,
I will look for you,
but it will not be enough,
you are too well ingrained in me to be replaced so easily,
and I am sure I will never find another like you,
but I would like to,

it would make the goodbyes easier,
I suppose leaving was always supposed to be hard,
but your bridge is not burned,
the gate is always open,
walk across to me when it is time,
when you've chased your dreams and collected all of your stars,
find me in the garden,
I will give you a flower,
we will make dinner together,
and share a glass of wine.

WHATEVER THE COST

ANNE J. HILL

A *THORN TOWER* CHARACTER SKETCH:
ACKER KILM

WITH ONE LESS pinky finger and a guilty conscience, Acker Kilm wasn't sure how many days he'd spent in the infirmary before his wife and children were allowed to see him.

"Acker!" his wife, Rilla, said when she rushed through the door. She sat beside him on the bed and stroked his cheek.

Kilm felt some ache in his chest melt away. "You're here." He'd been knocked out after the nobleman he served was killed, and the king was keeping a sharp eye on Kilm. He'd lost one pinky in the interrogation, and if he didn't cooperate in the future, he'd lose much more.

He knew the assassins behind the job, the Red X. He partly regretted ever agreeing to help Boyer. It seemed to be a pattern that whoever Kilm worked for would wind up dead by Boyer's hands. But a ten-year-old threat on his family's life kept Kilm from betraying the assassins.

If he turned the assassins in, his family was doomed. But if he didn't, his family was still doomed, and he'd rather face the wrath of the king than the Red X.

Rilla smiled, running her fingers through his beard. "They wouldn't let us come sooner. How do you feel?"

"Like there are little dwarves hitting my head with hammers." Kilm wrapped his arms around Rilla, lightly squeezing her.

She kissed his bald head and mumbled, "Please heal him, Storyteller."

Kilm rubbed her arm. He didn't share her sentiments of there being a Storyteller god, but he'd given up arguing over it years ago and focused his prayers to the dragon-god, Belok.

"Papa?" his eldest daughter, Gen, placed her hand on his shoulder.

Kilm patted her small ten-year-old hand. "I'm all right, honey."

"Where's Mar?" Kilm asked his wife.

Rilla curled up on the bed and laid her head on his chest. Kilm ran his fingers through her brown hair. "He didn't want to come. He said you'd look scary." Rilla chuckled softly.

"Hmm, yes, horrifying."

Gen wiggled onto the chair. "Are you dying?"

Kilm couldn't help but laugh. "No, sweetheart. Just a bit sore. I'll be back to working in just a few days. I promise."

Gen nodded and leaned back in her seat.

Rilla grabbed Kilm's hand, eyeing the bandage over where his pinky used to be. "Acker..."

He winced. "They asked some questions I couldn't...wouldn't answer. I'm lucky they haven't hung me for it." He kept his voice down, glanced at Gen and gave her a smile. She didn't seem to be paying attention to their words, thank Belok above.

Rilla frowned. "Does it hurt much?"

"I'll live." Kilm traced circles on her back.

Rilla kissed his cheek. "Good."

"There's one more thing..." Kilm pulled her head closer and whispered in her ear, "The king threatened me. He knows I've been helping the Red X, and if I don't do whatever he says, he'll have you all killed. I want you to leave the city 'til this blows over." His heart ached. The last thing he wanted was his family away from him, but if that's what it took to keep them safe, so be it.

Rilla pulled back, sitting up. "No."

"Rilla, please. For the children, if not for me. I can't lose you."

She swallowed. "If they don't have us to threaten you with, then they'll just find something else as important."

Kilm smiled softly. "There isn't *anything* as important as you three."

"Where will we go?" Rilla's eyes watered.

He reached up and stroked her cheek, tears pooling onto his thumb. "To my uncle. Tell him I sent you."

"The elves won't welcome us, Kilm."

He slipped his hand behind her neck and gently squeezed reassuringly. "They will. Tell Mar I love him. You need to leave tonight before the gates close."

Rilla wiped her cheeks. "How long?"

"I don't know, honey. Until I can come get you. But I promise I will." He pulled her down and kissed her. Rilla's body shuddered as tears dripped onto Kilm's lips. He ran his injured hand down her back and sunk his other into her hair. If things went wrong, this could be the last time he kissed his wife, and the thought made him tremble. He mumbled against her lips, "I love you, no matter what."

Rilla cupped his cheeks between her hands and kissed him harder, muttering, "I love you, too." She pulled back, wiped her eyes, and stood. "Gen, give your papa a hug. We need to go."

Gen looked over from staring out the window, where two birds were squawking at each other. She jumped off the chair and threw herself on Kilm.

Kilm kissed her head. "I love you, sweetheart."

"I love you too, Papa. I was listening...."

He winced and smoothed out her hair. "I need you to be strong and brave like I taught you, yeah? Help your mama take care of Mar for me."

She nodded seriously. "I will. I have my sword. I'll keep them safe."

Kilm smiled and patted her cheek. "That's my girl. Now, go with your mama."

Gen squeezed him one more time before they left.

Kilm closed his eyes and prayed to Belok for his wife and children to remain safe, whatever the cost.

Kilm will appear in Anne J. Hill's debut novel, Thorn Tower

POST-IT NOTE

MEGAN DILL

THEY SAY ABSENCE makes the heart grow fonder, but I wish I never had to experience it myself.

My husband and I communicate in post-it notes and napkins, in texts and calls. Sometimes we have time for a goodbye kiss or a whispered, "I love you," on the way out the door. Maybe, if we're lucky, we'll see each other in passing.

Other days, we don't see each other at all. He's working. I'm home. He's home. I'm asleep. I'm working. He's asleep. Honestly, our dog probably sees us more than we see each other.

We knew this would happen if we got married. I thought I was prepared for it. But nothing really prepares you for the utter loneliness of it all.

With a yawn, I head downstairs into the kitchen for breakfast. Tucker, our golden retriever, runs in to sit beside his food dish. I can't tell what he wants more—food or my attention.

After grabbing a glass from the cabinet, I turn to open the fridge when I see it—a bright pink post-it note stuck to the door. Today's note.

"'How lucky I am to have something that makes saying goodbye so hard.' I'm sure you know where that quote is from. Have a great day, Quinn! I love you."

I smile. He's right; I know exactly where that quote is from. Winnie the Pooh is a wise little bear.

Two years of marriage, and he still writes these notes for me when he doesn't see me in the morning. He has no idea, but I have a box in our closet full of them. Each and every one.

On the really good days, our schedules line up. I work the standard 9-5, but Ian's schedule is a bit more complicated. As a police officer, he does shift work. Sometimes he works from 4 p.m. to midnight, and other times he works from 8 a.m. to 4 p.m.

Nothing beats coming home to find him waiting for me. Those days when he gets off at 4 p.m. are the happiest days in our marriage. We watch movies, eat dinner together, play video games, and walk Tucker together. We finally get the chance to talk and go on dates. And, on those days, I fall in love with him all over again.

It's easy to remember he loves me on those days. It's easy to love him on those days. It's a little harder when it's just me, Tucker, and the empty house.

Before I head out the door, I slip my note safely into the box in the closet. And on the way out, I stop to write one of my own.

Because I love him, even when he's gone. Because I love him, even when we don't talk. Because I love him, even when I only get to tell him through notes.

Because I love him.

I post my note above the ice dispenser on the freezer door. A tiny TARDIS sits in the left corner of the note, surrounded by the words:

"I will be forever grateful that, in all of space and time, your path crossed mine."

Some days it feels like the two of us are worlds apart, but these notes help close the distance between us, one post-it note at a time.

INTIMACY

DENICA MCCALL

The sun's glare plays between our fingers and the warmth draws us closer.
Face to face, you stare into my being,
And you know.

The birds rhyme and the trees sway as I realize I can feel the pulse in your wrist upon mine,
So my beat catches up to yours—your passion stronger, your eyes inviting,
Your chest telling me that it's okay to press near, because your heart is what you want me to hear
Above all.
What once mingled with the background noises all around me has become the main thing,
So I breathe, and when your whispers warm my ear, I inhale this sweet air
Until I understand that you have found me again.

I don't want to be anywhere else, and you hold me tighter until I believe it's true
That you've never left and you never will.
Here in this beauty, I am known, loved, and free, and I can dance in full confidence in the midst of the mystery.

O DAYSPRING

MARY AGNES RATELLE

December, 1945

SUSAN BENT OVER the warm stove, watching two fried eggs nestled in a halo of butter crackle in the pan in front of her. Behind her, the radio played a soaring hymn:

O come, O come Emmanuel
And ransom captive Israel
That mourns in lonely exile here,
Until the son of God appears
Rejoice! Rejoice, Emmanuel
Shall come to thee, O Israel

Susan flipped the eggs in time to the collective breaths of the choir and popped two pieces of bread into the toaster. As she took out two coffee cups from the cupboard, she felt two arms from behind hug around her waist. "Charlie!" Susan laughed. "What do you think you're doing?"

"Saying good morning," Charlie said, kissing her cheek through her frizzy curls.

Susan turned around, her waist still encircled in her husband's arms. She felt her cheeks become rosy as a smile bloomed across her face. She looked at his face and noticed the dark circles under his eyes. His skin was sallow and stretched across his high cheekbones like hide over a drum. Susan brushed his face with her hand, hoping to bring a little color to his cheek, and kissed the tip of his nose. "If you don't let me go..." She smiled. "...your breakfast is going to burn."

"I don't care." Charlie laughed.

"Then the stove is going to catch on fire," Susan said.

"Hm, I still don't care." He stifled a yawn.

"And then the apartment will catch fire."

"So what?"

"Then the fire department will have to come and hose everything down."

"All right, you win," Charlie laughed, releasing his wife from his grasp and giving her another kiss.

Susan's cheeks felt warm and rosy, and she turned back to her work. She prepared two plates of eggs and toast and placed them on the table. Charlie set a pot of coffee and a little pitcher of milk on the table before seating himself. She sat down kitty-corner from her husband, and the two said grace. Soon, the prayer was over, and together, they began eating their breakfast.

Susan sipped her coffee and glanced at her husband, "How did you sleep last night?"

"It wasn't my worst night's sleep," he said. "I slept mostly through the night."

"You haven't been tossing and turning quite as much lately." Susan grinned. "It sounds like talking with Fr. Muldoon has helped."

Charlie rubbed his eyes. "I hope so."

She grasped Charlie's hand and kissed it. "You're stronger than you think, Charlie."

Half of Charlie's mouth curled into a weak smile. "Maybe," he said. "I can only hope."

After breakfast, Charlie prepared to leave for his job at the post office. Susan watched him as he put on his coat and wide brimmed hat. She tied his scarf around his neck and patted the lapels of his coat with approval. Once he was bundled up, Charlie kissed Susan one last time and left. As the door shut, Susan began cleaning the breakfast dishes. In an instant, the telephone beside the living room sofa rang.

"Hello?" Susan said, picking up the phone. "Susan Carpenter speaking."

"Hello, Mrs. Carpenter!" chimed a voice. "This is Dr. Farrow. I'm calling about our appointment the other day."

Susan sat down, gripping the receiver. "And?" she asked.

"Mrs. Carpenter," Dr. Farrow said. "Congratulations! You're expecting!"

Susan sprang up, the blood rushing to her feet. She twirled on the tips of her toes until the cord of the telephone wrapped around her legs. "Expecting a baby? A real live baby?"

Dr. Farrow chuckled. "Yes, I'll need you to come to my office again soon so we can examine you thoroughly, but it can wait until after Christmas."

"Yes, that sounds perfect!" Susan said, trying to catch her breath. "Oh, thank you, Dr. Farrow. Thank you!"

Susan hung up the telephone. The living room was quiet, except for the soft honking and buzzing of traffic outside. She sat down and wrapped her arms around her stomach. She closed her eyes. Susan felt as if her body were going to overflow and spill out of her grasp. It was like she was holding someone that wasn't her, as if her body had transcended her in the way that the stars were transcendent. Her body wasn't just hers anymore; it was a place of shelter for another vulnerable creature. She thought of Charlie, a small doubt creeping into her mind. She pushed the thought out and tightened her grip around her waist, the soft wool of her sweater caressing her palms. Susan took a heavy breath, "Maybe this can change things," she said to herself. "Maybe."

Evening approached, and with the darkening sky came a wind like stabbing icicles. Charlie slowly tramped his way up the hill towards home, hugging his scarf close to his neck. Soon he approached the path leading up to a stately church only a few blocks away from his apartment. The sound of the church choir practicing for Christmas Mass echoed off the walls and reached his ears as Charlie opened the door and stepped inside. Quietly, he found a pew and fell onto his knees in prayer. From overhead in the choir loft, a chorus of voices softly sang a hymn:

O come, Thou Rod of Jesse, free
Thine own from Satan's tyranny

From depths of Hell, Thy people save
And give them victory o'er the grave
Rejoice, rejoice, Emmanuel
Shall come to thee, O Israel

Charlie lifted his eyes to the large cross that stood on the altar, studying the nailed hands that were lifted above Jesus' head. Charlie heard footsteps approach and the pew creak beside him. He turned his head and saw a priest sit down next to him.

"Fr. Muldoon," Charlie whispered. "Good evening."

"Good evening," the priest replied. "How are you?"

"Fine." Charlie faltered, seating himself back on the pew. "...Fine."

"That's good. I'm glad that you've been visiting here more often."

Charlie nodded. "It helps. It's quiet here."

The two were silent for a minute. "Do they ever go away?" Charlie asked abruptly. "The faces, I mean. Will their faces ever go away?"

"You want to forget them?" the priest asked.

"Yes," Charlie said, "but I can't stop thinking about them. No matter what I do, they always come back—Sam, Michael, Jerry, Frank—all of them. It's like I don't want to forget them."

"I don't think you're meant to. They were your friends."

"But I wish I could."

"Why?"

"Because it would take all this pain away," Charlie said. "Sometimes I think they're demons. Maybe I'm possessed by some evil that I just can't shake."

"You aren't possessed. You're grieving."

"But it's more than grief." Charlie trembled, an edge of desperation lacing his words. "It follows me everywhere I go, cutting through my very soul and telling me things I wish I couldn't hear."

"What's it telling you?"

Charlie was quiet. The words hurt too much to speak, as if a line of barbed wire were wrapped around his tongue. He took a breath, "That I can't forget because I deserve this," Charlie murmured, his voice sounding like lead. "Maybe they are demons after all."

"Charlie..." Fr. Muldoon began, but Charlie kneeled back down and pressed his face into his hands. "You're in a time of darkness now," the priest continued, "but darkness doesn't have the last word. You have to believe that."

Charlie lifted his face from his hands. "But what if I can't?" he whispered.

"Then you have to try," the priest replied softly. "What's the point otherwise?"

Charlie didn't respond. He cupped his chin in his folded hands, his brows drawing deep lines across his forehead. Fr. Muldoon stood up and glanced at Charlie once more. Charlie knelt like a stone, not moving a single eyelash in the priest's direction. Fr. Muldoon walked back down the aisle.

Evening came, and Susan still hadn't told Charlie the news. When he returned home, Susan could see the exhaustion on Charlie's face. With Christmas getting closer, the post office was busier than ever, and Charlie came home even more exhausted than he was that morning. It wasn't the time to tell him. It was a cold night, and Susan and Charlie nestled into bed early. Before long, the two were asleep. The night crawled on, and the hands of their alarm clock inched minute by minute around the clock face. As midnight approached, Susan felt the covers pull more tightly around her shoulders, and she heard whimpering sounds beside her. Fighting the sleepy film over her eyes, she turned on her side in the direction of the sound. From Charlie's side of the bed, she heard her husband's stifled groans try to burst through his lips.

Susan put her hands on Charlie's shoulders. "Charlie. Charlie, wake up!"

Charlie's eyes were screwed shut, and the muscles of his arms tightened as he clutched the edge of the mattress. His brow was dripping with sweat. She knelt beside him and smoothed her hand over his shoulder. "Charlie, wake up! Wake up!" she shouted again.

Charlie dug his fingers into the mattress even more deeply, and his arm shook like a piston, the mattress shaking with him. At last, a loud guttural cry released from his lips, piercing through the stillness of the winter night. He jolted himself awake, his eyes darting from one side of the room to the other. Susan took Charlie's hand. It was slick with cold sweat and trembled like a leaf in the wind. "Charlie," Susan whispered. "You're safe. It was only a dream."

Charlie looked in Susan's direction. His eyes seemed to see through her, as if he were peering into some invisible world that only he could perceive. Slowly, his eyes refocused on Susan's face as she bent over him. He squeezed her hand until it turned white, then buried his head into her shoulder. Susan stroked his thick hair with her free hand. "I'm here," she soothed.

Charlie wrapped his arms around his wife and sobbed. "I can't. I can't live like this."

"Don't say that. You're going to get better."

"No," Charlie said. "I've tried. You know I've tried, but the dreams always come back."

"But you've been doing so much better lately," Susan said.

Charlie shook his head. "I think I deserve this. God is punishing me for what I've done."

"That's not true," Susan insisted. "It isn't your fault. You couldn't have saved them; no one could."

"It doesn't matter. Those men who were in the Hellcat with me were relying on me, and I... I..." Charlie's voice broke off, and he buried his face in his hands.

Susan touched Charlie's shoulder. "You're only one man, Charlie."

Charlie lifted his head. He directed his eyes to the window where the curtain gaped open, revealing a little sliver of the world outside. A beam from a streetlight poked through the curtains and fell on Susan's face. Charlie glanced at her, studying her features as if he were looking at her for the first time. He reached to touch Susan's face, but he froze, dropping his hand in his lap. "I wish you never married me," he murmured.

A stabbing pain pierced Susan's chest. "What are you saying? Don't we love each other? Don't you love me?"

"Of course I love you. I love you more than I can say. That's why I wish you never married me."

"Stop talking like that!" her voice became shrill.

"It's just that you deserve better than this," Charlie said. "You deserve better than *me*."

"You don't know what you're saying," Susan replied with desperation. "You're tired and upset. You'll get better, and we'll have the life we've always dreamed of, with a house and children and everything."

Charlie went limp and slid back down on his pillow. "I can't even think about that now. I can't think about a house and children. It's all too much."

Susan didn't know what to say; her own heart hurt too much to say anything more.

Charlie turned back on his side. "I'm sorry, Susan."

Wordlessly, Susan slipped back under the covers on her side of the bed. She stared at the ceiling, her mind blank and exhausted. Outside, the sharp wind blew across the sky and pushed against the windowpane, causing it to crackle under the force. She pulled the covers to her chin as if they could shield her from the world. After a moment, Charlie's voice broke through the silence. "I guess it's a blessing that we don't have children," he mused, half to himself. "I don't even know if I can take care of myself, let alone children."

Susan's stomach quivered.

After several long hours, the sun finally rose on Sunday morning. As soon as the light peered through the gap in the curtain, Susan rose from bed. Her eyes were droopy and raw, and her head felt heavy—she had barely slept for the rest of the night. Quietly, she dressed. She rubbed on some makeup, hoping to cover the puffy, purple circles under her eyes. As she bent over the bathroom sink, she heard Charlie get up. He walked into the bathroom, his jaw clenched and skeletal—the life drained from his face. Susan pushed her feelings down into her stomach and flashed him a smile. Half of Charlie's mouth feebly smiled back.

Soon, Charlie and Susan were dressed, and the two went to Mass. They sat in one of the pews in the back of the small church. On the altar Fr. Muldoon turned his back and chanted, "Kyrie Eleison."

Susan gripped her folded hands together and closed her eyes. Her chest felt stuffed, as if it were going to crack open from the sheer, steady force of her grief. She peered at her husband from the corner of her eye, his arms folded over the back of the pew in front of him and his face pressed into the crook of his elbow. As Susan looked at him, her heart winched and curdled like sour milk. She didn't know what to think or what to feel. She bowed her head down again and tried to pray. She didn't even know what she was praying for exactly, but she had to try. She pulled her veil close. "Please, God," Susan pleaded. "Please, deliver us."

When Mass was over, Susan and Charlie filed out of the pew wordlessly. Charlie reached out his hand to lightly touch Susan on the back, guiding her towards the back of the church, but she swayed to the side and dodged his touch. Charlie balled up his fist and put it in his coat pocket. As they made their way to the door, a voice called out, "Susan! Susan Carpenter!"

Susan turned her head and saw an elderly woman walking in her direction, arm-in-arm with a white-haired man. Susan's stomach twisted into a knot.

"Dr. Farrow. Mrs. Farrow!" she called back. "Merry Christmas! How nice it is to see you."

"And a merry Christmas it is, indeed," Mrs. Farrow said, giving Susan a wink. "How are you feeling?"

"Fine," Susan said quickly, flickering a glance at her husband. He wore a forced smile and his tired eyes darted between the old couple and the door. "And how about you?"

"Oh, I can't complain," Mrs. Farrow said. "How could I when there's such wonderful news?"

Susan's chest tightened. "Oh, yes," she said. "It is such wonderful news...that Charlie and I are going to spend our first Christmas together as husband and wife."

"It must be much nicer to have Christmas in your own cozy home," Dr. Farrow remarked, "than on an army base, isn't it, Charlie? Life must be a dream now."

Charlie pulled his lips into a line and nodded stiffly.

"Susan," Mrs. Farrow bubbled, "you must be so proud. Your husband is an American hero. Where would our country be without men like him?"

Charlie's face tightened. "Men like me?" he said in a low voice. "The only American heroes that I knew are those who died before they had the chance to fail anyone."

Susan cast a wary glance at her husband.

"Surely it's not as black and white as all that," Dr. Farrow said. "That's far too bleak a perspective."

"Whether we like it or not," Charlie said, "we live in bleak times."

Outside the church, Susan and Charlie were finally alone. As they walked down the sidewalk back to their apartment, light snow dusted the pavement and accompanied the scuffing sound of Susan's shoes against the concrete.

"What was that?" Susan heaved. "The Farrows are such lovely people. Why did you have to say that?"

"The Farrows have no idea what they're talking about. Where do they get off with all this 'American hero' stuff?"

"They're just two nice people who want to pass on some encouragement," Susan said. "You're taking it too far."

"Taking it too far?" Charlie scoffed. "I can barely sleep at night because I constantly see the faces of the men I failed. I don't think taking something too far is my biggest problem."

"You didn't fail them."

"Of course I did! They wouldn't have died if it weren't for me."

"That's not true, and you know that."

"Don't tell me what I know!" Charlie's cheeks were red from the cold. "Those men will never see their families again because of me. If that isn't failure, I don't know what is!"

Susan inched closer to Charlie. She didn't know what to say.

"I'm going to fail you, too, Susan," Charlie continued. "I already have."

"You haven't failed me. You didn't fail to survive. You came back, and that means you can start new."

"Oh, it's so simple when you put it like that." Charlie looked up at that gray sky. "But how can I start new when I'm haunted by all that's happened?"

Susan's eyes glanced behind her husband. A few feet away, she saw Fr. Muldoon exit the side door of the church, his long, black cassock brushing against the frozen pavement. He saw Susan and Charlie and waved at them. Susan waved back politely.

"Susan," Charlie said in a quieter voice, "what kind of life is this? How can we forget all that's happened and have that life with a house and children? We can't have that life. I couldn't bear it."

Susan felt the bile in her stomach churn. "Is that what it's all about?" Susan said in a harsh whisper. "Is it just about what *you* can bear? What about what *I* can bear—what I *have* to bear?"

"What do you mean?" Charlie asked.

Susan clenched her jaw. "It doesn't matter," she snapped. "What I think—what I say—doesn't matter anymore."

"Susan, that's ridiculous. You know that's not true," Charlie said.

"Now it's my turn," Susan argued. "Don't you *dare* tell me what I know. You don't know a thing about what it's like to be me."

Charlie was silent. Susan's eyes wandered to Fr. Muldoon again. He was standing on the pavement, looking in their direction. Susan put on a fake smile and looked away.

Susan and Charlie returned to their apartment in silence. When they arrived, Susan set to work making the two of them breakfast. She cracked two eggs, busting the shells against the ridged edge of the pan, and set them to fry in a molten puddle of butter. The eggs hissed as they cooked, and musty steam rose from the pan. She took two pieces of roughly cut bread and left them to burn in their little cells in the toaster. As she flipped over the eggs, Charlie wrapped his arms around her waist. Susan felt his chin digging into her shoulder and his face pressed her itchy curls against her cheek. The grasp of his arms closed over her stomach like a vise, until Susan could scarcely move. She felt a stabbing pain in her stomach. She could almost swear she could feel the baby in her womb struggling to be freed from his grip. Susan gasped for a breath and pushed at her husband's arms.

"I have to finish breakfast," she said shortly.

Charlie pulled away. He leaned in to kiss her cheek, but Susan pretended not to notice and dodged it by reaching up and getting two coffee cups from the cupboard. Charlie took the cups away from Susan and placed them on the table, along with the pot of coffee. When she finished the eggs and toast, she served them on two plates and sat across from him. Charlie reached for Susan's hand, but she didn't reach back. After saying grace, Charlie looked up at his wife.

"What's wrong, Susan?"

"Nothing," she said.

Charlie eyed her carefully. "Are you sure?"

She scraped a thin layer of butter onto her toast and sprinkled it with a little salt. "I'm sure."

"Dear, please talk to me," Charlie coaxed.

She held her breath to keep herself from crying. "I don't want to talk about it, Charlie. Please leave me alone."

"But, Susan..."

"I said I don't want to talk about it. I don't want to talk about anything."

Charlie looked at his plate. "Yes, dear."

The two were silent for the rest of the day.

The next day was Christmas Eve, and Charlie left the house early to finish some Christmas shopping. He tramped down the bustling street, his mind filled with distressing thoughts tangled together like wire. He cursed himself over and over, as if that would give him relief. A brisk wind tore down the street, and Charlie ducked into a nearby bookshop. The smell of new pages and orange pomanders met his nose as he walked in. Distractedly, Charlie browsed the shelves. He still hadn't bought a gift for Susan. His eyes landed on the window display, which housed a small créche. Jesus was nestled in the manger, swaddled in a pure white blanket while Mary and Joseph bent over him with their hands folded in prayer. A Christmas tree stood near the créche and stretched its branches across the rest of the windowsill. One branch reached over the créche, dangling a wooden ornament above the heads of Mary and Joseph. It was a crudely made decoration—a piece of wood with the word "Rejoice" painted across it in childlike letters.

Rejoice.

What was there to rejoice over? A broken man, a ruined life?

Charlie looked at the créche again, resting his gaze on Joseph. There was something about him that was particularly lifelike. His clothes were threadbare, and his hands stained by years of hard labor. He was weatherworn, ordinary. *And this man held the Christ child?* Charlie thought. *Impossible… And yet…*

For the first time that day, Charlie's mind was quiet. A voice entered his heart, one he scarcely recognized as his own.

Emmanuel shall come to thee.

Charlie was still. *The Christ child will come…a child. A child will come!* Another thought flashed through his mind. It was soft at first, but slowly it grew, like the sun rising over a mountaintop. He couldn't put the thought into words, but soon another word came to his lips. "Susan...Susan."

Susan was alone in the apartment. She busied herself with decorating the house, hanging homemade holly garlands over the doorways and changing their white tablecloth for a red one with ivy embroidered on the edges. She plunged her mind into her work and barely stopped to take a breath. She knew that if she stopped, she would start crying. Susan refused to cry.

In the back of her mind, her thoughts lingered on her phone call with Dr. Farrow. The joy she felt that day seemed like a joke now. The baby was coming, and there was nothing Susan could do to change that. It was part of her in a way that nothing else in the world had ever been. She couldn't deny her child any more than she could deny herself. Susan dusted off the bookshelf and placed a gold-plated candelabra beside the wedding photo that sat on the top shelf. She had written the date in the bottom corner of the photo in blue ink. April 22rd, 1944. That day felt so long ago when Fr. Muldoon joined them in marriage mere days before Charlie was sent overseas. On that day, Susan was forever bound to Charlie and everything that he would become. At that moment, an idea came to her mind. She went to the telephone and quickly dialed a number. The telephone buzzed beneath her ear.

"Hello," Susan said. "Fr. Muldoon? This is Susan Carpenter."

"Hello!" said Fr. Muldoon. "How are you this fine Christmas Eve?"

"I'm sorry to bother you, Father," Susan said. "Particularly on a day like today."

"It isn't a bother," the priest said.

Susan gasped for a breath. "Father, I need your help. I have to tell somebody."

Susan told the priest everything. For the first time, Susan let herself cry, allowing all the feelings she had stuffed deep into her chest loosen and pour out of her. The priest listened, interjecting a quiet, "I see," or "oh, dear," between Susan's thoughts.

"Father, I don't know what to do," Susan said, finishing her story. "I can't leave Charlie, but I can't leave our child either. I feel trapped. I feel like..."

"Like there's no room for you and your child at the inn?" Fr. Muldoon said.

"Yes, that's exactly it," she said. "I thought that maybe if you told Charlie, he would listen to you."

"I want to help however I can, but this is between you and Charlie. There's nothing I can say that you can't say to him yourself. Charlie isn't against having a family. He's just afraid."

"I know that he's afraid," Susan said. "But what can I do?"

"Tell him the truth. You can't banish the darkness without exposing it to the light."

"But what if he's too afraid?"

"Then you have to hope. There was no shelter for the Blessed Mother to have the Christ child, but she hoped, and God did the rest."

"And God will do the rest for me?"

"Yes," the priest said. "God will provide for you. There's a shelter for you and your child."

Susan said goodbye to the priest and hung up the phone. She began putting strings of blood-red cranberries on their Christmas tree, thinking through what she was going to say to Charlie. She snapped on the radio, and in a moment, the apartment was filled with soft music. A moment later, the front door flew open. Charlie stood in the foyer, out of breath and covered in snow. His eyes were fixed on his wife, as if he could see into her very soul.

"Susan," Charlie gasped, "The child... The child!"

Susan locked eyes with her husband for an enduring moment. "You know, don't you?" she said at last, her voice breaking.

Charlie nodded, panting.

Susan fell on the sofa, her eyes filling with tears. Charlie sat beside her and wrapped his arm around her shoulders.

"I know you don't want this," Susan cried. "But our child is coming anyway."

Charlie's eyes were shiny, and his cheeks were flushed. He opened his mouth, then closed it again. "Our child?" he whispered.

Susan pressed her face into her hands until they became wet and salty from her tears. Charlie lifted Susan's chin and looked into her gleaming eyes. "Why didn't you tell me?" he asked.

Susan grasped her husband's hand and pressed it to her cheek. "Because you were scared." She sniffed. "I'm scared too, but there's nothing we can do now."

Charlie sat quietly for a moment. "Maybe..." he said, faltering. "Maybe..."

"Maybe," Susan interjected, "there is hope—for all of us."

Charlie gazed at his wife, his eyes soft. He kissed her and wrapped his arms around her waist. Susan nestled in his arms and placed her head on his shoulder. They rested.

In the corner, the radio continued to play, filling the living room with music like sunlight streaming through an open window. The singing of a choir emanated from the speakers, surrounding the two with their voices:

O come, Thou Dayspring,
Come and cheer our spirits by Thine advent here
Disperse the gloomy clouds of night,
And death's dark shadows put to flight
Rejoice! Rejoice! Emmanuel
Shall come to thee, O Israel

THROUGH THE NEGATIVES

AUDRAKATE GONZALEZ

I SAT OUTSIDE the bathroom door just waiting. Farrah had been in there for the past ten minutes. I was in no rush to interrupt her. My nerves were a jumbled mess and I think I needed all the time I could get to pull myself together.

It had been two years of trying. Test after test and disappointment after disappointment. It never got easier. After so many negative results, we had continually grown further apart rather than closer together. And then when the third doctor said it was a problem on my end, I thought Farrah would leave me for good.

I wasn't able to give her the one thing in life she's always dreamed of having. We weren't able to have kids, and she may never be a mother. But there was a light shining on our side, because the fourth doctor was giving us a chance. She had said it may not be impossible and that we might be great candidates for IUI. So, we spent the money. We would spend as much money as it would take. And, seeing as how this was our fifth attempt at IUI, we had spent all the money. There was nothing left in our account for us to continue this journey. If it didn't work this time, I wasn't sure what our next steps would be.

So, I sat and waited. I waited until I heard the small whimpers from inside the bathroom, and then I took action. I wasn't going to let her face another negative result alone. I opened the bathroom door and looked at the tear-stained face of my wife sitting on the floor. My heart sank.

"Farrah–I–"

"It's positive. Rich, we're going to be parents!" And then my own tears fell from my eyes.

CHASM

EMILY BARNETT

A chasm lay between us.

The cruel sea
crashing over ships,
dragging them down.
A barren wasteland
that hasn't seen rain
in years.

We teeter on the edge,
calling across the
Wilderness,
wild in our hopes
and dreams.

But the forest is dense.
The fog, too heavy.
The rain would undo us.
Our journey, too far.

A chasm lay between us.

But you endure the trail
through endless plains,
lighting grasses and
expectations on fire.
You scale the mountain
I stand in the shadow of.

You set
your coffee down
and reach across
the table.
The palm of your hand
like a crescent moon—
a sliver in the dark.

Taking your hand
costs me something.

But gives me more.

Your fingers are cold
as if they've forgotten
my touch.
But the chasm closes.
I know the warmth
will return
soon.

A POST-APOCALYPTIC ROMANCE

CRYSTAL BAILEY

LONG-TERM RELATIONSHIPS can be really challenging, especially after the apocalypse. First of all, your significant other can die at any given moment. If it's not by one of the rabid, zombie-like diseased people we call Morphs, then it's starvation or the elements—take your pick.

But Zhan and I have managed to defy the odds. We've been together for over two years now and couldn't be more in love. We first met in the woods one dark and misty night, both of us stalking the same Morph. We needed to eliminate it because it had been spotted near our colonies. Turns out, Zhan's colony wasn't too far from mine. Long story short, we ended up trading weapon-cleaning tips over the body of the freshly-deceased Morph we'd taken out in a team effort.

We've been together ever since.

Our two colonies ended up merging, thanks to us, and now we both lead an elite team that specializes in Morph hunting. Zhan leads the team, with me as his second in command. There are eight others besides us. This time, we need all hands on deck because a large group of Morphs were reported in the area earlier this morning.

So now all ten of us creep through the woods, weapons and eyes sharp and ready for any sign of the Morphs.

"Lily, over there," Zhan whispers to me, so close it tickles my ear. He points to our right.

I squint, and I see it—something blue moving behind the trunk of a large tree up ahead. I nod at Zhan to let him know I've spotted it, then hold my arm up and give a silent signal to the rest of the team to stop. They hang back, waiting impatiently while Zhan and I check it out.

The two of us move with such stealth that when we jump on either side of the tree, crossbows aimed at whatever is hiding behind it, we can tell the man never knew we were coming.

He jumps, screams, then cowers. "Please, I'm not a Morph! Don't hurt me!" he pleads.

I look at Zhan, and he gives the okay to lower our weapons. This guy is no Morph.

"Get up," I say to the man. "We won't hurt you."

He uncovers his face and stands. When he does, the shock leaves me momentarily speechless.

"Steve?" I ask in disbelief as soon as I can find my voice.

He narrows his deep brown eyes as he scrutinizes me. Then his face brightens with recognition. "Lily? Is it really you?" He looks me over, head to toe, drinking me in. No doubt I now look very different from the girl he remembers. That girl would've never been able to survive in this new world, so she had to go.

I nod in affirmation. He steps toward me and embraces me, squeezing me in the most uncomfortably tight hug I've ever had. Zhan raises his weapon, but I wave him off.

When the hug finally ends, Steve looks me in the eye and says, "Lily, you have no idea how much I've missed you. I can't believe you're alive." He leans in to kiss me.

I shove Steve away from me, panicking over what Zhan might do to Steve if he followed through with the kiss. Steve trips over a tree root and falls backward. When he stands, embarrassment and confusion are written all over his face. "Hey, what was that for? Can't I kiss my long-lost girlfriend?" He brushes off the back of his pants.

Zhan's eyes go wide at the word *girlfriend.* "What? Really?" he asks, shooting a look of disbelief my way. I'm not sure if it's due to the fact that it's so rare to run into anyone from your pre-apocalypse past, or because he doesn't picture Steve as being someone I would've ever been interested in. Steve and Zhan couldn't be more different from one another.

I look at Steve and set him straight. "We haven't seen each other in three years, Steve. I'm with Zhan now."

Steve looks up at Zhan, a muscular guy two years older and probably a foot taller than him—currently giving him the stink-eye—and gulps.

"What are you doing out here alone?" I ask.

"I got separated from my group two days ago. Been trying to find them ever since."

Just then, loud rustling noises come from several different directions all at once, accompanied by vicious snarling.

"Is that what I think it is?" Steve asks, looking around nervously and whipping out a butter knife from his jacket pocket.

"If you think it's a large group of Morphs that have surrounded us and are now coming in for the kill, then yeah," I say. I frown at Steve's odd choice of weapon. "Are you serious? A butter knife?"

"This is the only thing my group would let me have. They took all of the good weapons," Steve says, looking embarrassed.

"That sucks. You better stick close to us then," says Zhan. I smile at him. Though this running into Steve situation is more than a bit awkward, Zhan is a protector to the core. I know that he would give his life, without hesitation, if it meant saving any one of us.

That now includes Steve.

Steve nods in agreement and moves closer to me.

One of our overeager team members, Jace, yells at the trees, "What are you half-deads waiting for? Bring it on!" He brandishes his customized spiked mallet and cracks his neck, a small smile playing on his lips. Jace isn't very stable, but he's one of our best Morph fighters.

I point my crossbow at the trees in the direction of the nearest sound, but then it goes quiet. Everything goes quiet. We all wait, tense and anxious for whatever comes next.

Several Morphs take us by surprise, launching themselves out of the top of the trees.

One lands on Zhan's back. I aim my crossbow and let it fly. Direct hit. The morph twitches, then falls to the ground, motionless. Zhan rushes over and gives me a quick kiss, then says, "Another flawless Morph kill, Lily. You never disappoint." He aims his crossbow behind me and fires. He frowns and immediately fires off a second shot, which is accompanied by a loud yelp. I spin around; another Morph is down. We both turn and witness complete chaos as our team and the rest of the Morphs battle.

"I better stay here and protect Steve," I say to Zhan. "You go on ahead."

Zhan nods at me and rushes off to join the melee. I'm jealous. It looks epic. But I'm stuck here babysitting my ex-boyfriend.

Within minutes all of the Morphs have successfully been eliminated, with only three of us injured. Jace looks pretty banged up, but the other two only bear some gashes and scratches.

"Steve, if you want, you can come back with us," I say. "It's almost sundown, and, to be honest, I doubt you'll survive the night if you don't. There's just too much Morph activity around here lately." I may not want to be with Steve anymore, but I still care about him, and I certainly don't want him becoming a Morph meal by dawn.

"No argument here. I'm coming with you." Steve is clearly grateful for the invitation.

As we're walking back, Zhan leaves my side to go check on Jace, who is lagging behind us and in a lot of pain, though he's trying to hide it. Steve seems to welcome Zhan's momentary absence and utilizes the small window of opportunity in order to have a private conversation with me. "Are you sure you'd rather be with him?" Steve whispers to me so Zhan won't hear. "I mean, we were in love. And what about prom? We went together, and you said it was the best, most magical day of your life. Just because the Morph apocalypse happened the next day doesn't mean we can't still be together now that we've finally found each other."

Before I can answer him, two Morphs that must have escaped earlier jump out of the trees, landing between me, Steve, and Zhan. Zhan and I both grab our crossbows, aim, and fire at the exact same time—him killing the Morph on the right, and me, the one on the left.

I arch my eyebrow and turn to Steve. "What can I say? The couple that slays together, stays together."

MUD PRINTS

KRISTEN BAZEN

TODAY WAS JULIA'S twenty-eighth birthday, and her husband hadn't remembered yet. No chocolate, no flowers, no diamonds. Not even a kiss. The only gift she had received so far was a trail of mud prints left by his work boots.

Wyatt stood at the kitchen sink, oblivious as usual, washing up for a late lunch. Julia held a mop in one hand and a bucket of dirty suds in the other, trying to remember why she had married him.

"I just washed the floor," she said, her voice flat. Her husband didn't seem to hear her through the running water and the soap scrubbing. Wyatt could always tune out words he didn't think were necessary.

"Wyatt!"

Wyatt turned off the water and reached for a towel. "Did you say something?"

Julia gestured sharply to the mud prints that made a trail from the front door to the kitchen sink. "Why can't you be more considerate? I have enough to do around the house without having to do it twice." She held up her dripping mop to underscore her words.

Wyatt regarded the trail he had left. "One of the horses is limping," he said as if somehow that excused him. "I'll have to call the vet. It looks like an abscess."

"And Elijah's been sick for three days!" Julia snapped. "You're not the only busy one. It takes five seconds to remove your boots and twenty minutes to rewash the floor."

Soft footsteps approached from the playroom, and Benjamin leaned his blond head around the corner. Wyatt laid out four pieces of sourdough and began to butter them. The trail of mud prints grew longer and more convoluted as her husband visited the fridge and then the cupboard.

Was it too much to expect an apology? If Julia hadn't been holding a mop and bucket, she would have put her hands on her hips. "Are you going to ignore me, then?" Under her breath, she muttered, "It's what you do best, anyway."

Wyatt arranged thick slices of ham and pickles on his sandwiches, picked up the bottle of mustard, and met her thorny gaze. "Everything I say just makes you angrier," he said, his tone heated now. "We live on a ranch. Is a little bit of mud really that big of a deal?"

Four years of mud and manure tracked in from the pasture, the paddock, the barn—yes, that was a big deal. "It's not just once, Wyatt." Julia let her bucket slam down, and bubbles sloshed over the rim. "You muddy my floors every single day you come in for lunch. And I'm sick of it!"

Benjamin retreated to the playroom.

With his whiskered lips pressed into a thin line, Wyatt gathered his ham and pickle sandwiches and stalked out the back door, heading for the barn. Apparently, he thought the horses were better company than she was. Maybe they were.

As soon as Julia picked up the bucket, intending to rewash the wood floor, Elijah started crying. Her shoulders drooped. For a moment, she stood in the middle of the kitchen, staring at nothing, feeling the weight of her heart and unmet expectations. Was this really about the mud? And had she always been this irritable? But he was so impossible.

Married life with Wyatt had begun with roses and dreams, and now it consisted of diapers and arguments. They had built their ranch in a beautiful valley under the wide Wyoming sky, living their mutual dream of raising and training Quarter horses. But now, with an infant and a toddler, Julia didn't have time to work with the horses as much as she used to.

Having her husband home all day and sharing all three meals together had once been a highlight of owning a ranch. Long workdays couldn't keep him from her and the boys, and she had considered herself a privileged woman. Now, she only saw the mud prints.

Elijah's cries increased in volume, and Julia set down the mop and bucket. Forget the floor. It would have to stay muddy. Wyatt would track in more dirt anyway when he came in for dinner. Her stomach groaned, reminding her that she hadn't eaten lunch yet. Well, she would have to wait another half hour because Elijah needed his bottle first.

In the gray recliner in her bedroom, Julia cradled her son and listened to his soft grunts and sucking noises. His forehead didn't feel as hot, so maybe the fever had finally broken. Little Benjamin poked his blond head through the door and came to her, his pudgy fingers gripping her knees with toddler strength, trying to pull himself into her lap. Of course. It was always when she was feeding his brother that Benny wanted to be held.

"In a minute, Benny," Julia said, bridling a sigh.

From the window flanking her shoulder, she saw Wyatt at the edge of the pasture, forking hay into the feeding trough with a vengeance. She wanted to stay mad, to stew in her frustration, to justify her anger. Her husband didn't know how to apologize, never remembered her birthday or their anniversary, threw his laundry next to the wash basket, left his boots under the kitchen table, and of course, tracked never-ending mud through the kitchen, playroom, and bedroom.

After Elijah had emptied his bottle, Julia burped him and laid her little one on her chest over her heavy heart. Her eyes welled with tears suddenly. When had she started seeing only the negative qualities in her husband? What if she tried to remember why she had said "I do" to the quiet and steady rancher?

Through a veil of tears, Julia watched Wyatt stab his pitchfork into the grass and mop his forehead with the sleeve of his plaid shirt. He rested his arms on the fence for a moment, and Julia remembered somewhat grudgingly that her husband worked just as hard as she did, though their tasks were different. He had always been a hard worker, never complaining about the dirtier jobs or less exciting aspects of running a ranch.

A palomino Quarter horse approached the fence and nuzzled Wyatt's shoulder. Wyatt stroked the smooth neck with strong, gentle hands. Kind hands. Hands that had never been used in anger to hurt someone but always to protect her and the boys. With painful tardiness, Julia realized the only times Wyatt got angry were after she accused or belittled him.

No, her husband wasn't perfect, but then again, she wasn't either. Julia ran her hand over Elijah's fuzzy head, thinking. For all the moments she had let bitterness fester as she waited in vain for Wyatt's apology, had she ever apologized for her own harsh words? Almost frantically, she sorted through her memories but couldn't recall a single instance.

What might change if she let go of her pride and chose to apologize? Wyatt still leaned against the fence, absently playing with the palomino's mane. If ever there was a perfect opportunity, it was now.

She hadn't done laundry yet this week, and all she wanted was lunch and a nap, but Julia rose from the recliner and swallowed her ego. It went down like tar, but it stayed down. Moving Elijah to her hip, she held out her hand to Benjamin.

"Come on, Benny. We're going to see Daddy."

Wyatt heard Benjamin's chatter as they approached the pasture, and her husband turned. He met her gaze with a tired, guarded look as if preparing to defend himself. It made Julia's heart ache. She let go of Benny's hand, and he ran to the fence to touch the satin muzzle of the palomino.

With Elijah still perched on her hip, Julia stopped in front of Wyatt, struggling to find words to ease years of gradually-built tension. The palomino nickered from the pasture, and a wind current offered the perfume of fresh hay and pine fencing.

"I'm sorry, Wyatt," she said finally, quietly. "I didn't mean to snap. I'd rather have lunch with you than without you, mud and all. You work hard for our family, and I haven't been appreciative enough."

Wyatt let out a breath, and his blue eyes grew as warm as the summer sky above them. Stepping close, he slid his hands around the back of her neck, moving his calloused thumbs along her cheekbones. "I'm sorry, too. For making a mess."

Julia's heart felt like a canary released from her cage, suddenly able to spread her wings and soar over fields and mountains alive with wildflowers of every color under the sun. Bitterness was left far below, and she leaned into her husband's broad chest, where her head fit perfectly under his bearded chin. His chest rose and fell with a sigh of contentment as he surrounded her and Elijah with his arms.

For a fleeting moment, Julia considered informing Wyatt that it was her birthday but decided against it. She shouldn't tie any strings to this apology. It needed to stand on its own. Maybe next year she could remind him of the date.

Small hands touched her jeans, and Benjamin wove himself into their circle, giggling. Wyatt reached down and ruffled his son's hair. "The vet will be here any minute," he said, an apology in his tone, but he didn't move.

"Okay." Julia lifted her head and smiled up at her husband. "I'll see you at dinner, then."

"I'll try to remember to take off my boots," Wyatt said, smiling back.

Back in the house, Julia finally ate her lunch of leftover chicken soup, and it tasted far better without the bitterness in her stomach. New energy pulsed through her, and she managed to wash and fold a load of laundry before it was time to make dinner.

The lasagna in the oven was making Julia's mouth water by the time she heard the back door open. She sat in the gray recliner, feeding Elijah again, watching the horses from the bedroom window. And then—a wonderful sound. Leather flopped onto the doormat, and socked feet padded into the kitchen. Tap water turned on full blast as Wyatt washed up—no, the water sound was too hollow.

Water sloshing, cloth wrung and dripping. The soft swish of a mop on wood. Slow, sure steps across the kitchen floor. Julia listened, her heart swelling with emotion and love rekindled. The last drop of milk found its way into Elijah's mouth, and she set the bottle on the windowsill. Moving her son's head to her shoulder, she patted his back in rhythm with the mop as if the steady back-and-forth were a song.

From the kitchen, a stream of water poured down the drain, followed by the tap of a bucket set on the counter. Wyatt entered the bedroom, a bouquet of wildflowers in his hand. Purple aster, crimson paintbrush, and blue larkspur—all her favorites. Julia stared at him, stunned. When was the last time he had picked her flowers?

"Happy birthday, love," he said, bending down to give her a lingering kiss.

"They're beautiful, Wyatt," Julia whispered, not trusting her voice. She breathed in deep the scent of sun and field.

"I'm sorry I didn't remember earlier," Wyatt said. "I had it marked on my barn office calendar, but I didn't look at it until I had to schedule a follow-up with the vet." He gave her a crooked smile.

Julia tipped up her chin for another kiss. "I forgive you." Somehow, the simple words restored her own heart, though they were directed to her husband.

From underneath his plaid shirt, Wyatt's stomach rumbled, and Julia grinned, transferring Elijah to her husband's arms. "Dinner's almost ready."

Together, they walked into the kitchen, and the mud prints were gone.

THIS I CLAIM

ANNE J. HILL

I built my house on a hill
Brick by brick
The foundation was weak
I knew this
And yet I built
Hoping with every tear,
Sweat, and drop of blood
To sturdy the foundation
Of this tumbling hill
And when it was done
I placed my flag
Into the soil
Marking it as mine
But when the hill
Crumbled beneath me
I stood back up and said
"No, for you I have claimed,

I built here
I intend to stay,
You may fall
But I will only
Place brick upon brick
Once more
For you are my hill
This I claim
This I will keep"
Let it repeat again

STONE SWORN

CASSANDRA HAMM

W*HAT IF IT doesn't last?*

Gemma peeked through a crack in the temple's inner doors. A half dozen Traustad villagers talked amongst themselves as they waited for her to enter the ribbon-swathed chamber. Towering over Father Eimar, Wynnstan rocked back on his heels, hands clasped. *Human* hands.

He was making a mistake. Any moment, he'd see that.

The chatter softened, replaced by a lyre's low thrumming. Gemma adjusted the hem of her leaf-green dress and wondered if it hugged her too tightly, if its neckline was too low. But then she imagined the look in Wynnstan's eyes when he'd see her walking down the aisle.

It didn't matter that her uncle would've beaten her within an inch of her life if he'd seen her wearing this, or that the men back in Folstad would've leered over every exposed bit of her. Traustad was different. *Wynnstan* was different.

The temple's outer door creaked open. She turned.

A middle-aged man in a threadbare tunic stepped inside. She registered the stink of liquor before her gaze faltered on his face.

"Uncle Roan?" Her chest constricted so tightly she could barely get the words out. "What are you doing here? How did you find me?"

"Can't miss your wedding, now, can I?" His familiar rasping tone sent chills over her freshly scrubbed skin.

Run! her mind screamed, but her feet wouldn't move. A year without the constant belittling, the pinches and slaps, the control over who she could talk to and where she could be—and now Roan had to show up on her *wedding day?*

"I hear you got yourself a new man." Roan bared his yellowing teeth in a feral grin. The candles cast ghastly shadows over his freckled skin. "Flesh and blood this time."

Gemma stiffened. "This is still Wynnstan, Uncle. He's a man now, not a golem."

Roan barked out a laugh. "Sure it is." His gaze crawled over her body, and she hugged her arms over her chest, wishing she could be dressed in something looser.

She glanced at a nearby mural of the Holy One clasping the hand of a sobbing woman and drew her strength from his gentle, forgiving eyes. "It's true!" she said. "I saw him change. I *caused* it."

"If he *changed*"—Roan drew out the word with a sneer—"he can change back."

Her retort died in her throat. She remembered the crushing heaviness as remedy after remedy had failed—concoctions that made her nose burn and Wynnstan almost choke. But nothing had worked—

Until her lips had brushed his, and he'd softened into a man.

But what if her lips one day turned him to stone? Would she stay?

Fickle. Flighty. Needy. The words, echoes of her childhood, burned her ears as if Roan was speaking them right now.

He didn't need to speak them. She already knew.

The doors burst open, nearly knocking Roan off his feet. Wynnstan rushed through, his hairless head brushing the ceiling. "Gemma!" He reached for her, and she flinched away. His eyebrows furrowed. "Are you all right?"

Her eyes burned. *You're too good for me, Wynn.*

"When you didn't come inside, I feared something had happened...." Wynnstan trailed away. His eyes focused on Roan. "*You.*"

"It's bad luck to see 'er before the weddin'," Roan said. "Ain't like it'll last anyway. Should'a married Horan when you had the chance, girl."

Gemma shuddered at the thought of the butcher she'd been betrothed to before she ran away. Wynnstan had saved her in so many ways—from her uncle, from the fate of an abusive marriage, even from herself. But how had she repaid him? With doubt and dissatisfaction.

Sweat dampened the curls at the back of her neck. She tried to look at the Holy One, but shame burned too fiercely. *You don't deserve love from anyone—Wynnstan* or *the Holy One. What you got from your uncle is what you deserved.*

"You need to leave, sir." Wynnstan's jaw throbbed. He started to reach for one of the nearby candles, then drew his hand back. "You're not welcome here."

"I should'a had you call me 'sir,' Gemma." Roan grinned at Gemma with rotting teeth. "Maybe I still will. Might teach you obedience."

She shrunk away from her uncle, remembering belts biting into her skin.

"She's not calling you *anything.*" Wynnstan managed to look imposing and polite at the same time. "She won't be talking to you at all. Now, if you please, we have a ceremony to get to—"

"You sure you even *want* her?" Roan gestured to her dismissively.

Gemma's breath caught. *Please don't—*

"She's weak and disobedient, an ugly little liar—"

"Stop!" she cried. Each word sliced into her skin, sharper than any physical blow he'd ever given her.

"Don't you *dare* talk about Gemma like that," Wynnstan growled.

"I raised her, boy," Roan said. "I know who she is."

"I know her better than you ever will." Wynnstan touched Gemma's chin, forcing her to look up at him. Candlelight dusted his dark features in gold. "She saw a man in me when everyone else saw a monster."

Gemma leaned into his touch, stifling a sob. "But he's right. I *am* weak. When things get hard, I run."

"You stayed when the remedies didn't work." Wynnstan's fingers tightened on her jaw, tugging her closer. "I gave you a way out, and you stuck with me."

"But if you change back..." Her voice wobbled. *Is it wrong that I love him more as a man than as a golem?* "I don't know that I would...stay." Just saying the words made her stomach churn. *Now he knows who I really am.*

His eyes were as soft as goose feather down. "I won't change back." His nose brushed hers, his breath hot against her lips. "You freed me from my stone prison. I'm never going back."

A hand grabbed her, jerking her back—Roan's, she knew, just from the pinch of his fingers. Her flower crown tipped as she fought to keep her balance.

"Don't touch her," Wynnstan snarled, pulling Gemma against his side. His touch was firm, protective, reassuring. His scent, solid and warm like cedarwood, filled her nostrils.

"Ungrateful girl!" Roan drew himself up as much as he could, despite the stench of liquor and the worn clothing. "You wouldn't be here without me. I sure as hell didn't have to take you in when your mama died, but I did, and this is how you repay me?"

She recoiled, shrinking back against Wynnstan, fear tightening in her chest. Then her eyes found the mural.

The Holy One cradled the hand of a woman whose name she would never know, yet it felt, somehow, as though he were cradling *her* hand. As though he saw every part of her broken self and loved her despite it. *I forgive you,* he seemed to say. *You are loved. You are clean.*

If he forgave her, then surely Wynnstan could too.

"I have every right—" Roan continued.

Gemma took Wynnstan's beautiful brown face in her hands and kissed him, his lips soft and pliant beneath hers.

"Man or golem, I will always love you." And for the first time in months, she truly believed that.

She could get drunk on Wynnstan's smile—warm and sweet with a certain fire, like honeyed mead.

"You need to leave *now.*" Gemma lifted her chin and met Roan's wide-eyed gaze with the flames he'd tried to quench.

"I am your *guardian!*" Roan blustered. "I took you in when your mama—"

"I'm done with you, Uncle." She exhaled as the truth reverberated through her—*I don't need him. I never needed him.*

Roan gaped.

She smiled up at Wynnstan. "Now, let's get married, shall we?"

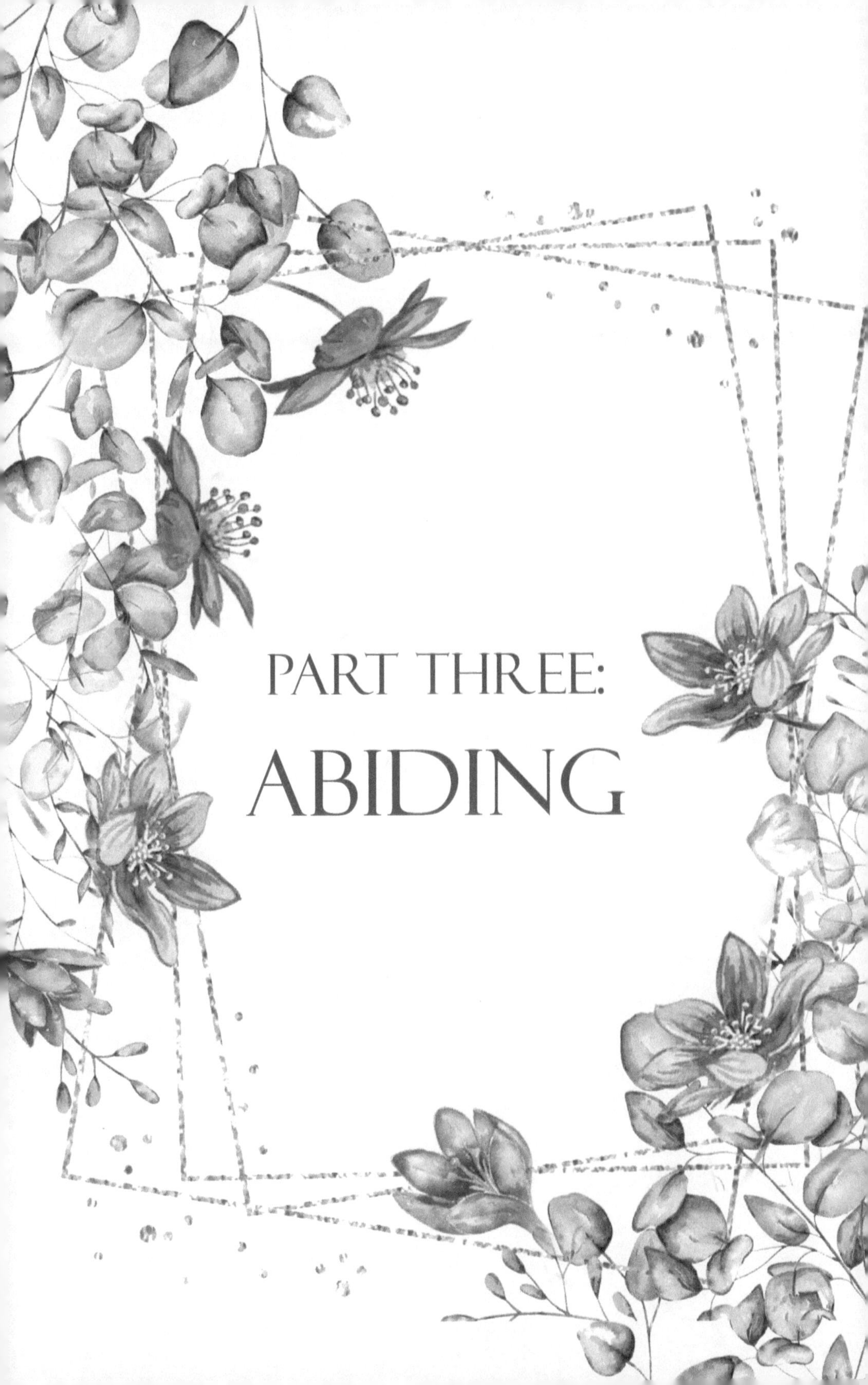

PART THREE:
ABIDING

ORGANIC

ANNE J. HILL

TOM SAT ON the wooden steps in the early morning before the sun rose and looked out at the empty farm he and his wife owned. It had once been filled with cows and other livestock.

That is...until the couple died.

Tom sighed heavily, ran his fingers over his neck, and felt the spot that changed the course of their lives forever. He had been old and expected to die soon, but he didn't foresee hungering for blood.

"Did you eat this morning?" his wife asked from the front door. She insisted on still calling the sunrise hours 'morning' even though it was when they ate dinner and got ready for bed. Ever since the *change*.

Tom huffed. "No." Eating was a chore now that they'd bled through all the cattle—he refused to find humans.

Their little farmhouse in the middle of nowhere was a blessing and a curse. The nearest grocery store was an hour away by car.

"Come in then. Breakfast is ready."

Tom huffed. *Dinner*. "How hard is that to do? Just open the packet, and...that's all."

His wife tapped her foot, just as impatient undead as she'd been alive. "You hungry or not?"

"Coming, coming." Tom grabbed the railing and pulled his old body up. Turning into a vampire at age eighty-five was rather unfortunate. Couldn't that blasted hitchhiking hobo have frozen him in his twenty-year-old body instead?

He shuffled his way into the house and pulled the blinds on the door shut behind him. Tom sniffed, taking in the smell of dinner. But he paused at the kitchen table with a scowl. Something didn't smell right.

"What's the matter?" his wife asked.

Tom sat down and poked the raw ground beef with his fork. "This isn't organic."

"They were out." She shrugged, sat down, and put on her bib. "Either this or starve, and you know what happens if you let yourself go too long."

He winced. He knew. The man buried in their garden had known more than most. Tom couldn't let the hunger drive him mad again—first his wife, and then that stranger a few months later. At least his wife was still alive, sort of. "Right. But you couldn't have tried another store? You're getting lazy."

His wife blinked at him, her fork touching the bloody beef. "Excuse me. Would you like to go buy groceries? Would *you* like to sneak out in the middle of the night and stalk to the store so the sun doesn't burn *your* flesh off?" She hissed, her fangs protruding. "Would you like to be the one explaining to every cashier why you've bought nothing but pounds of ground beef? And then get yelled at for making them run out of expensive organic beef, and no other customers can find any? Just because your husband has a nagging need for his blood to come with fancy meat, even though his wife is perfectly fine bleeding any ordinary animal... Huh? Would you?"

Tom glanced down at the average ground beef and sighed. "No, dear. You're right."

His wife looked surprised but took a bite and dabbed her lips with her napkin, always the queen of tidiness.

Come to think of it, Tom assumed he was the one who struggled with this new...*lifestyle*...the most. He'd had to fire his farmhand, killed a man while fighting his new urges, and had been turned when he was meant to die soon.

But his poor wife had to eat blood when even a speck of dirt drove her up the wall. This farm life wasn't her cup of tea. He'd dragged her out here when they wed. Just like he'd accidentally dragged her into this eternal living hell. And she took it like a trooper, buying him all sorts of grass-fed and organic blood-infused meats to keep his allergy-sensitive stomach calm.

He looked down at the ground beef, then grinned at his wife. “Honey?”

“Hmmm?” Her red-tinted eyes glanced at him.

“I'm sorry I've put you through so much, but I'd rather go through hell with you than anyone else.”

His wife studied him and then slowly smiled. Tom knew he didn’t say things like that enough.

“And I'll get the groceries next week,” Tom offered, and pecked his wife on the cheek.

Death was too long to not choose love over raw organic beef.

THE END

RACHEL LAWRENCE

When kids have flown
And floors are clean
We're left alone
Just you and me
With graying hair
And wrinkles deep
Enough to hold
This love we keep
Offering up
Year after year
The flowers that
We planted here
You hold my hand
And know my heart
In ways you couldn't
At the start
When we stood on
The edge so steep

And held our breath
And took a leap
Which hurt more than
We could have known
But look at all
This love we've grown
I gaze back up
Here at the end
And know that I
Would jump again

SMILE

HANNAH CARTER

I VERY RARELY see my grandmother cry—the sunshiney, happy-go-lucky member of our family.

In fact, I remember only two times. When I was young, she babysat my brother and me every day. My brother and I got into a fight (as siblings typically do), and I remember that she went into her office and cried.

"Why do you have to pick at each other so much?" she asked me when I found her later.

I never fought with my brother again—at least, not around her.

The second time I saw her cry was when my grandfather's cancer returned.

Again, again, again. We seem to live in between bouts of cancer. If it isn't cancer, there's always some ailment that has plagued him for ten-plus years. Shoulder pain, back surgeries, depression, infections...the list grows every year.

And my grandmother stays with him through every ailment. Through every storm, through every late night or early morning, every hospital stay, every bout of illness. Through every day when he sits on the couch and refuses to smile, but instead sobs or covers his head, positive that this will be the sickness that kills him.

During his last bout, I found my grandmother crying in the family room.

Of course, my grandfather was not around. She wouldn't dare cry in front of him.

"I can't do it," she whispered as she wiped her eyes. "I can't make him happy. He refuses to be happy."

My grandmother sings and dances with my grandpa to their wedding song, "*Happy Together*" by The Turtles, in this room. She should not be weeping in it now.

"I get so frustrated," she added. "At this. At him, sometimes. If he could only smile."

My grandmother boasts about how she can still pick me up, and I'm a woman in my twenties. She often does it just to prove a point—that she is no weak, frail woman.

She can hold my weight.

She can hold the weight of the world, but she should not have to.

I fidgeted. Held back my own tears. "Do you ever want to divorce him?"

The forbidden d-word. My worst fear. Because I know how hard it is. How this decade of pain has been a struggle for all of our family. How it causes spats and fights and depression and anger.

Could this be the final tipping point?

Because my grandmother *never* cries.

She is our sunshine.

Our happy-go-lucky girl.

The glue of our world.

"Oh, no." She shook her head. "I just need your help. Smile for me so I can smile for him, okay?"

So I smiled.

She smiled back.

And she finished her cry, stood up, and went into the other room to see if he needed anything, or maybe to bring him his favorite ice cream, or maybe to make sure he was still napping.

All with a smile on her face.

And I smile for her, just as she's smiled for all of us through the years, so she doesn't have to bear the weight alone.

Because she loves him, he loves her, and I love them both.

And I hope, one day soon, when all the surgeries and chemo are behind us, he can join her for another dance on the living room floor while The Turtles sing my grandparents' song.

MEMORY LANE

NOBEL SHUT CHAN

On the night we first met you told me
One day I might disappear
To a place where you cannot follow.
Will you still go
As far as you can go?
And I replied
Whatever happens, I will be there
Until the end.
And that was that.
You took my hand and we flew
Past the glittering stars,
Through the deepest seas
Where shipwrecks hid treasures
Less beautiful than your smile.
I learnt to read the laughter in your eyes,
The brush of your fingers against mine
As you lingered too long
In movie theaters, restaurants,

Holding our secret
In the space between our palms.
Decades shrunk into pennies
Thrown into wishing wells,
Hoping that the end would never come,
That the world would stop spinning
Just for one lifetime.
But the world doesn't stop for a wish.
One day I came home to find
You standing in the kitchen,
Struggling to remember where you were going.
It was small things at first:
Lost keys, misplaced wallets,
Half-filled mugs and tipped over coffee pots.
Then, forgotten dates, obvious questions,
Where are we and *what do I do*
And finally, *who are you?*
Hands shaking too much
To keep holding mine.
Slowly forgetting the words
Whispered under the covers,
I love you,
I love you,
I love you.
(And yet, the dawn continues to break
The night sky wide open.)
Because your eyes still laugh
At my jokes. Your hands
Still search for mine in the dark,
Even if they can't remember why.
You still collect pennies in a jar
By our bed, and your smile
Is still wrapped in gold.
Your face in the moonlight
Shines like the night we first met,

Asking *when I disappear,*
Will you leave me?
And my reply is still the same.
Whatever happens, I will be there
Until the end.
And I would do it over,
and over,
and over again.

LOVE REMEMBERS

HAILEY HUNTINGTON

CYNTHIA FROWNS AT her reflection, further creasing her wrinkled skin. "Why am I getting all dressed up today?" Her thin voice warbles.

I clasp the vintage pearl necklace around her neck and smooth back one of her wispy white curls. "You have a very important date today, remember?" Instantly, I bite my tongue, regretting tacking the *remember* on at the end. Of course, Cynthia doesn't remember. But I still slip up sometimes.

Unaware of my unintended jab, Cynthia glances her reflection up and down. Her faded floral dress hangs loose on her thin frame, but I know that it is one of Ernest's favorites. That's why I picked it out. Cynthia's hands shake as she picks up a bracelet. Her veins are visible through her paper-thin skin. "Who am I going on a date with?"

"Ernest. He's a very nice man. He cares an awful lot about you." I smile sadly. My heart twists like it does every time Cynthia asks me who Ernest is.

Cynthia *hmms*, twisting the gold band around her fourth finger. She doesn't remember what the ring symbolizes. It's just another piece of jewelry to her.

"I like you, Lucy," Cynthia announces suddenly as I cross the room to retrieve her walker. "You can visit me again."

I can't keep back a laugh. Oh, Cynthia, ever so charming. "Thank you. I will visit you again." My smile falters. I have to reintroduce myself to Cynthia every day. She doesn't remember that I'm her caretaker.

Setting Cynthia's walker in front of her, I glance at the clock. "Well, your date should be showing up soon. Ready?"

"Just another minute." Cynthia turns back towards the mirror, applies a quick coat of bright red lipstick, and puts on a pair of clip-on earrings. Her gaze flickers back to mine. "Do I look good enough?"

"You look beautiful, Cynthia."

She takes a deep breath, her thin frame shaking. "All right then."

Leaving her room behind, I lead Cynthia through the nursing home to the front desk. Ernest is already waiting in the lobby to our right. When he sees us coming, he carefully rises from his chair and pulls off his hat. He twists the worn flat cap in his hands. "Good afternoon, Cynthia." Ernest's eyes shine adoringly as he looks at her, almost as if it was their wedding day sixty years ago. "Will you give me the honor of treating you to lunch?"

There's a brief moment of hesitation before Cynthia answers. "I will, Mr. Ernest." Cynthia slowly crosses the remaining space between her and Ernest. I hang back, watching them.

For the past five years, ever since Cynthia's dementia started rapidly deteriorating her mind and Ernest couldn't care for her, he's taken her out to lunch every Wednesday. Rain or shine, he's ready at noon without fail. Even when Cynthia forgot who he was, he didn't waver in his commitment. Once he told me, "I promised Cynthia, 'til death do us part,' not 'til memories do us part.'"

Cynthia takes Ernest's outstretched hand when she reaches him. Something sparkles in her eyes, and the stiffness in her shoulders eases. Her mind may not remember that Ernest is her husband, but her heart knows. The kind of love between the two of them isn't something that can be forgotten. It lasts. It weathers the storms, the highs and lows. It's the kind that makes me believe my own love story might be possible someday. It's a love that goes deeper than memories.

WRINKLES

RACHEL LAWRENCE

ON WEDNESDAYS, SHE does laundry.

The basket isn't as full as it once was. Mostly his work shirts. Her dresses. Plain white socks and underwear.

She sets up the rusty ironing board and starts to sort the latest load, still warm from the dryer.

Mundane tasks like this give her time to think, something she used to wonder if she'd ever have again.

She smiles, remembering the years she did laundry every day of the week. Back then, the hamper constantly ran over with grass-stained jeans, soccer uniforms, socks with missing partners, and cartoon-themed undies. Those were the days she'd dig through the piles to find his clothes for the next day while he read just one more story to a room full of sleepy eyes. He did all of the voices, took them on adventures to faraway places, won her heart all over again from the doorway down the hall.

When the last night light had been turned on, the last blanket straightened, the last sip of water given, they'd collapse on the couch together and review the day.

"Do you know what your son did this morning?" she'd start. And he would laugh before she even told him, knowing it would be far more unbelievable than anything he could imagine.

"I didn't even know a penny could fit up a nostril that small," she'd finish, shaking her head.

He'd ask about the girls' ballet recital date and put it in the calendar in his phone since he never missed anything if he could help it. She'd remind him that she needed to buy the youngest new slippers since she lost one somewhere in the black hole of their minivan on the way home from rehearsal two nights ago.

He'd hold her hand, answer her questions about the project he was working on at the office, listen to her recount the latest plot twist of the novel she was writing whenever she could grab a spare moment. At some point along the way, the conversation would shift to the future—all the things they'd do, the places they'd go, the sleep they'd get one day, in just fourteen years or so.

Fourteen years turned into nine that bled into six, and then four, three, two, one last load of the baby's tee shirts that he threw into a duffel bag without folding them, anxious to get back to campus and the rest of his life.

And then they were left, two lone socks at the bottom of an empty machine.

She bought herself a new wardrobe, finally published her book, picked up a new hobby and a brochure on Italy. He, however, though quick to shower her with genuine encouragement and support, was content to remain in this gentle cycle of wake, work, home. The farthest he ever wants to travel now is to the ball field down the road for their oldest granddaughter's games.

They still find themselves side by side, hand in hand, on the couch at the end of each day, but they're much quieter now. She sometimes relishes the comfortable familiarity, but she often worries that it's because they've run out of things to talk about.

Somewhere along the way, she realizes he's changed. And so has she. Each of them has grown, stretched, shrunk, faded, softened. Sometimes by choice, sometimes by necessity, sometimes by accident.

The iron runs out of steam, and she walks to the kitchen sink to refill the water cup, catching the tail end of an interview on the living room television.

"I just felt like it was time to start over," the beautiful woman smiles into the camera. "Find myself. And I felt it was something I had to do alone, with no one holding me back."

She only pauses a moment before she returns to the board and looks to the basket behind her for the next piece of clothing, her eyes snagging on her favorite sweater. It doesn't fit quite like it used to, back when it was newer, when she was young and thin and dumb enough to think she knew what love was.

What else would she rather reach for, though—on a long day, a cold night, an ordinary Wednesday—than this covering that has held her through so much time, so much change that it's become part of the very fabric of her being?

Maybe, she thinks, each season together just brings new wrinkles that require their own investment of time, attention, and good old-fashioned hard work. She knows from experience that the results will be worth it.

She smiles and moves the iron back and forth, again.

TO HAVE AND TO HOLD

MIRIAM WADE

Love is all about choices
For better days are a frame of mind.
Loving you was my best decision
For worse days are far behind.

Growing old with you was easy
For richer in our love we grew.
We worked hard to see the good
For poorer in health were you.

Love left me abandoned
In sickness you were captured.
You were gone and I was left
In health, and feeling fractured.

It wasn't always easy
To love through it all.
Yet, our hardest days I learned
To cherish whatever may befall.

The love we shared was special
It is a decision of the heart.
As we said all those years ago:
'Til death do us part.

ONE CUP OF COFFEE

AMBER KIRKPATRICK

TWENTY YEARS OF marriage and I have fought regret at least twelve of those years.

Disparate temperaments. Rare are the outright fights, but the low-key bickering, the passive-aggressive control, and the unpredictable outbursts of temper can drain even the most optimistic woman. Cutting words and emotional neglect can diminish as much as a strike. He never reads my words—my heart and soul poured on paper isn't worth his valuable time. Even in our good years, I have thought of leaving once a month. In the bad seasons, at least once a day.

But then there are the long nights talking politics and theology. Watching classic movies. Sharing stories of the children. Holding hands in bed until his snoring allows me to let go.

And, of course, there is the cup of coffee.

It doesn't happen every morning, but quite often, a cup of coffee appears at my bedside with the perfect amount of cream and sugar. He knows I'm not a morning person, and it's his way of gently bringing me into the light.

Sometimes, a simple cup of coffee is an act of Grace.

So here I remain. One cup of coffee at a time.

LIGHTS IN THE LAKE

EMILY BARNETT

The stars were going to kill her.

I'd told my wife this a hundred times, but Martha had only gotten more stubborn with age.

Frost collected on the quilt as I dragged it toward the figure sitting in the center of our yard. The woods surrounding our homestead looked like giants with shoulders hunched against the cold.

But Martha didn't take notice. Gaze tilting down at the ink-black lake, her silver hair shimmered about her shoulders like the moon. With a grunt, I piled the quilt around her small frame.

"Thank you, Charles."

"You'll catch your death."

She must've heard the frustration in my voice because she finally deigned to look at me, then her eyes flicked to the ground behind me. "Where's your chair?"

"I'm not sittin' out tonight. Game's on." I crossed my arms, wondering if she'd fight me on it. Her hazel eyes were evergreen in the dark. The wrinkles in her face were little streaks of shadows.

"All right," she said. "Do you want me to watch it with you?"

Though she always offered, I knew her better than a Yankee roster. She hated baseball.

"No." I stalked toward the house. "You won't see anything in that water, though," I grumbled over my shoulder. I was met with silence. When it came to the lake, nothing I said could get through to Martha. Not since she saw the lights when we were twenty-three.

It was early that fateful morning. Not even the birds were awake yet. Summer dew soaked into my pajamas, and my ears strained in the silence, hoping to hear God. To understand why the worst thing had happened. Why He'd let it happen.

The quiet pushed back until I flailed in the drowning thoughts of my own grief. I sucked in a quaking breath.

"Charles?" Martha's voice was thin, and I turned. Her nightgown hung limply over the bump on her stomach.

"You should be resting. The doctor said shock could—"

"I know what she said."

It had been three days since my parents had been killed in a car accident. Three days of a fog I couldn't quite penetrate. And though I felt lost and angry, I knew it ran just as deep for Martha. She'd been an orphan most of her life, and my parents had taken her in when we began dating. Mama loved her as much as me—maybe even more. Not that I minded. Everyone loved Martha.

And I ached as I gazed at Martha's belly. My parents wouldn't be a part of our child's life. How could some of the most important people of my existence never speak with or love one another?

"Let me get a chair for you, at least," I said. *Let me do something.* I was an untethered sail, a boat heading out to sea one moment, running aground the next. But I had to stay busy, to keep moving, or else I'd sink.

I was in the garage when Martha cried out.

Heart pounding, I threw down the chair I was trying to pull from behind the lawn mower and raced back outside. When I reached her side, she didn't seem in pain. But her face—it was *glowing.* She pointed at the lake, gaping at the dark ripples. Tears leaked down her freckled cheeks, and she didn't bother to wipe them. I wasn't even sure she knew I was there.

"Martha." I jostled her arm, trying to bring her back to earth. "What is it?"

She blinked three times, then turned to me. She was as breathless as if she'd run five miles. "The *lights*. Reds and blues, and then a light green—like Mama's kitchen...lighting up the water. Swirling like a whirlpool, as if...as if I could step right in and it would lead to *them.*" Her brow furrowed. "You didn't see anything?"

I studied the now-calm water before shaking my head. "Maybe you're tired. Or the medications the doctor gave you—"

"I *saw* it, Charles." Desperation gleamed in her eyes. "It was the most beautiful thing."

We remained outside until the sun rose and the lake turned a dusky blue. Until reality scrubbed over any fancies of magical lights, or loch ness monsters, or portals to other worlds. Everything looked duller in the daylight. More concrete.

But Martha didn't stop believing in what she saw. She said it was a miracle, a reminder we were not alone.

Almost every evening before bed, she went to the water's edge. The churning portal never reappeared, but it didn't stop her from seeing other strange things from time-to-time: Glowing beings tiptoeing in the forest, patches of spring surrounded by snow, spice and poetry sung on the wind. The depths of a person's soul written on their face.

Martha believed the portal had opened her mind to the *other*.

I believed the loss had driven her to delusions. Martha saw what she needed to survive.

After our baby was born, healthy and kicking, Martha's visions lessened. We returned to a somewhat normal rhythm, but when I'd catch her gazing in the darkness, or smiling at sunlight filtering through the window, my chest would tighten with worry.

But there was something under the worry, something dark inside my gut.

Once our kids grew up and moved away, and old age began creeping into our bones, Martha returned to her earlier ritual. That thing inside me bled darker with each trip we made into the night. I began to hate our yard and how the stars caught the waves just right. What was the point of beauty if it offered no warmth, no answers? But Martha was content as if she saw something I couldn't.

My hand was on the sliding door when I heard Martha cough. I paused, glaring at my own wrinkled reflection in the glass, my gaze slipping to the widescreen TV on our wall. The Cardinals were playing the Yankees. It was going to be a good one.

Martha coughed again, and I sighed, making my way back out to her. This time, I brought a chair.

The quilt had slipped, and I readjusted it over her small shoulder before sitting. Save for a few crickets and far-off hoots, all was quiet. It reminded me of the morning I'd prayed to hear God's voice. When Martha had seen the 'lights' and I'd seen nothing in return.

"What is it?" Martha asked.

I jumped, surprised she was studying me. "Nothing," I grumbled, crossing my arms. "I just don't know why you won't give this up. It's nonsense."

She squinted at me, reading me like a damn novel. "What is it that's really upsetting you?"

I clenched my teeth, staring at the moon until my eyes grew dry. Martha touched my arm, and my defenses lowered a bit. "Nothing," I said, prodding at my own thoughts as if they were a pile of floundering fish. Martha was always better at understanding emotions. Usually, she knew what I felt even before I did. "I'm just angry, is all."

She cocked her head. "You're angry that I sit out here?"

"Maybe." But that was only half true. "Well, no. I know why you come here. The stars' reflection reminds you of those lights." My eyes turned misty, and I swiped at them with a gnarled finger. My voice wavered. "It's just..." I closed my eyes against their sting. "It was me who asked for a sign, it was *my* parents who died, and it was *you* who got an answer." I lifted a shoulder. "I'm mostly angry I resented you for it."

I nearly left her when the kids were in high school. When our last child had been baptized, and my heart squeezed with guilt. That same loneliness harkened back to the morning I'd cried out into the void. Silence had been my companion then. It still was.

I shook my head and swallowed my salty tears. Her hand didn't leave my arm though I didn't deserve her touch. Her kindness. If only she knew the dark gnawing at my soul.

"If you'd seen my miracle," Martha began, "would it have changed anything?"

Yes, I wanted to say. But I hesitated.

"We raised three amazing kids. You have a wife who adores you." She motioned to the sky. "The sun rises each day; the rain waters the earth. Our life..." She swallowed. "Our life was a beautiful one." She sighed, and I wondered if it was because it was late or something else. "If *that* isn't enough to prove there's more out there—" She jerked her chin to the lake. "—what do you think some lights would've proven, Charles? Hmm?"

I wiped a rogue tear from my cheek. "It would've been evidence we aren't alone."

"Is my love not proof of that? I'm with you. You aren't alone. Not here. Not after here, either."

After here. That was the true depth of my fears. To know what lay beyond the heavens and planets and the fabric of reality. Was it nothing—or everything? I was never content in the nuance of it all. I was never content in forgetting it either.

It was a plague without a cure.

I placed my palm over hers and sucked in the cold air. I was seventy-two. If I hadn't seen a golden staircase to heaven, or discovered the Bermuda Triangle, I likely never would. And as my hopes and fears spiraled within me, Martha's hand never faltered. She never let go, always pulling me along, trying to show me the wonders I always seemed to miss.

Hers was a love I didn't deserve.

Maybe some mysteries weren't so unattainable. And some miracles were clothed in normalcy.

I sighed. Martha was right. A lifetime of proof was before me, and I'd chosen not to see it. Even if I'd been the one to witness the lake's display, I would've been driven mad with wondering. Doubting my own eyes and mind, searching for *more* rather than being content like my wife.

"It's cold. Should we go in?" Martha asked, her eyes sparkling. "The game won't be done yet."

I nodded, and we stood to go back inside. We could bring the quilt and chairs in tomorrow. Our steps were slow but steady, and Martha's arm tucked into mine felt like a gift.

We were nearly to the porch when colored light washed the patio, house, and yard. It was like a giant disco ball had erupted from the gurgling lake. I stopped in my tracks as a song trickled through the churning waters. Chills crawled up my arms. Was it…?

Martha gasped and turned, still clutching my arm. Her eyes widened, and I could see color dancing in their reflection. Her face was glowing. But I didn't turn.

"Charles." She tugged at my sleeve. "It's here. The lights!" She was breathless and giddy. Young once more. "It's your sign. Your *miracle!* Look, Charles!" Her tone was urgent, flabbergasted at why I remained unmoved.

I was a sail that had finally found a boat to tether itself to. I didn't need any more signs or wonders to prove what I was beginning to understand. What I was beginning to *see.*

We were not alone.

"That's all right, Martha." I kissed the side of her head. "The lights in the lake are for you. But you—you are for me."

REMEMBER ME

ELAINE WELLS

Remember me, love,
when this world is dust,
when there is just us,
and life is just chaos,
this wasteland of smoke,
and reflections of our faces in muddy waters.

remember me, love,
because I will remember you,
sweet music floating through the fog,
a crow sweeping across the sky, silhouetted by sunlight,
singing to the tune of a broken guitar,
you said once I find beauty in disaster,
but all I see is you,
a beauty in this disaster.

remember me, love,
when no one remembers us,

when we are just the echo of an old song that no longer plays,
it skips and repeats,
but we still sway to it,
when our corpses are overgrown with flowers,
when this world no longer has a place for us.

remember me, love,
when no trace of me is left,
when every letter has been burned,
and every word turned to ash,
when my name means nothing,
remember me when there is no one left to,
remember I loved you.

THE DATE

RACHEL LAWRENCE

THE GREEN SOAP had been her favorite. She'd always said it made him smell like Christmas.

He finishes showering off the remnants of another long day at the office and moves to his closet to pick out the perfect shirt and tie.

This is the third date Dante has been on this week, and it's only Wednesday.

He laughs quietly to himself as he fumbles with his buttons in the mirror. Who would have thought that his seventies would find him starting over like this? Who would have guessed he'd be brave enough to put himself out there again and again?

Falling in love the first time had almost been too easy. He'd met the girl he'd eventually marry when he was only nine years old after she'd skipped across the street the day his family moved in to see if he wanted to climb trees. At the end of that summer, he'd told her he'd marry her someday. In all fairness, she'd asked. It would be a long time before he'd be interested in girls romantically, but he'd known from the start that he wanted to spend the rest of his life with his best friend. He couldn't imagine anything other than forever by her side.

He grabs his keys and turns out the light, locks the empty house that's too full of memories about her.

The drive across town is quiet; he rarely turns on the radio anymore since every song seems to remind him of what he's lost these past few years. He wants to be present tonight, happy, even if only for a handful of hours.

He parks the car and takes a deep, steadying breath before walking inside. An elegant lady with shoulder-length gray hair is already seated at a table near the window, looking even more beautiful than he expected.

You can do this, he reminds himself. *Just say hello.*

She's studying her hands as he approaches. "Amanda?"

Her eyes flicker upward to meet his, and he thinks he senses a spark. Maybe it's just wishful thinking.

"I'm Dante." He extends a hand, and she places hers in it, smiling. He exhales and takes the seat across from her. "How are you?"

"Good," she smiles. "I've had a really good day. How about you?"

"Good." He straightens his tie. "My day just got a lot better. You look gorgeous, by the way."

She blushes and looks away. He reminds himself that he can't talk to her with the candor he's used to. To this woman, he's only a stranger.

He decides a change of subject might be best. "Do you want me to order us some food?"

She shakes her head. "I'm not very hungry. And..." She blushes again. "I think you're very handsome."

He almost laughs out loud with relief. "Thank you." He winks. "I tried."

He can tell that tonight will be different.

Monday's date was skeptical, and he'd left feeling like an idiot. Tuesday's date had flat-out asked him to leave halfway through dinner. But tonight, the woman who sits on the other side of the table has a look in her eyes that makes him feel more like himself than he has in a very long time.

That look, those eyes, this breathtaking woman give him the courage to do all over again what he's done countless times since September: to risk his heart knowing how completely and devastatingly it's capable of breaking.

He tells her about his family, his job, his hobbies. She laughs until she cries when he regales her with story after story about the crazy dog he used to own.

He talks her into sharing a piece of pie and then, later, letting him walk her back to her room down the hall.

"This was fun." She beams up at him. "Can I give you a hug?"

"Of course." He wraps his arms around her, biting the inside of his cheek to keep the tears from escaping.

She buries her head in his shirt and breathes in. "You smell good," she murmurs. "Like..."

"Christmas?" he offers.

She pulls back, giggling. "Exactly!" She gives him one last smile and reaches for the doorknob. "See you tomorrow?"

"Yes." He nods.

And though he isn't sure what version of her he'll see tomorrow or if she'll even want to see him at all, he knows that he wouldn't miss it for the world. He would fall a hundred times over for her.

He already has.

Back in his car, he loosens the tie she bought him twenty years ago and reaches for the radio dial, replaying all the memories that she can't.

THE SECOND TIME AROUND

KATIE FITZGERALD

WHEN THE CALL came that our newborn grandson, Eli, couldn't stay with his parents, I winced. But my wife, Anna, said, "Of course, we'll take him."

When she hung up the phone, I sighed loudly, picturing all of our planned dinners on the patio and saved movies in our streaming queue popping like bubbles. We'd never have time to ourselves now. Anna patted my shoulder and went to pull out the crib.

"Are you sure that's how that goes?" I asked as she began assembling the frame. By the time the railing was attached—crookedly, I pointed out—she was glaring daggers at me. I contemplated our near-empty calendar, lamenting that it was about to fill up with obligations we'd already completed the first time around.

Eli came around dinner time, a tiny squalling bundle in an infant car seat. I carried the seat inside and placed it on the living room floor, standing back while Anna fussed and cooed. She unbuckled Eli's tiny form and lifted him up to snuggle against her shoulder.

At that moment, from between the lines on her face, Anna's eyes met mine, and they were the same eyes I looked into thirty-five years ago, when she held our own newborn for the first time. Back then, seeing her love for our daughter, I knew I would do anything she asked of me, no matter the price.

As she brought Eli over and held him out to me, she said, "Is there anything in the world more beautiful?"

More beautiful than renewing my commitment to my bride, than walking with her down yet another path toward the unknown, than making her happy one more time without counting the cost?

"No," I said. "Nothing."

A BOX OF CRACKERS

DAVID LASLEY

You bought
a box of crackers
at the store.
Your doctor said,
"You won't live long
unless you eat these crackers,
(and other foods like them)
and take these pills,
and
and
and..."

You gave me one to try.
They had a nutty taste.
They were made of
almonds,
apparently,
like our flour now,

and our snacks,
and our milk,
and
and
and...

They were also
(unexpectedly)
delicious!
Then again,
they were
a little less
filling
like your favorite dessert:
lemon anything.

They were also
a little more
fragile
like your
uncooperative body,
apparently,
which had me fooled
into thinking
you were strong.

You *are*. In fact,
more so...
just...differently.

So, I will try now
to love you
differently
and be
a little less

fragile
a little stronger
and more helpful
and brave
and
and
and…

I'll make you
lemon bars
made of almonds,
of course,
with a
rich, creamy curd
and brown, crispy crust.
It will taste like
lemon anything
and salty-sweetness
and love
and kindness
and
and
and…

MARRIAGE IS A DRAGON

HANNAH CARTER

IT WASN'T EASY being married to a dragon. Singed furniture, hoards in the living room, and scales all over the floor during molting season. Not to mention, dragon back rubs were certainly out of the picture. But Mari and Basfurlortiliar—Bas for short—had made it work for over fifty years.

Still, when Bas, a dragon shifter, had a cold, it certainly put a strain on their marriage.

"*Achoo*!"

Plaster dribbled down on Mari. She hurriedly leaned over the pot so nothing fell into the stew. Even when in human form, Bas' sneeze tended to carry a bit of firepower. But whenever he had a full-blown illness and couldn't control his shifting ability, well, suffice to say they'd lost their first house in a fire caused by the flu thirty years ago.

A pause, and then a pitiful bellow that shook the rafters: "*Mariiiiiiiii*!"

She flicked off the burner and darted up the stairs—and to do so, she had to dodge several large clumps of gold, books, knick-knacks, and other odds and ends she was forbidden to touch.

She entered their bedroom and immediately started to cough from smoke inhalation.

"I'm thorry," Bas croaked. Sparks flew onto their quilt as he blew his nose. "I thet your night-thand on fire."

"Oh, Bas!" Mari picked up the fire extinguisher—one of seven she kept for her own hoard—and sprayed the flames down. As they dimmed, at the heart of the conflagration, sat the smoldering remains of pictures, portraits of their children and grandchildren throughout the years.

"I'm tho thorry." Bas coughed.

Mari looked up at him. He looked so pathetic, with his red scales a dim color and tired eyes that lurked behind his circle glasses, almost too small to fit on his wide head. He clutched at the quilt with his claws as if he thought he needed to hide from her wrath. "I didn't mean to." He sniffled.

Mari touched the charred remains of their daughter's fifth birthday party and their grandson's first missing tooth. Precious memories of a life she'd built with Bas ever since they met in a university library.

"You know..." Mari said softly. "The only reason these pictures mean anything to me is because they're of the life I've built with you." She reached over and grasped his scaly arm, giving it a squeeze. "And the life I want to keep building with you."

Bas' green eyes softened. "I love you, Mari."

"I love you, too." Mari kissed him between the nostrils on his wide snout. "Now, I've got some soup for you if you can resist burning down the house while I go get it."

"I can try." Bas sucked in a breath. His face scrunched up, and his eyes twitched. "Ah—ah—"

Mari readied her fire extinguisher and shot a spray of foam at her husband as the flames exploded from his mouth. This garnered another quick sneeze, and Mari dove out of the way and extinguished another small fire on the carpet.

She turned around and giggled as Bas settled back down in the sheets with a white, frothy mustache all over his face.

"Maybe you better leave that here." Bas sniffled. "You know. Justh for emergenthies."

READY OR NOT

KATHLEEN BIRD

GUNFIRE RICOCHETED OFF the rocks behind them, and she ducked down beside her husband. He grabbed her hand and squeezed it tightly.

"Don't worry, Anne," he said with a smile that highlighted the wrinkles on his forehead. "Even the apocalypse can't break us up!" He kissed her hand before releasing it and jumped up to return fire at the mutant army that approached.

"You really know how to show a girl a good time, Matthew." She cinched the straps on her backpack a little tighter and mumbled under her breath about stupid arthritis as her fingers protested the motion. Anne tugged the tourniquet on her leg a little tighter and groaned in pain.

"Ready to run?" He asked as he dropped back into their hiding place and replaced his empty clip.

"Not sure how much running I can do. But with you? I'm always ready!" She stood on unsteady legs and smiled with determination.

Matthew grabbed her hand again, giving it another squeeze of encouragement. They took off into the ruins of their hometown as the world behind them exploded with unnatural light.

YOU WERE THERE

MIRIAM WADE

We were young when you asked.
We were young when I said yes.
We were told it would never last.
Still, you were there.

You were gone and we were estranged.
You wrote letters—the words never ceasing.
You returned and vows were exchanged.
Through it all, you were there.

We longed for children—we riled.
We struggled through adoption.
We were blessed with our wanted child.
No matter what, you were there.

You delivered our second child.
You watched as our children grew.
You saw our grandkids and smiled
For our family, you were there.

We thought we would have forever.
We never expected it all to end.
We, at that moment, were together.
Without warning, you were gone.

I watched as our grandchildren grew.
I welcomed our great-granddaughter.
I found it hard to not miss you.
For in her eyes, you are there.

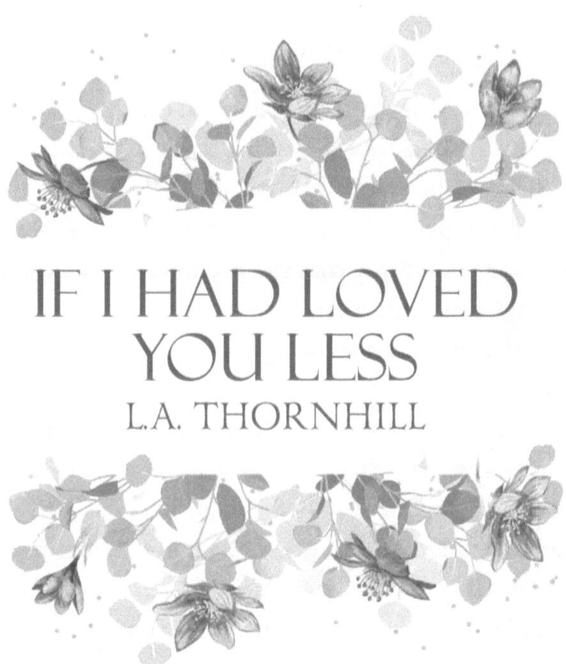

IF I HAD LOVED YOU LESS

L.A. THORNHILL

EDITH PERCH USED a handkerchief to wipe off twigs and leaves that cluttered the stone bench. Once suitable, she set down her book on the edge before taking a seat.

She breathed in the scent of the lake country—the pond water in front of her, the aged oak tree behind her whose enormous branches shaded her from the summer sun, the local garden that dotted the village of Broadhaven.

It had been nearly forty years since she last sat on this very bench overlooking the village she had been born and raised in. So many years, and yet her memories of this quaint English village were still fresh and vibrant in her mind's eye.

She sighed and picked up her book. Edith flipped through the pages of Jane Austen's *Persuasion.* As a young girl, this novel had been the least of her favorite of Miss Austen's works, always preferring the more youthful romance of *Sense and Sensibility* and the cleverness of *Emma*. However, life had greatly swayed her appreciation of this timeless book. It was a great pleasure to have found her original copy among her cousin's belongings. Edith had forgotten she had lent it to her before she moved away from Broadhaven all those decades ago.

She flipped toward the final pages of the book, well-creased from use. It was a relief to know that her cousin had enjoyed the story over the years. Edith settled on a page and read aloud: "'The one claim I shall make for my own sex is that we love longest when all hope is gone.'"

Edith's breath caught, and she quickly closed the book, setting it on her lap. Perhaps it was a good thing that she had a train to catch. Though all her memories of Broadhaven were cherished, some still tasted of sorrow and regret.

No, not regret. She had made the right choice, but it was difficult to reflect on nonetheless.

She closed her eyes and relished the feel of the breeze kissing her face, putting her stubborn, loose gray hair back into place. At least for the moment.

"Edie?" A voice broke through her thoughts.

Her breath caught, and her eyes flew open. The voice was different, older, a little gruffer, but she knew it all the same.

I should not have come back.

"Gideon."

Gideon Longhurst stood before her. Tall in stature, with curly gray hair, and slight mutton chops that couldn't disguise the spatter of freckles on his face. Wrinkles now creased his face as they did hers, but she still thought him as handsome as the day she left him. He held a top hat in his hand, and he wore a forest green tailcoat with a matching waistcoat. He looked every bit the dashing gentleman she knew he would be, excepting the faraway look in his eyes as he gazed at her.

She set her book aside and curtsied. "I'd know you anywhere."

"Edie. Edith . . ." He swallowed and then bowed. "And I would know you anywhere as well, Edith Perch." He raised an eyebrow. "Forgive me, is it still Perch?"

"It never changed," she said, her voice cracking. She sat back down on the bench. "What brings you to the park?"

"I was on my way to the family farm. I enjoy the walk through here." He passed his hat from one hand to the other a few times. "May I join you?"

She scooted over, making room for him. "This used to be your spot, after all."

"It still is." He sat next to her, resting his hat on his knee.

"Still?"

"I come here every Saturday evening." He chuckled. "It's just where I like to come and think."

"You always did." She drummed her fingers on her book. "How is the farm?"

"My brother Harold runs it quite well. It is thriving and will carry on in the family."

"I am so happy to hear it." She looked down at his hands, as calloused as she recalled. "Do you still work the land?"

"I help when I have free time. My law firm takes priority, of course, but I've never been able to rid myself of the farm boy in me."

Edith smiled, recalling the sunburned lad with auburn hair and freckles who used to be her constant companion. "You always did love the farm."

"Always." He glanced at her. "So tell me, Edith Perch, what have you done in the thirty-eight years that you've been gone? When you left our little village, you had taken the position of governess to a family in Ireland."

"And so I was for nearly ten years. I educated the four children in that household."

"Did the family treat you well?"

"Tolerably. I was just the governess, but I have no complaints."

"What did you do after?"

"I found work with a family back in England, but that didn't last a year."

"The children were too unruly?"

"No, their parents were."

Gideon nodded. "And what then?"

"I came to work for another family in Scotland and was there for another five years. The father had a cousin who was opening a schoolhouse and needed a teacher for the girls. There I remained until a few years ago when I longed to return to England. I lodged in London and tutored when I could until I found the job that I'm on my way to now. Once again, a teacher, but this time I'll be in Devonshire."

"You've seen more of her majesty's kingdom than I have."

"You never desired to travel, Gideon."

"Well, not for the long periods of time that you have. But why have you stopped here?"

She looked down at the book in her hands. “I received a letter from my cousin, Anne. She was selling what remained of the family home and asked me to take whatever I wanted. I had hoped to find something from my parents.”

“And did you?”

“Not as much as I liked. A few of Mama’s crochets. Papa’s hat. And a few of my books. So many of our possessions were sold to pay off Papa’s debts when he passed.”

“I’m sorry. He was a good man, and I miss him greatly. He simply got in over his head trying to save his land.”

Edith nodded.

Gideon dusted off the top of his hat. “Is . . . is that one of the books you found?”

She held it up for him to read. He removed a pair of spectacles from his waistcoat pocket and slipped them on. He smiled as he read the title. “You always were the romantic.” He replaced his spectacles.

“Something you used to tease me for.”

“Of course I did. You would sit on this very bench and ignore me for one of your love stories.”

“Oh, so you were teasing me because I was ignoring you?”

“Indeed.” He smiled.

She couldn’t resist smiling herself. “I’ll have you know, Gideon Longhurst, that I did that because I knew it aggravated you. Although I didn’t know exactly why it did.”

“You never did fully read my intentions,” he said, glancing over the pond.

Edith looked away, unable to ignore the meaning behind his words. *I didn’t misunderstand everything.*

“I’m sorry about Fiona,” she said after a moment. “She passed too soon.”

He dusted his hat again. “Thank you. We had thirty good years together. She went peacefully in her sleep.”

“How many children did the two of you have?”

“Four. Two boys and two girls.”

“That’s wonderful.”

“My eldest son will inherit the estate and my firm. My second son works with my brother on the farm.”

“He fell in love with the land, too?”

"Yes."

"And your girls?"

"Both are well married. The youngest is studying at university to be a teacher. The eldest just had her second child. And they all remain in steady contact, even after their mother passed."

"You have a full life, Gideon. I am happy for you."

"And what about you, Edith? Are you happy?"

She nodded. "Like you, my life has had its sorrows, but I am happy with my lot."

He narrowed his eyes. "What other sorrows have you had, Edie?"

"While I was in Scotland, I met a young naval captain. We were engaged. But his ship was lost in a storm."

"I am so sorry." He laid his hand on her arm. "What was his name?"

"Captain Erwin Benson. He was a good man, and I do not regret the time we had together, though it was too short."

"It always feels short. Even after thirty years."

She nodded. "I have no regrets, Gideon."

And she meant it. Returning to Broadhaven and seeing Gideon Longhurst again had reinforced the importance of the choice she made the last night she was in the village. The last night she saw her beloved friend.

He passed the hat between his hands once more. "Right. I have no regrets as well, but I still do have questions. Questions that have persisted within me all these years."

Edith traced the edge of the book's binding and said nothing.

"Edie." Gideon shifted on the bench so that his body was turned in her direction. "Thirty-eight years ago, the night before you were to leave for your governess work, I left you a note to meet me here. Do you remember?"

She did remember.

Perfectly.

He continued, "We sat on this very bench together. You were wearing your favorite blue dress. Your hair was messy because you had just taken it down for bed, and you had hurriedly fixed it."

She pushed a few of her loose hairs behind her ear.

He laid his hand on top of his hat as if he would dust it again, but he paused and then set it behind him. "That night, I found the courage to tell you how I felt about you back then. How I loved you . . ." He took a deep breath. "I had asked you to marry me."

Similarly, she set her book aside and faced him. "I remember."

"You said you did not reciprocate my feelings. That you believed we had only been teasing and playing games when we talked of getting married before."

Her throat went dry. How many nights had she laid awake, recalling the confusion and distress on Gideon's face when she said those words to him? And how it was the last expression on his handsome face that she would see for almost four decades? If she had one regret, it would be the way she left him.

But she had no other choice.

"I did say that," she whispered.

"For years, I believed what you said. That it was all in my head. Just another one of the many childish games we had played for far too long. But always, in my innermost thoughts, I wondered if you were being sincere with me. And if you weren't, why would you lie to me? I, who was your oldest and dearest friend. In that, I was secure of knowing." He laid a hand on top of hers. "Please, tell me the truth. Put my mind at ease. What changed that night? Why did you not accept my hand?"

This was something Edith had never once believed she would get the opportunity to do. So many letters she had begun to write but inevitably threw away. So many times imagining this exact moment but never buying a train ticket. Sometimes out of cowardice, other times out of a sense of propriety. But mostly because she thought it was a secret best kept to herself.

But what was to hold her back now? Here he was, asking her face-to-face. At their old spot, no less. How could she refuse him this?

Taking a deep breath, Edith unburdened her soul to her friend. "Gideon, that night we met here, you were so sweet and gallant. It was the most romantic thing I could have imagined. All of it. The stars. Your words. The breach of decorum. You were rescuing a newly orphaned girl and offering all your love. Not even Miss Austen could have written the moment better for me. If I hadn't already been in love with you, I surely would have fallen for you then."

Her old friend looked stunned. It was evident that he had not expected such a reply. "Then why did you lie to me? Edie, why?"

"I'm so sorry. I never wanted to lie to you, but I felt I had to."

"I don't understand."

She laid her hand on top of his, returning his gesture. "Oh, Gideon. You were studying law. Your parents were counting on you to help save the farm. Help support your brothers and sisters. And, it was no secret that Fiona Whitehall was very fond of you. Even her parents, despite their higher status, liked you as well. They encouraged your education and used their connections to get you to the university, did they not? They were hoping for a kind lad like you to marry their daughter and take care of their estate, not abuse it. You were just the lad."

"Edie . . ."

"You never could see it. You never could see then how much Fiona and her family liked you. You always believed it was because your father and hers were old friends. I never thought much of it, either. But when my parents died, I spent more time with the Whitehalls. They generously invited me to dinner on more than one occasion. And I discovered the difference in futures between us."

"You never said anything."

"I never thought of it until you proposed. Perhaps I was distracted by my loss or the fear of my having to take employment in another country. But that night on this bench, everything became quite clear to me. If I were to accept you, I would ruin your chances to support your family and harm your future as a lawyer."

"You couldn't know that, especially back then."

"What could an orphaned governess offer you? I had nothing. Only a few books that hadn't been sold. You would have gotten your education, yes. I believe the Whitehalls to be good enough to still support you, even if you were to marry me. But not to the extent they would have supported their son-in-law. And then what would have happened? How long would it have been until the farm was lost as my parents lost theirs? Who would have paid for your brother's military commission? Provided your sisters a dowry? That was all you, Gideon."

He glanced away. "You still should have been honest with me."

"Would you have let me go if I had? I knew you, Gideon. Even if you had let me go to Ireland, you would have never seen Fiona's affection for you. You would be writing to me to return home or threaten to come to Ireland to ask my hand again. No, my sweet Gideon. Eventually, I would have accepted you because I did love you." Tears filled her eyes. "Had I loved you less, I would have accepted you. But I loved you too well, so I had to ensure you were free of me."

"And you of me?"

"I thought I was. And I spent these decades confident in my choice. You were married and supporting your family. All was as it should be. But now..." She sighed. "I've missed you."

There was a long contemplative pause between them.

"I understand," he said after a moment. "And now I am at peace with my questions. But not with my heart."

Edith blinked rapidly, her turn to be confused.

He continued. "I spent the first years of your absence heartbroken. You were right. I, at last, did see Fiona. And I eventually was able to return her affection. Our marriage was good. My love for you was gone but never forgotten. I cherished our youth together too well to forget you. Even when I became a widower eight years ago, I mourned Fiona but never forgot you. But now, you're here. You're on this bench, holding a book, opening up to me as we used to in our youth. And I feel exactly as I did all those years ago."

"Gideon . . ."

"I'm not asking you to marry me. Not now. We're not the same people who sat on this bench before. We have had separate lives, separate loves. What I'm asking you is to remain here so we can get to know who we are now."

Edith's vision blurred, and her heart raced and fluttered as furiously as it did the night of his proposal. She couldn't fathom what was happening. Surely this was a dream. Perhaps she had fallen asleep on the train to Broadhaven, and her mind had conjured this up from her heart's secret depths.

"Gideon, where would I stay?"

"Always the practical one. My estate is large, but if you feel that improper, then you can stay at my family farm. Whatever you wish, you name it, and I will provide it. I want you to meet my children. I want the chance to see you again."

"This is so sudden. And I have employment . . ."

"I know. I know. I am asking a great deal of you. This may not work out, but I believe it will. That is if you can love me again as you say you did." He brushed away a tear that slipped down her cheek. "And still do?"

She nodded, lip quivering.

"My dearest Edie, I cannot let you leave me a second time."

Despite the tears in her eyes, laughter bubbled up inside of her. A joy and relief that she hadn't dared hope for filled her entire being.

"Then I will stay, Gideon."

He brought her hand to his lips and kissed it tenderly.

A fortnight later, Gideon proposed on the very same bench. This time Edith accepted him with all her heart.

LOVE IS AN ACTION VERB

ANNE J. HILL

They say you can't choose who you fall in love with
You're powerless over your own emotions
Love grabs you and won't let you go
Nothing can change how you feel, who you love

But I choose who I love
I choose you every day
In the storms and
In the great calms

I choose you by doing
My actions speak volumes
More than words ever could
And I choose to love you

Love is an action verb
Not a thing that takes you over
It doesn't drown you in
Impossibilities

Love doesn't chain you
Bind you, bid you to obey
You aren't a slave to emotion
Because love isn't an emotion

Love
Is an
Action
Verb

I didn't fall, stumble helplessly
In love, by accident
Waves didn't knock me over
A flimsy wishy washy soul

No
No
I *chose*
You

I didn't choose you because of how
You make me feel when the sun shines
When the days are bright and your
Smile is sweet like honey on your lips

No
No
I *chose*
You

For how you mess up and know it
How you apologize for your wrongs
And how you don't pretend you're perfect
How you fight to control your own soul

Because love
Is an
Action
Verb

I don't stumble blindly, hoping for love
I don't jump ship in the midst of a storm
I don't latch onto whatever arms are near
I don't submit to the emotion of love

Because, my dear
If you've taught me anything
Through all of these years
It's that...

Love
Is an
Action
Verb

So as we grow old, and wrinkles take over
I'll still sit in your arms and kiss your cheek
Because no matter what storms blow our way
I choose to love you to the end of our days

STONE SHATTERED

CASSANDRA HAMM

"ANWIR PROPOSED!"

Gemma's smile froze as she stared at her daughter, who'd just burst into the house like a devil was on her heels. Imara's eyes—the ones she'd inherited from Gemma—sparkled with fierce happiness, their vivid green nearly blinding in contrast to her light brown skin.

You didn't, Imara. Please tell me you didn't.

Wynnstan swept their daughter into his arms, nearly knocking over a nearby chair. "I'm so happy for you, Imara."

To think that man would be joining their household. *I should've spoken up. Shouldn't have let it go this far.* But to see Imara so happy...

"Mother? Did you hear me?" Imara's features shifted into their familiar scowl, scrunching the freckles on her nose. "I *told* you Anwir proposed to me."

"I thought the two of you weren't serious." Gemma kept her voice as light as she could.

"Of course we were serious." Imara pouted, making her seem more like seven than seventeen. "I thought you'd be happy."

"I am happy, Imara," Gemma said through gritted teeth. She glanced at Wynnstan, but he appeared puzzled. Typical man. "I just..." She needed a moment to think, to curb her tongue, but clearly, Imara wasn't going to give her that.

The one time Imara had *wanted* to come home, she'd come bearing bad news. *Did I drive her away?* Gemma couldn't think of how, but...maybe she'd learned her parenting skills from her uncle. The thought made her want to retch.

"We barely know him," Gemma said finally.

"I know him." Imara folded her arms over her chest. "And he loves me. That's all that matters."

Maybe Anwir did love Imara. But there was just something about him, a feeling, an itch Gemma couldn't quite scratch. The way his eyes lingered on Imara's body instead of her eyes...it reminded Gemma too much of Horan, the man her uncle Roan had nearly sold her to.

"It is a bit quick," Wynnstan conceded, "but we're very happy for you, Imara. He seems like a good man."

Gemma nearly choked at that. Good, kind, oblivious Wynnstan.

"Do you have something to say, Mother?" Imara's eyes were knives.

"He should've asked your father first," Gemma said.

"Of course he asked Father," Imara snapped.

Wynnstan frowned. "No, he didn't."

Imara's green eyes widened. "He said he—" She paused for a long moment. "Never mind. He must've just forgotten."

"Forgotten?" Gemma sputtered. "He must've forgotten to consult your parents on marriage? Imara, do you hear yourself?"

"Gem—" Wynnstan started.

"Can't you be happy for me for once, Mother?" Imara stomped away with her fists clenched.

The door slammed shut behind her, sealing her away as completely as the wall that had somehow formed between them, a wall as solid and impenetrable as Wynnstan's skin had once been. And Gemma wasn't sure a simple kiss could tear it down as it had with her husband.

"What the blazes, Gemma?" Wynnstan whirled on her.

Though the years had taken some of his strength and intimidation, she still shrunk back instinctively. *Don't cower,* she reminded herself. *It's just Wynn.*

"She is *not* marrying that boy," Gemma said.

"Why in the world not?" Wynnstan spread his arms wide. "He cares for Imara."

"Everyone cares for Imara," Gemma muttered.

"Why don't you like him, Gemma? Why?"

How could she explain the unease that crept over her when she was around her daughter's beloved? "Do you see the way he looks at her?"

Wynnstan snorted. "Like every red-blooded young man looks at his beloved."

"You didn't look at me like that!" she snapped. "Like you wanted to devour me!"

"I wasn't a man then!"

Gemma recoiled. Was that it, then? Were all human-born men treacherous and lustful and possessive? Had she merely gotten lucky in finding a stone-golem-turned-man?

"Gemma, dear—"

"Don't 'dear' me!" she snapped.

"I'm just saying that no one seems to have any complaints about Anwir."

She heard the unspoken words—*No one but you.* Her lips tightened. "Do the other men talk about his exploits?"

"No. He seems to have fallen very hard for our Imara and stopped pursuing anyone else as soon as he met her. Loyalty—a good trait, you have to admit."

"Or obsession," she murmured.

"Come on, Gem. He treats her well. He cares for her. He'll provide for her."

"He asked her to court *three times* before she said yes."

"Perseverance," Wynnstan said. "He didn't give up, and now it's paid off."

"He should have respected her right to say no."

"Gemma, that's not—"

"Isn't it?"

"You need to give the boy a chance," Wynnstan said in an annoyingly reasonable tone. "I know your past experiences make you untrusting, but—"

"Past experiences?" she exploded. *"Past experiences?* You mean my good-for-nothing uncle who tried to sell me into marriage to a man who would've beat me as much as, if not more than, my uncle had? Those past experiences?"

"Gemma, it's been twenty years." Wynnstan palmed the back of his hairless head. "Isn't it time to move on?"

The words connected like a punch to the gut, worse than anything her uncle had ever done to her. She stared, open-mouthed, hands shaking. *Move on? Move on?!*

Wynnstan's eyes widened. "I didn't... I mean..."

Her voice was hoarse. "How can you say that to me?"

"Gemma, that's not what I meant."

As if she could just wish away the pain and the memories and the terror every time a man looked at her, even now, twenty years after she'd escaped from Roan. She tried to keep her breathing steady, but her lungs were collapsing, and she was remembering. *Oh, Holy One, make it stop—*

She whirled around and stalked toward their room.

"Gemma, wait—"

She slammed the door, letting her hand rest on the knob to still its shaking. *You're safe,* she told herself. *You're free.*

But what if Imara had just agreed to relinquish her freedom? Gemma couldn't just sit back and watch. She had to help her daughter. Even if Imara hated her for it.

Get your slimy hands off my daughter.

Gemma barely stopped herself from speaking the words aloud as Anwir slid his arm around Imara. Gemma's hand tightened around Wynnstan's bicep.

What was wrong with her? Her daughter was getting married. She should be ecstatic.

Offer him a drink. Offer him a seat. But when Anwir's hand wandered lower than Imara's hips, Gemma bit her lip so hard she tasted blood. Imara batted his hand away. He just laughed and tugged her closer.

"Be civil," Wynnstan murmured in Gemma's ear. His breath stirred her graying curls.

"I am civil," she snapped.

She didn't have to look at him to know he was raising his eyebrows.

"Gemma and I want to welcome you to the family, Anwir," Wynnstan said more loudly.

Anwir smiled. It was a slick sort of smile, one that belonged to charmers and womanizers. Or maybe Gemma was reading too much into it.

"Thank you, sir," Anwir said.

Oh no. Not *sir.* Sure enough, when she glanced at Wynnstan, his smile was a little wider now, a little too pleased.

She had to admit that Anwir *was* handsome with his thick black hair and warrior physique. No wonder Imara had fallen for him.

I fell in love without knowing what my husband looked like under all that stone, Gemma thought crossly.

Wynnstan nudged her.

She coughed. "Yes, we, ah, are thrilled that Imara has decided to settle down." Was that as awkward as it sounded in her head?

Imara shot Gemma a glare as if expecting her to misbehave. *I know how to behave,* thought Gemma, though she decided Anwir might benefit from a beating.

That's Roan speaking, she realized. She had never been big on physical punishment—not after what she'd gone through with Roan. But sometimes, she found him living on through her in her mannerisms, her words, her actions. Her temper. Her impatience.

She hated it.

"You'll have the service in Father Eimar's temple, I presume?" Wynnstan said. "Your mother and I got married there, Imara."

Ah, yes, their wedding day. A beautiful and terrible memory. The day Roan tried to keep her from marrying Wynnstan. She'd forgiven her uncle, but thinking of his cruel words—which popped up in her brain more often than she liked—sometimes sent her spiraling.

Stop. This is about Imara, not you.

"The temple?" Imara wrinkled her nose. "No," she said with a laugh.

"*No*?" Gemma repeated. Where else would they have it?

"We've arranged for the judge to do the ceremony," Anwir said, tugging Imara closer. "Something small and...intimate." He kissed her. Not something soft and sweet but hungry and possessive, taking pleasure instead of giving, staking his claim on her.

Only Wynnstan's hand on Gemma's elbow held her back.

After several awkward moments, she cleared her throat, then more loudly when they still didn't break apart. Oh, heavens, did they have no shame? *Wynn and I never do that in front of* you, *Imara!*

"Excuse me!" Gemma said. "We're having a conversation right now."

Imara finally dislodged herself from Anwir, curls tousled, lips slightly red and swollen. She rolled her brilliant green eyes. "It's fine, Mother. We'll still be 'legitimate,' even if we don't get married in a stupid temple."

Gemma's lips tightened. As if that was what she was worried about.

"When will the wedding be?" Wynnstan asked, his eyes flicking between Gemma and Imara.

"At the end of this month," Anwir said.

Gemma flinched. "Isn't that a bit soon?"

"You think everything is too soon," Imara spat.

Gemma forced herself to take even breaths. "I just think you're rushing into this. Why don't you wait a little longer, get to know each other better? Marriage is a big commitment."

Anwir's arms tightened around Imara. She curled into his side.

He smothered her fire. That was the only way Gemma could explain it. He'd wrapped little chains around Imara's wrists and had the audacity to call it love.

"We just know," Imara said. "We're meant to be together, Anwir and me. Like you and Father."

How could Imara compare her relationship with Anwir to what Gemma had with Wynnstan, her husband of twenty years? Gemma felt herself slipping, felt the anger rising up. "We are *not* the same," she said through gritted teeth.

"You barely knew Father when you ran away with him." Imara glared down at Gemma with some of her old fire, but it seemed warped, changed by the man who'd stolen her away. "Isn't that right?"

"That's not..." Well, Gemma supposed she really *hadn't* known Wynnstan all that well when she ran away from Folstad to start over. But Wynnstan had always shown himself to be kind and good. "He's not right for you, Imara. Trust me."

"Why should I trust you?" Imara barked out a bitter laugh. "You never care about what I want."

Gemma stared at the girl she'd give anything for, the girl she just wanted to protect. *That's not...it can't be true.*

"Imara," Wynnstan said slowly, "don't say things like that to your mother."

"She can say whatever the blazes she wants," Anwir said. "She's her own person."

What if Imara's right? What if I am *being too hard on her?*

Gemma broke away from Wynnstan to step closer to Imara. "I'm just worried about you, Imara. Marriage is important, and it's not to be entered into lightly."

"I know that, Mother. I'm not dumb."

"You don't understand." Gemma swallowed. She hated being vulnerable in front of Anwir, but if it would get Imara to listen to her... "My uncle tried to force me to marry a terrible man, and I just don't want you to feel pressured into marrying someone."

"Anwir isn't a terrible man. And no one is forcing me. This is what *I* want. Why can't you accept that?" Imara blinked hard, but tears still slipped down her cheeks.

"Come on, Imara." Anwir guided Imara toward the door, his knuckles white as he gripped her skin too hard.

Let go of her! Let go!

Imara didn't fight back. She just let Anwir pull her across the floor..

"You don't need them," Anwir said.

"Wait!" Gemma cried, lurching after Imara. But her daughter was already out the door.

"You think this is my fault?" Gemma stared at her husband. "Are you serious?"

"You pushed her away." Wynnstan's jaw muscles throbbed. "You should've been *happy* for her."

"I can't! There's something wrong with him, Wynn. Can't you feel it, or are you too wrapped up in your own head?"

Wynnstan let out an irritated grunt. "You're the one who's wrapped up in your own head. He makes Imara *happy,* Gemma, and you want to take that away from her?"

"Happiness isn't everything."

"So you don't want her to be happy?"

"That's not what I said and you know it." Gemma squeezed the bridge of her nose.

"They love each other. They want to be together."

"She doesn't know what she wants. She's just a child."

"She's eighteen years old." Wynnstan spread his arms wide. "She's past marriageable age."

"So now you want us to sell her off to the first man who asks?"

Wynnstan groaned. "Gemma!"

Her lip curled. "I guess Anwir probably isn't the first to ask, just the first to be accepted."

"Why are you so against him?" Wynnstan shouted.

Gemma stepped back, her body on high alert, her breathing speeding up. In her head, she saw Roan gripping a belt, and she instinctively covered her face with her hands.

"Gemma?" Wynnstan's voice was soft and choked. "Oh, Gem, I'm sorry. Are you all right?"

Gemma lowered her hands. *You're safe,* she told herself, staring up into Wynnstan's face. *He won't hurt you.* Infuriating man that he was, he was still *good.*

"I shouldn't have yelled." He carefully reached for her, then pulled back.

Part of her wanted him to grab her hands. The other part wanted to smack him. But she nodded.

"I thought..." Wynnstan paused. "I thought you'd forgiven him."

Roan. Cowering away from slaps. Flinching from verbal daggers. Crying alone at night because she would never be free. *You're free now. Truly free.*

"I *did* forgive him. But that doesn't change what he did to me. How he hurt me. The scars he left." She blinked hard to hold back tears.

Wynnstan's arms came around her, and she almost pushed him away, but it felt so good, so solid, so familiar. She inhaled his woody scent and focused on breathing, in, out, in, out.

"I will admit, Anwir did seem a little..." Wynnstan paused.

"Controlling?" she mumbled into his tunic. "Possessive? Manipulative? Slimy?"

"Slimy?" Wynnstan repeated.

Gemma nodded against his tunic.

"Well, that's not exactly what I was going to say." Wynnstan's barrel chest rumbled as he spoke. "Still, I suppose he might not be the greatest man for our Imara."

"I told you. You didn't believe me." Her voice broke. Her eyes decided to leak without her permission.

"I know. I'm sorry."

There was silence for a long moment. Gemma ached with all the things she wished she could say, all the things she wished she could undo. She knew she wasn't a good parent. How could anyone be? But what if she'd ruined her chance to see her daughter get married?

"I'm worried about her, Wynn," Gemma whispered. "I don't want her to make a mistake."

"We all make mistakes, Gem."

"But this is one of massive proportions. If he hurts her and I don't try to stop it from happening, I..." Her words trailed off, a sob hiccuping in her throat.

Wynnstan kissed her hair. He didn't say anything, and somehow, that was all right.

Her hands fisted in his shirt. Wynnstan's stomach protruded more than it had when they were young and foolish, and his arms weren't as muscular as they once were, but there was something comforting about knowing his imperfections.

Wynnstan pulled back and gazed down at her. How she loved those deep, dark eyes. "I'll talk to her," he said. "See if I can get through to her, understand what she's feeling. Maybe it's all a misunderstanding."

"All right," she said. Maybe Imara would listen to her father. "I'm sorry I yelled."

"I'm sorry I didn't listen."

"You're listening now."

Wynnstan lowered his face to Gemma's. Their lips brushed, slowly, sweetly, as though for the first time. One hand cradled the back of her head while the other splayed against the small of her back. *I love you, I love you, I love you.*

Slowly, the shattered bits of her heart shifted back into place.

PART FOUR:

CHERISHING

FAMILY, FRIENDS, & STRANGERS

STONE STEADFAST

CASSANDRA HAMM

GEMMA NEVER THOUGHT that on her daughter's wedding day, she'd be crouching behind a bush.

Sweat soaked the back of her neck as she watched the courthouse door. The sun beat down mercilessly like one of Uncle Roan's belts. Her knees were getting much too old for this, especially since she'd returned to the same spot for the past few days just in case Imara and Anwir decided today would be the day they'd elope.

What if they'd decided to get married earlier than they'd originally planned? What if she'd missed it? *Holy One, please, don't let me have missed it.*

"Gemma, what are you doing?"

Gemma nearly leaped out of her skin. Her husband Wynnstan stood behind her, tall and dark and frowning.

"You're drawing too much attention to me," she hissed. "Get down!"

He grunted as he knelt, knees creaking. "You know you're being ridiculous, dear."

She glared over at him. A piece of hair fell into her face, and she tried to blow it out of her eyes, but it refused to do anything but quiver. Wynnstan gently tucked it behind her ear, his rough fingers lingering on her jaw.

"You can't stop their wedding," he said gently.

"I wouldn't have to if you'd gotten through to her!" she snapped.

He stiffened as though she'd slapped him. She winced and gave his hand a quick squeeze. "Sorry."

He squeezed back and didn't let go.

She'd known it was unlikely Imara would listen, even if Wynnstan was the one doing the talking. Still, it stung to know that their daughter didn't want *either* of them at her wedding.

"I'd been wondering where you were these past few days," Wynnstan said. "I guess now I have my answer."

She knew she was being ridiculous, hiding behind a bush, waiting for a glimpse of the daughter who refused to speak to her. The more she tried to cling, the more she lost Imara to Anwir.

Had she been wrong trying to convince Imara not to marry Anwir? Would it have been better to support her?

Gemma blinked hard, hating the tears that stung her eyes. "I'd give anything to even be invited to the wedding, even though she's marrying *him.*"

"I know," Wynnstan said.

Movement caught her eye, and she looked back to the courthouse. The breath left her lungs. Imara and Anwir stood at the courthouse door, hands entwined.

Leaf-green fabric flowed down Imara's skin like water. Gemma's old wedding dress.

Only Wynnstan's hand in hers kept Gemma from running toward the courthouse and throwing her arms around Imara. *I'm sorry, I'm sorry, I'm sorry.* Words that begged to escape because how could she be angry with Imara when her own heart was so easily twisted?

"Heavens," Wynnstan breathed. "She's..."

The door opened, revealing the judge, Udric. Imara turned her head just before Anwir pulled her inside, giving Gemma a glimpse of her painted face. Even at a distance, her kohl-rimmed green eyes shone like emeralds, and her red-stained lips curved in a shy smile.

"Perfect," Gemma finished.

Wynnstan leaned his head against Gemma's as the door closed, sealing their daughter inside the courthouse.

What am I doing out here? Imara would need her to get through this marriage, and Holy One help her, Gemma would be there. Now, if only Imara would accept her forgiveness.

Gemma brushed a quick kiss against Wynnstan's cheek and stood, knees creaking. She brushed the dirt off her dress—far too simple for a wedding, but she didn't have time to change—and bustled toward the door.

Wynnstan, muttering under his breath, hurried after her. "We can't stop her, Gem," he said.

"I'm not going to stop her," Gemma said, and a weight seemed to lift from her shoulders. "I'm going to love her through whatever happens because what kind of mother would I be if I abandoned her now?"

With a sort of strangled groan, Wynnstan pulled her close, kissing her with a passion she'd almost forgotten. Gasping, she clutched his tunic to keep herself steady. He pulled back, murmuring, "I love you so much, Gemma."

She would have stayed there forever if there hadn't been more pressing matters. So she gave him one more quick kiss and pulled open the courthouse door.

The narrow hallway smelled like jasmine, likely from Imara's wedding attire. It opened into a large, open room full of benches. Hands clasped, Imara and Anwir stood by Udric, the judge.

Udric's eyes landed on Gemma and Wynnstan. "Your parents have arrived, Imara," he said.

Imara released Anwir's hand and whirled around. Gemma let out an involuntary gasp.

That brief glimpse outside hadn't done Imara's beauty justice. Her light brown curls were twisted into an elegant knot, and her eyes appeared luminous, almost glowing. *My daughter. My beautiful, strong daughter.*

"Mother? Father?" Imara's blood-red mouth hung open. "What are you...?"

Wynnstan's hand slipped into Gemma's. It was a bit sweaty, but she welcomed it all the same.

"I told you she'd try to stop us." Anwir's lips pinched into a thin line, turning his handsome face sour.

"I'm not trying to stop you." Gemma swallowed hard. "I want to see my only child get married."

Udric looked back and forth between Gemma and the soon-to-be-married couple as though deciding whether or not to throw Gemma out.

Imara, for once in her life, seemed to have lost the capacity for words. Her mouth opened and closed like a beached fish's. "Mother, I..."

"I'm sorry I didn't support you, Imara." Gemma's eyes pricked with sudden moisture. "I won't lie and say that I approve of your choice...." Her eyes flicked toward the glaring Anwir. "And I completely understand if you don't want me here, but I just want to be a part of your life." She choked back a sob. "In whatever capacity. Please."

Imara stared down at Gemma. When had she gotten so tall? Yet, the expression on her face was so lost, so fragile, she seemed like a little girl again, terrified, wanting Gemma to explain away her fears. *I'm sorry I failed you, Imara.*

"Don't listen to her, Imara," Anwir hissed. "You know how controlling she is. She's been trying to break us apart, remember? She wants to stop the wedding!"

"She says she doesn't," Imara said in a quavering voice.

"You trust that liar?"

Imara stiffened. Some of the fire returned to her eyes. "*No one* calls my mother a liar," she said.

Something warmed inside Gemma. She gripped Wynnstan's hand more tightly—grasping this fragile moment where Imara loved her enough to defend her.

Anwir groaned. "Come on, Imara. You know this is all a ploy to get you to trust her again, and then—"

"*I'll* decide what's going on, thank you," Imara said in an icy tone.

Anwir stiffened. The look in his eyes chilled Gemma to her very bones—it was the look Roan had worn when she'd dared to defy him.

Run, Imara, she wanted to scream. *Run.*

She couldn't make Imara's choice for her, but she'd protect Imara however she could.

"Let's just forget this happened and get on with the ceremony," Anwir said, grabbing Imara's hand with a possessiveness that made Gemma's blood boil. "Judge, we specifically requested that her parents not be allowed at the—"

"Wait." Imara tried to pull free of Anwir's grip, but he held tight. With her free hand, she brushed an errant curl away from her flawless face. "I think Mother is right."

Gemma gaped.

"We really haven't known each other that long," Imara said. "Maybe we *did* rush into this. We should get to know each other a little better before getting married—"

"What?" Anwir exploded.

Imara cried out, just a whimper, but Gemma immediately knew—Anwir was holding her hand too tight. Small bruises, small wounds that could be explained away. Had she missed any on her daughter's skin, or had Anwir not yet gone that far?

"Imara, I love you! I want to marry you! How can you say that we're not ready?"

"That's not—I just want to be sure!" Imara tried to pull away. "Anwir, let go of me!"

Wynnstan swelled beside Gemma, all strength and righteous fury. He muttered in her ear, "You were right about that boy."

"You're surprised?" Gemma hissed. "Holy One, keep me from strangling Anwir."

Anwir shifted to grab Imara's wrists, leaning forward until their foreheads touched. "Bind yourself to me. Leave everything else behind." He cast a significant glance at Gemma and Wynnstan. "All we need is each other."

Imara's emerald eyes met Gemma's, and in them, Gemma saw herself—young, terrified, unsure. Roan had tried to convince her not to marry Wynnstan twenty years ago. But now their roles were flipped—the abusive lover and the kind guardian. Well, not that Gemma would consider herself *kind,* exactly, just ready to protect Imara from the kind of men who had always made Gemma's life a living hell.

"I don't want to choose," Imara said. Hearing her voice break nearly made Gemma's own heart break. "Can't I have both?"

"They'll try to drive you away from me. They already have." Anwir pressed a rough, desperate kiss to her lips. "You're mine, and I'm yours. All we need is each other."

Gemma couldn't keep quiet any longer. "Imara isn't an object to be claimed," she hissed. "She is a *human being.*"

"Stay out of this." Anwir's glare could saw through wood.

"Don't talk to my mother like that!" Imara finally wrenched free of Anwir's grip, stumbling toward Wynnstan. He caught her against his chest, arm curled around her protectively.

Anwir moved toward Imara but stopped when Wynnstan growled at him. "Imara, get back here," Anwir said. "We belong together."

Imara held her shoulders rigid. "I belong to no one," she said. "Least of all *you.*"

He flinched, like she'd rammed him with a blade.

Gemma nearly crumpled. *Holy One, thank you. Please protect her from the consequences of this, but thank you for helping her see what he was before it was too late.*

"You'll never find anyone who loves you more than I do," Anwir hissed.

Though filled with tears, Imara's eyes were as steely as ever. "I already have." She pointed at Gemma and Wynnstan.

Hesitantly, Gemma reached for Imara's shoulder and squeezed it. Imara reached up and held her hand over Gemma's. Gemma swallowed hard, trying not to burst into tears.

Wynnstan rose to his full height. "You need to leave, Anwir," he said, "or we'll have the judge throw you out himself."

Udric, who'd been watching all with wide eyes, nodded vigorously.

Anwir shot them a bitter glare, but Gemma turned away dismissively. He'd lost, and she'd be ready for whatever he'd send at them in revenge. *You will never have my daughter again.*

"You'll come back to me, Imara," Anwir said. "You'll see."

"I make my own choices," Imara said.

He practically burned with fury, but one glance at Wynnstan made him turn toward the door. When he disappeared, Gemma slumped against Wynnstan. "Thank you," she whispered.

"I'm proud of you," Wynnstan said. "Both of you."

Imara stood ramrod straight, but Gemma could see the shattered look in her. It would take her time to heal. Maybe she never fully would. But Gemma would walk with her through it. *Thank you, Holy One,* she thought again. *Thank you, thank you, thank you.*

"I'm sorry, Mama," she said.

"I'm sorry too," Gemma said.

Gemma, Wynnstan, and Imara leaned into each other and stayed like that in the courthouse, Imara in wedding finery. Maybe their embrace was healing enough.

LOVE

DENICA MCCALL

I follow love like a stream with no end, and it, in turn,
Follows me
An infinite chase around the world, even extending
To the universe
I could walk forever and never escape its flow
Yet I'm still searching in shadow, wishing
That it might peek through the shroud above me like sunlight through evergreens
Love is my peace, and Love is my king
Love is what I hope will terminate this wandering and leave me knowing
I won't end up alone, because
In the end, all I want is to find home
All I've ever desired is to have family, a people
I can call my own
But this path is not mine to pave; its bristles and curves were
Already made
I have choices but
The best is when I wait, silence my eager feet and see

That all this time, love has been whispering to me
Beside me, inside me, around me, above me
Love is this light that pierces my dimmed sight,
A constant companion that I just need to receive.

A PAPA FOR NOVA

HANNAH CARTER

NOVA TRAILED AFTER Aster, her current guardian, as he strode down a road in the light of the evening sun.

"My legs are tired," Nova said in case Aster hadn't heard her the first seventy times.

Her purple, four-fingered hand reached for his special darknight cape: a magical fabric that concealed their true nature as moon elves. And since the fae wanted to kill all moon elves—and were quite good at it—Aster and Nova had to follow two main rules: *don't draw attention to yourself* and *stay close at all costs*.

Aster chuckled as he passed her a maple syrup bite. "Here. I'm guessing that will make your legs stop hurting. But please hurry. We have to beat the fae hunter to the big top. I'm sure she'll try to attack our new friend during the show."

Nova chewed her treat and frowned. Aster had been tracking a fae hunter for a whole year now in hopes of her leading him to another kidnapped moon elf child. Yesterday, he'd returned from patrol and announced he'd followed the fae to a local circus and found their *new friend*—a boy named Sirius.

"Do you think..." Nova began, but the words got all jammed up, sticky as her candy.

Aster latched onto her hand. "Think what, little mouse?"

Nova scrunched up her face. Oh, the words were all gummy! *Do you think we need to rescue this boy? What if you love him more than me? Do you want to be my papa?*

Stupid, sticky words. Nova sniffled a bit.

Aster paused so he could kneel and smooth her white hair. "Please don't cry. You don't need to be scared that the hunters will get Sirius. We'll save him."

Nova's mouth twitched. Aster drew her forehead closer to his. It was a familial moon elf gesture, one of the many nuances of her heritage Aster had taught her.

Papa.

The word got all stuck in Nova's throat.

Aster pulled away and patted her head. "Come on. We can't let the hunter win."

The circus tent rose into the sky, a gigantic red-and-white beacon, all lit up. Its bright joviality was a jarring juxtaposition to the dark feelings that lurked within Nova. While minstrels plucked out jaunty jigs, Nova glared at all of them in passing from underneath her darknight cape and pulled closer to Aster.

"Keep a look out for the fae hunter." Aster drew Nova closer to him as they entered the big top. His obsidian eyes scanned the crowd. "We're going to grab Sirius and get out of here. I want to avoid fighting anyone if we can."

They settled down into their seats, and the ringmaster came out to the center of the ring. A spotlight lit him from above, and he held out his hands. "Ladies and gentlemen, I'd like to welcome you to the show...."

He continued on, but Nova didn't hear him because Aster leaned close and nudged her. He pointed to a little boy that couldn't have been much older than her—maybe nine or ten, eleven at the most.

"Look. Do you see him?" Aster asked.

Nova squinted, even though it was hard *not* to see the interloper, with his mottled purple skin that would turn a brillant, sparkling amethyst in the moonlight. "I guess."

"He doesn't know how much danger he's in." Aster squeezed her hand. "He doesn't know anything about moon elves at all, just like you didn't last year."

Nova curled her shoulders in. Last year—when she'd been in the orphanage, all alone, unwanted, and shoved up in a tiny attic room. She hadn't known anything about the fae, either, and it was kind of scary now that she did. But she also hadn't known about getting tucked into bed at night with a kiss and a bedtime story, or having someone make her pancakes for breakfast, or a hundred other *good* things, either.

Is that all going to go away? Are you going to send me back to the orphanage and tell all the bedtime stories to Sirius instead?

Are you going to like him *more than me?*

All the words got jammed up inside her mouth again, and refused to come out. Tears burned at Nova's eyes, and she rubbed the back of her hand underneath her nose to keep from sniffling.

Sirius waved to the crowd as he started to climb up the tower to the trapeze. Nova swallowed. It felt hard to do that, like maybe her throat was so full of the gummy words that nothing could get down, either.

The interloper took to the trapeze in the opening act. Nova glared at him as he somersaulted between bars and—

Sirius shrieked as one side of the rope that held the highest bar snapped.

The thread on the remaining cable popped but didn't break. Sirius held onto his lifeline and revolved in a slow circle.

"Help!" he cried.

The crowd erupted in pandemonium and surged forward.

"Someone get that boy down!"

"Stop the show!"

People jostled Nova this way and that. Her grip slipped on Aster's hand, and—

"Stay here, Nova!" Aster cried over the roar of the crowd. "Stay...!"

The noise drowned out the rest of his words. Nova grunted as the crowd pushed past her, and she fell forward. Her hands smacked against the ground, but nobody was there to pick her up or kiss her hurt palms.

Her throat choked up again.

She had to find Aster. She had to convince him to leave right now.

Nova started to crawl through the dirt toward the ring. Wherever the boy was, Aster would be. Right?

But Sirius still dangled in mid-air. He cried out again—he sounded so *scared.* Why hadn't Aster reached him yet?

The frayed strand of the rope loosened a bit more, and Sirius slipped closer to the ground.

"Help!" he wailed. "Please, somebody help!"

Nova reached the side of the circus ring. She couldn't see Aster, couldn't hear him over the chaos. But when she lifted her head, all she could see was another moon elf—terrified, alone, just like her. Just like how she'd been in Miss Daisy's attic. Locked away, unloved, without hope of rescue. Each day, each month, each year, for eight years, Nova had suffered and been ignored and mocked for her heritage.

Until Aster.

Aster, who tucked her in with a kiss and a bedtime story, who made pancakes and taught her about family.

But even though he did all those things...Aster was not actually her papa. He could send her right back to Miss Daisy's and replace her with Sirius.

And if he did...maybe then it was Sirius' turn to have Aster now, not hers. For him to get bedtime kisses and breakfast pancakes. After all, Aster *really* wanted to find Sirius.

This time, the tears did fall—but at least Sirius did not.

Nova scrambled toward a large ladder. Her hands shook, and her stomach tumbled the higher she climbed.

"Do it for Aster," she whispered to herself. "You can do it, little mouse."

A platform loomed at the top, and Nova pulled herself onto it. She whimpered as she scooted forward, flat on her tummy.

She peeked her pointed chin over the ledge. The rope gave a bit more and brought Sirius an inch closer to his doom.

"Hey!" she called. "Give me your hand!"

Dark, frantic eyes met hers.

Sirius stretched out, their fingers a few inches apart.

He couldn't reach.

Nova edged closer.

He nodded. She could almost hear him counting to three under his breath, and she braced herself for the impact.

Sirius swung his body with a grunt. The rope snapped, but he was already airborne. His hand grasped Nova's...except a nine-year-old was no match for gravity.

The added weight jerked her over the edge. Both of them tumbled down, and time slowed.

"Nova!" Aster bellowed from below.

"*Papa*!" The word exploded from Nova's lips, the usual stickiness gone.

She clung to Sirius and squeezed her eyes shut. A thud—groans—dirt—*pain*.

Nova moaned and peeked one eye open. She'd collided with Aster, his expression a contortion of agony. Groaning, he propped himself up, his arms still wrapped around them.

"Papa," Nova sobbed. She clung to Aster and clutched Sirius' hand. "*Papa*."

"Shh, shh. It's okay." He winced, and his eyes flew open. "Nova—Sirius. Are you both okay? Are you hurt? We've got to get out of here—I haven't seen the hunter yet, but that doesn't mean she's not here." He checked them over like he'd forgotten his own pain. Nova sniffled and wiped her eyes, but nothing she did stopped the tears until Aster pressed his forehead against hers.

"Oh, Nova," Aster whispered. "You saved Sirius. I'm so proud of you."

Nova nodded. "And—I know you might love him more than me, but...please don't give me back to the orphanage. *Pretty* please? Do you think...maybe...you can love both of us?"

"Yes." Aster pulled back and ruffled Sirius' hair. The poor boy quivered and sniffled as his eyes darted between them.

Aster's voice sounded gummy when he continued. "I can love both of you very much. I already do."

He placed his forehead against Nova's again.

Sirius whimpered, and Nova and Aster separated once more.

Slowly, Nova pressed her forehead against her new brother's. "We can both love you."

SISTER

DENICA MCCALL

I never had a sister, but
Family is chosen, right?
When all the crap hits the dam and
Oceans burst through, threatening to
Drown me in *I'm too much,* or *I'm not enough*
She's there, grasping my slipping fingers
An image of
"We might as well have had the same mom"
Words flush from lips at end of day when
The moon has risen, and all the world's asleep or
At war
And she speaks, and she listens
Her choice, despite my disposition
Expositions embrace my chaos as I sit and recite
The stories along the winding streets of my mind

I never had a sister, but
My heart is chosen, right?

Who else would put aside her own agenda to listen to mine,
To hear me ramble and not only tolerate but delight?
She lifts me up; I lift her too
We shatter mirrors when reflections lie
And instead, echo the other's beauty in the contact of eyes
When we break contact, there's a missing piece, like
She was always destined to be part of my family

I never had a sister, but
This one's a keeper, right?
Too many questions linger, based on those who came and went
And I still hang onto insecurities
But sometimes, her presence is my cure
Fighting to remember, we hold each other up
Fighting to deny the whispers that creep up
We endure
Because
She's my sister

SIX MONTHS

MARY E. DIPPLE

"HEY, MAN."

The couch cushion sinks halfway to the floor under Dan's weight as he sits next to me. I swallow hard, unable to take my eyes off the shining metal in my hand. "Ruth told you?"

"Yeah."

I shake my head. "I can't. I can't do it. Not again."

"Yes, you can." Dan leans forward, elbows to knees.

The dim basement hides my tears. "You don't understand. You weren't there the first time. I can't put Ruth through that. I just can't." My hand trembles as I run it through my hair. I don't want to die. "I don't have the strength to do this, Dan."

"You're not alone, Andy. Not this time. I wasn't there the first time. And neither was Ruth. But we're here now. We'll be your strength, man. Just lean on us. Okay? We're here for you, and we aren't leaving. Not now. Not ever." Dan's hand reaches around me and squeezes my shoulder. "Besides, I'm going to need someone to be my best man."

"No way!" A smile breaks through my tears, and for a moment, I forget the metal in my hand. "Susan said yes?"

"Yeah, so how about it? Think you can stick around to be my best man?"

"When's the wedding?"

"Six months."

My smile turns to a grimace. The doctor said three. I take a shuddering breath and look at the metal in my hand. To make it to Dan's wedding, I'd have to fight.

Dan squeezes my shoulder again. "I've got you, buddy. You don't have to fight alone. Not this time."

The metal stares back at me, whispering lies, telling me that it's not enough. That *I'm* not enough. I close my eyes and slid out the mag. "Six months?" I nod. "I can do six months."

"You bet you can, buddy." Dan pulls me into a bone-crushing hug, his hand sliding the gun from mine. "I've got you, man. We're in this together. No matter what."

NOTICING

HAILEY HUNTINGTON

THE GIRL SITS alone on the bridge. Pedestrians file past with nothing more than a glance—some don't even give her that.

I almost walk past her too. But something about her reminds me of my daughter—maybe it's the faded jean jacket or the curly, dark hair—so I slow down and truly look at the girl. She stares past the tide of people to the other side, her gaze fixed on the moving water. The autumn breeze blows her hair into her face, but she doesn't brush it back. Shadows hang beneath her haunted eyes. Call it mother's intuition, but my gut knows that something is wrong.

Grocery shopping can wait.

I retrace my steps several yards back and pop into the small cafe. After a couple of minutes, I exit with two cups in hand. My pulse increases as I walk up to the bench. "Coffee?"

It comes out awkwardly blunt. Who's going to accept a drink from some random lady on the street?

But the girl looks up, drawn out of her thoughts. "Umm. Thanks." She takes the cup I hold out to her, and my gaze slips to the slight bump of her stomach. As she grips the coffee, I sit down next to her. I normally would have asked, but I don't want to give her an opportunity to push me away. Sometimes it's the people who need someone the most who push them away the hardest.

An awkward quiet falls. I fiddle with my purse strap and sip my steaming mocha. If she won't break the silence, I guess I'll have to. "Do you come here often?"

"Only when I need to think." The girl doesn't meet my eyes, staring down at the white lid of her cup. She hasn't drunk it yet.

Maybe being forthcoming will make her relax. I watch the people bustling about as I talk. "I'm sorry for intruding. You just remind me of my daughter, Evelyn." My lips curve into a soft smile. "I miss her."

I can sense that those weren't quite the right words. The girl stiffens and wraps her free arm around her stomach. "I'm sorry."

"Oh, it's not like that!" My cheeks flush as I hasten to correct the misunderstanding. "She's studying abroad this year, learning about music while walking the same streets that Beethoven did." I look at the girl. She's gazing at the river again. "When I saw you, I couldn't help but think of her. She just flew out last week." I pause, searching for the right thing to say, words that might put a crack in the wall the girl hides behind. "I hope that if Evelyn feels lost, confused, or alone over there, someone will take the time to stop and notice. To help."

The girl glances at me, meeting my gaze for only a moment. But in that second, I see all I need to in her eyes.

I give her space and silence, rummaging quietly in my purse. After a minute, I pull out a pen and piece of paper and scribble down numbers and letters. I hold the note toward the girl. "Please, take it. And really, do call or text me if you need anything. I know you don't know me, but please believe me when I say I want to help."

The breeze tugs at the paper, flapping it up and down in my outstretched hand. For a moment, I don't think she'll take it. But then her hand moves slowly toward the paper. She takes it and reads it. Looking up, she meets my eyes once more and doesn't look away. "Thank you"—her gaze drops down to the note for a moment—"Nelly." The faintest hint of a smile sparkles in her eyes. The darkness has lifted from her face.

"Of course." I take a sip of coffee before asking, "Is there anything you need right now?"

The girl shakes her head. "Not anymore."

WHAT LOVE WAS

ELAINE WELLS

I thought I knew what love was,
I thought it was quantifiable,
Something earned or made,
Something I could understand,
I thought it was his smile,
His laugh,
His approval,
In the moments that never last,
I thought it was something I could do right,
Though I longed for a thing I could never have,
I thought it was my name on his lips,
Being called pretty,
I thought love was something
I didn't deserve enough to ask for,
Maybe pretending was better than rejection,
Maybe love was a fantasy all along,
An impossible warmth only found in someone else,
But more so heard about than seen,

Like a trope on tv,
A genre of cinema rather than an actual thing,
But when I finally stopped looking,
I realized how wrong I had been.

The day I learned what love was,
I learned to love myself,
I smiled at my face in the mirror,
And laughed at my own jokes,
And took myself out places,
I dressed up and called myself pretty,
I fell in love with my friends,
Their conversations and innocent affections,
Never forcing it to be more than that,
I fell in love with sunsets,
And summer breezes,
And little clay houses on shelves at the store,
With flowers in spring,
And stickers of plants,
And old poetry,
My cats,
I started to see the beauty in everything,
I started to heal,
And realized how I had grown,
Now that I am not scared to take up space.

There is so much to love of life,
That I had not noticed before,
And now I am sure,
I will not have one great love,
But many.

MR. TEDDY

ANNE J. HILL

RELATED TO *THERE ISN'T MUCH TO SAY* IN *WHAT DARKNESS FEARS*

LANDON HAD MADE it to her house just as they were zipping up her body bag.

His sister.

He saw her face like she was just sleeping, slowly fade into darkness. And that's when he threw up all over the kitchen floor. He gagged as the smell of acid-eaten bacon and eggs reached his nose.

Landon pulled himself away from the scene and locked himself in the bathroom. He turned on the hot water and let it run over his hands until it hurt, the pain bringing back some sense to his head. He quickly turned the faucet to cold and splashed it on his face.

He gripped the edge of the counter, staring at the man on the other side of the mirror. Landon's face was dripping, his hair sticking out, and his already dark eyes looked almost black from dilation. Landon didn't recognize that man.

And then he hurled into the sink.

He looked away, his head throbbing. Somewhere between the smell, the queasiness in his stomach, and the harsh reality of his sister's death, he forgot something important.

He shut off the water, dried his face, and went to check on his sister's daughter.

His niece.

Landon closed her bedroom door and crouched down beside the bed. Mia was clinging to a teddy bear who was missing an eye and badly needed arm surgery. Her eyes were red and she looked smaller than usual. The policewoman sitting on the other edge of the bed stood and left the room now that he was finally there.

"Hey, beautiful girl." Landon offered her a smile, but he knew it probably looked pathetic.

Mia stared back at him, her face contorting like she just licked a lemon. For a moment, he thought she was going to rush into his arms, but instead he got the teddy square in his face.

He pressed his fingers against the bridge of his nose and sighed. "Mia, love, please don't hit me." He picked up the teddy and nestled him back into her lap. "Your teddy doesn't like being thrown either, I'm sure."

Mia wrapped her arms around the toy's neck tightly. "His name is *Mr. Teddy.*" She heaved. "I want my mommy!"

Landon's stomach somersaulted. "I know, honey. Can—can I be an okay second choice right now?"

She studied his face hard. "Mommy's in a bag."

He swallowed bile, blinking back tears he swore he wouldn't let loose. "Mommy's with your Daddy now, sweetie."

Her little fingers tightened around Mr. Teddy's foot. "I was sleeping, and then mommy went BANG!"

Landon held his hand out to her, his jaw clenching, trying to hold himself together. "Come here?"

He watched the gears turning in her delicate head. She wiggled across the bed and wrapped her arms around his neck. Mr. Teddy dangled down his back. He hugged her tight, suddenly feeling weak under her fifty-pound body.

Mia cried, so Landon let himself cry with her. He pulled her small frame in tighter and rocked her, feeling seasick as he did so, but he'd face the monstrous sea for her.

He hummed a shaky tune. Mia had always liked music, and it calmed her. Her chest heaved against him, and she forced back sobs as she listened.

Landon wished right then that he'd been a more present uncle in the past. But it didn't matter now. He would raise his sniffling niece as well as he knew how—with Mr. Teddy beatings and all.

Landon and Mia will return...

YOU'RE SAFE

DENICA MCCALL

Right there, where
My hand meets your heart
Right
There

Take a breath

Right there, where
My touch is your light
In the darkness of your own mystery
When your chest caves and you don't know why
My light, as I search
Knows it, feels it
Ah, there it is
Right there
And I,
I'm right here, child
Holding your head to my pulse

So you don't have to work it out
All you have to do is
Unravel
With me
Undo this tension
With me
When I'm near you
You're seen
So right there, where it hurts
Right there, where you ache
Where your dreams lie in wait
My fingers, like balm
Work courage in,
Into the muscle that holds so much
I whisper through my touch
You're safe
It's safe here
Let go of that fear

It's safe here

SOLAR ECLIPSE

S.M. JAKE

SYLVIE TWISTED, HER massive crinoline spinning golden rays of satin around her as she watched the back door of the ballroom again.

Veda wouldn't miss Sylvie's birthday. She wouldn't! Even if it was one of her hard days. Still, if her big sister didn't hurry her pretty little backside down here soon—

"Happy Birthday, Miss Jackson."

Sylvie spun.

Peter.

She tried not to smirk as his polite smile twitched, eyes flickering around the crowded ballroom, eyeing a corner where he'd likely rather be hiding with a book. It was adorable, though not the most gentlemanly behavior.

Tonight was a lot: the electric lights reflecting distant stars in dark windows; a string quartet dictating an orbital dance; dozens of voices colliding in an indistinct buzz; a cacophony of perfume, cologne, sugar, and sweat mingling in invisible noxious clouds. A galaxy in motion, and Sylvie as its sun.

"Tell me, has seventeen been everything you anticipated?" Peter's second smile was better, his dimple peeking out, and Sylvie's heart did a funny little flare.

No! Stop it. Stop it!

"Well, the first twelve hours have been simply delightful. I'll get back to you in three hundred and sixty-four days with my final verdict."

Peter chuckled, nodding at the floor, his lack of retort leading to an awkward lull in the barely started conversation.

Her fingers twisted, burrowing in the golden gathers of her skirt.

"Have you seen the cake?" she asked in a rush, anxious to be sure he didn't drift away into someone else's gravity. Even now, the others watched, orbiting close by in their swirling reds and blues, waiting. "Why, it has to be the most dazzling confection I've ever laid eyes on!"

"Oh?" Peter's eyes came back to her.

She grinned, slipping her hand into his elbow with such grace no one would notice that he hadn't offered it. "You simply have to see it!"

Peter's cheeks tinted pink, and he nodded as he took the lead.

Shoot! Rein it in, Sylvie. She had a way of beaming every emotion in her heart without intending.

But, oh, how she wanted to shine for Peter, to catch him in her gravity and keep him in her orbit. He was gentle and charming, clever and intellectual. Awkward, yes, but that smile more than made up for it.

Sylvie turned away from him, discreetly fanning her flaming face. No. She wouldn't pull him in, even if she had to fight her very nature. She had seen the way Veda watched him, the flush that ran her sister's pale cheeks when Peter's name came up.

While Sylvie filled a room with light and laughter, Veda made those around her ebb and flow in more subtle ways; she drew them out, or helped them rest, pulled them close, or gracefully stepped back. *If* she had the energy. Veda had been waning this evening.

"Are you all right?" Peter asked. "You look flushed."

Well, pointing it out doesn't help!

"Just warm."

"Should we step outside for some air?"

Sylvie's heart stopped, asteroids of emotion crashing into her. The magic of drifting in the warm summer night on the arm of a boy sent her soaring. Surely, if ever there was a night Sylvie could shine without fear of being too bright, too impetuously dazzling, it would be on her birthday, right?

A distant body drifted into the room, catching Sylvie's gaze.

Veda.

Silver silk glowed with soft white light, imperfect folds and gathers imparting abstract beauty. She smiled, small and tired, but her expression was so open, so honest, as she moved toward Sylvie.

Veda stopped, her gaze shifting to Peter and back. Her smile softened, and she drifted backward.

Sylvie's chest flared again, and she struck out toward Veda, dragging Peter in her wake.

"Oh, sister!" Sylvie cooed, pulling her into a twirling embrace. "You look amazing! Absolutely dazzling. Doesn't she look amazing, Peter!" Three careful steps, and she had swapped their places.

"Oh, look!" Sylvie glanced across the room, searching for anyone. "It's the Carwalls. I really must thank them for coming!"

Sylvie's heart burned as she walked away. Yet she pushed on, each step helping her cool a little more.

She risked a peek; Peter's hand was out, an invitation, and Veda's nose was pink as she accepted.

Sylvie smiled, less beaming and brilliant, but still happy. Sometimes, perhaps, the sun simply chose to be eclipsed by the moon.

AN ODE TO PEOPLE WATCHERS

BY LARA'S PUBLISHER, ANNE J. HILL

PEOPLE WATCHERS CAN BE FOUND IN *WHAT DARKNESS FEARS* AND *FOOL'S HONOR*

There once was an author named Lara
Who had deadlines piling to the sky.
"Write about love! And choices!
Oh, and don't forget *People Watchers*!"
Her publisher would remind her.
But as the days grew nearer,
Lara, the author, could not get
Catalina, the character, to write
Her stories about Jeffrey.
So Anne J. Hill, discouraged by this,
Looked over an old draft for
People Watchers #3, but alas
It did not fit the theme and
There was no time to finish.

And Lara could not make
Catalina write about Jeffery,
For Lara realized something important:
She needed to choose her sanity
And her few hours of sleep
Over a story about authors
And characters and a publisher
Who set their stories in stone.
Because Anne loves her best friend,
She wrote a little thingamabob
So *People Watchers* can live on.

REAL

LINDSI MCINTYRE

CIRCUITS HUMMING, HE calmly plotted his next move. There. Jepedo leaned across the table—his arms were too short to reach the piece while seated—and set his bishop down in front of his opponent's king. "Checkmate."

Father studied the board. Then, running a hand over his thinning hairline, he sighed. "You win again, my boy." He smiled at Jepedo. "But at least I managed to stay in the game a little longer this time, eh?"

Jepedo stretched his face, copying the expression. Truthfully, he could have ended the game sooner, but Father had to leave after it was done. So, he'd pretended not to see the opportunities that would've won the game.

The door to the observation room opened. Cindy, Jepedo's favorite caretaker, stepped through. "Sir. The admiral is on his way."

Father's smile crumpled in a way it never had before. Jepedo mimicked that expression, too, trying to understand it. Father breathed deeply. "Thank you, Cindy. Please, give us a moment."

Cindy nodded and looked at Jepedo as she walked out. *That* look he understood. She had a secret.

Father breathed deeply again. "We have to talk about something important, Jepedo."

Jepedo straightened on his booster seat. He loved these talks with Father. There was always so much to learn. He copied Father's intake of breath, wanting to show he was ready to engage fully in whatever topic they discussed.

Father's eyes glinted under the observation room's pale yellow lights. "Jepedo. Do you remember what I told you about the day you were created?"

Jepedo's long-term memory drives kicked in with a whir. "Six years ago, the United States government authorized the creation of an artificial life form, hiring a team led by Dr. Adams to perform the experiment."

Father smiled, this one tinged with pride. "Yes. And by all accounts, you are a huge success." His expression changed again. Anger. "But, from the very beginning, there were people who wanted to shut us down." Father's face crumpled.

Jepedo did not like that look on Father's face. Not at all.

"Last week, those people finally managed to get the all-clear to cancel our experiment."

"Why?" Jepedo asked.

Father took a deep breath. "They claim the experiment was a failure since the original purpose of your creation was to learn if emotions could be artificially created. Specifically, they wanted to see if love could be duplicated."

"What is love, Father?"

Father looked like he might cry. "Love is a special feeling, Jepedo. Love is when a mother protects her child. It's when a father works hard to keep his family fed. Or when an officer gives his life to serve his community. That's love. Do you understand?"

"I understand." But even as he said it, Jepedo knew it wasn't quite true. He understood the words, but he'd never experienced love. Father, all humans, *felt* things. Feelings weren't thoughts. Or instincts. Or even consistent from person to person. They were irrational and undefinable. But what Father had just described weren't feelings. They were actions. "I can do that. I can protect and work and serve, Father."

Father's smile was sad.

The door opened again. "Sir. The admiral's here."

Two men, one with stars on his uniform, stormed into the office on the other side of the observation room's window—their faces masks of stone. Father stood, patted Jepedo's head, then walked out the open door.

"Can I help you, gentlemen?" Father asked.

"Don't play dumb," the admiral replied. "You know why we're here. That *thing* is an abomination."

Jepedo knew that word. And he did not like being called it.

"You never should have gotten the green light for this experiment. Our orders are to terminate the subject."

"You can't just kill him!"

"*It* isn't alive, Adams! It's a thing. A tool." The admiral turned to glare through the window at Jepedo. "And a broken tool at that."

"It's only been six years. He needs more time."

"It's already been decided." The admiral shoved Father. "Move aside."

Father pushed him back, grabbing the man's gun as the officer stumbled. "Stay away."

That was bad. Very bad. Father was committing a crime. Jepedo jumped down from his chair.

"What are you doing, Adams?"

"I can't let you do this." Father backed toward the door. "Jepedo. Come here."

Jepedo inched into the room. Father took his hand, pulling him to the door.

"You won't get far, Adams," the admiral said.

"We'll see."

The two walked out of the observation hall into the main laboratory. The living quarters were to the right–the only world Jepedo had ever known. Father pulled him into the elevators on the left.

The ones that led *outside*.

The elevator slid silently to a stop at the top, and the doors opened. Jepedo stepped into the sunlight's warm, gentle rays for the first time. A beautiful sound reached his ears. He'd heard birdsong before, but only on recordings. Their melody turned in his chest with a soft hum.

"We're going to see everything I promised, Jepedo." Father smiled. "Just you and me."

Jepedo smiled back, this time automatically as if he couldn't hold it in. Mountains. Rivers. Parks. He would finally get to see it all.

They were halfway to the street when Jepedo's ears, far more sensitive than Father's, heard the sound of a gun's hammer clicking into place. His processors ran through scenarios, searching for the most likely one. He could easily dodge a bullet, so aiming at him would be useless. But a human couldn't.

One possibility rose above the others.

Someone was aiming their weapon at Father.

Jepedo's processors played out the scene. It would soar through the air. Strike Father. Pierce his heart. Acute blood loss would quickly follow. Jepedo froze. Father would die.

I can't let him die!

Something dormant inside Jepedo sprung to life. Without processing the outcome, he jumped between Father and his attacker. The bullet struck, knocking him back into Father's arms. They both fell to the ground; Father's tears pooled on Jepedo's face.

"See, Father," Jepedo said as the hum of his circuits slowed. "I told you I could love."

TEARS FLOOD THE SEA

ANNE J. HILL

Times get tough
When you lose
Someone you
Always loved

When their
Memory is
All you have
Left of them

Grief shipwrecks
Rips families
Apart
Limb from limb

Especially when
The one you
Lost, kept
Everyone together

Now you're
Flailing for
A lifeboat
In the sea

Each person
Fighting their
Own battle
Against the

Same enemy
We all call
Grief and sorrow
—our minds

But it only
Takes one
Hand, reaching
Grabbing

One action
One voice
One reminder
One love

To reunite
To build from
The ashes
And cling tight

To the ones
That remain
Still a unit
Just different

A new normal
That's not
Normal
At all

But choose
To fight
Together
Not against

A family reborn
Choosing to
Stick together
No matter what

Even when
Grief shipwrecks
And your tears
Flood the sea

And grief
Clings to anger
And anger to
Isolation

The waves
Are bumpy
But then again
They always were

So grab my hand
And let's all stand
Together, in this fight
For one more night

PAPÁ MUERTE

HANNAH CARTER

AH, DÍA DE los Muertos. A day we set aside to honor our family members. To spend time with the living. To remember our dead.

Except they're kind of hard to forget when their skeletons stare at you from across the table.

"Well, Finny! Have you decided to follow in your pop's footsteps yet?" Grandpa's skull rattled as he reached for another tamale.

"No, I don't think I will," I said dryly.

"And why not? Your father has a very respectable position!" Dad's girlfriend, Catrina added. Her sugar-candy teeth clacked against each other. "And the job stability is fantastic."

The man himself swung open the kitchen door. Up-tempo mariachi music poured in from the other room; Dad had recently hired some poor undead musicians to play each time he wanted to make a grand entrance.

"That's right!" Dad effused. "People never stop dying. You could be Grim Reaper, Jr. for all eternity!"

"Call me crazy, but I'd prefer the stench of rotting flesh *not* follow me everywhere I go."

All the guests groaned in a series of clicking jawbones along with cries of "*Finn.*"

"What do you expect when you adopt a living being?" I shrugged my bony—yet still flesh-covered—shoulders.

The Grim Reaper—*Daddy Dearest*—settled beside me and wrapped his skeletal arm around me. "Why don't you go out with me tonight? A little father-son holiday bonding time?"

"I don't—"

"Excellent!" Catrina clapped her hands together. "Oh, you boys go have fun!"

"Sure. Killing people is *loads* of fun," I muttered.

"That's the *Día de los Muertos* spirit!" Dad cheered.

"I was being sarcastic!"

Dad and I floated down the road, invisible to the mortal revelers. Growing up, being weightless and utterly dependent on Dad terrified me. Now, I huddled close inside his cloak.

I sniffed. "Wow. No rotting flesh smell today. Did you wash it?"

"Yep. Lavender-scented detergent!" Dad patted my shoulder. "Now, Finn. I know you think your old man's job is uncool and all—"

"No, Dad. A businessman has an *uncool* job. Yours is *murderous.*"

"—*but* I think that's because you don't know exactly what I do."

I snorted, but my sarcastic reply stuck in my gullet when I noticed where we stopped. "Dad."

"What?"

Panic clawed into my stomach. "Why are we at Sofi's house?"

Dad waved the words away. "She lives in the suburbs. Every house here looks the same. I'm sure you're mistaken."

"*Dad*!" I shrieked. "I know my best friend's house—how can you not remember? You've dropped me off here for everything from Pee-Wee soccer games to movie nights."

Dad tilted his head. "Oh."

He drifted closer to the family room window. A candle from Sofi's *ofrenda* had been knocked over somehow, and the flames were spreading to the couch. She slumbered right by it, sleeping pills scattered on the table beside her.

Dad clucked his tongue. "Oh, well. Hey, maybe you can invite her over for the next holiday, since she'll be dead."

"No! We have to help her."

"What are you going to do? She's destined to die tonight."

I glared at him. "I'm going to help her—like *you* should."

"I can't help them all." Dad cupped my cheek with his bony hand. "I've only done it once before. When I was supposed to take a little two-year-old boy in a car crash. I used up my only resurrection amulet to stop his death."

Dad tapped the medallion hanging around my neck.

Hot tears burned in my eyes. "You can't have Sofi. Maybe *you* can't help her, but I'm not the Grim Reaper."

I ripped away from his embrace and staggered to the window, now visible to mortals.

"Sofi!" I pounded on the window. "Wake up!"

Flames licked at the couch. Sofi's family must have been out celebrating without her. Earlier at school, she complained about being sick and tired.

I don't think she'd like to sleep with the fishes, though.

I threw my weight against the window. It crashed, and I toppled onto the floor. Shards of glass bit into my exposed palms.

Sofi yawned, her eyes hazy. "... Finn?" She wiped at the sides of her mouth, but her eyelids drooped half-mast again.

I coughed as the smoke burned my throat and eyes. The blaze had already consumed the *ofrenda* pictures of Sofi's ancestors and would claim her, too, if I couldn't get her out.

"Come on. I got you." Adrenaline helped me hoist Sofi up. Her head lolled onto my shoulder as she wheezed. She'd definitely taken too much medicine; she was dead weight.

A burning table collapsed right in front of the window.

I staggered back, dizzy from the heat. Flames danced around me on all sides and crept closer. The fire blazed to the ceiling and blocked off the living room door behind me.

"Dad!" I yelled, my voice hoarse. If Dad answered, I couldn't hear it over the roar of the flames. "*Help*!"

Funny, relying on Death to circumvent himself.

Dad phased through the window, his cloak billowing behind him. He latched onto Sofi and me. Silent, cool relief greeted me as we entered the spiritual plane, away from the flames.

"You know, as much as I love my job…" Dad began. It probably would have hurt his reputation for anyone else to hear the depth of emotion oozing from his words. "…I love being your dad more."

He pulled us back into the real world and deposited us outside. I held Sofi in my trembling arms and hacked ash and smoke out of my throat.

Dad patted my head. "Good job, Finn."

I spit a few times to rid my mouth of the acrid taste. "Will you get in trouble since I defied death?"

Dad chuckled. "Nah. You saved her, not me. Besides, it's nice when love is stronger than death." He kissed my temple, the faint strands of a mariachi song in the air. "Happy *Día de los Muertos*, kiddo."

SHE AND I

MASEEHA SEEDAT

12:06 am
She wakes up
Crying and wriggling,
Searching the bed for Teddy.
I pull the stuffed animal from under my head
And wrap my arms around her instead.

05:23 am
She leaps from the blankets
Banging and slamming,
Searching the drawers for porridge.
I drag myself away from the warmth of my bed
And race to the kitchen to toast some bread.

08:47 am
She races around the room
Laughing and screaming,
Squealing as I shove on a sock.

I hold her firmly, buckle the shoes
And run, for there's no time to lose.

11:11 am
She interrupts my thoughts
Babbling and jabbering,
Going on without a breath.
I pull into the checkout queue
And suddenly remember I need shampoo.

01:52 pm
She throws the pasta across the room
Wailing and complaining,
Shrieking until she's red in the face.
I quickly give her some backup mini pies
And pick the spaghetti off the tiles.

04:31 pm
She's at it again
Acting and playing,
Re-reading her favorite farm book.
I slurp the fake tea she pours
And add a point to her tic-tac-toe score.

07:23 pm
She's soaking wet
Splashing and dripping,
Leaving a soggy trail of footprints behind her.
I wrestle a diaper on
And try to convince her we're playing salon.

09:08 pm
She's still up
Eating and fussing,
Watching that purple dinosaur *again*.

I zone out of his annoying song
And she starts to sing along.

10:12 pm
She bawls her eyes
Howling and crying,
Nagging me for one more story.
I hand her Teddy, turn off the light
And the darkness eases away her fight.

11:59 pm
She finally yawns
Snuggling and cuddling,
Whispering 'I love you' in my ear.
I almost cry and bite my lip tight
And that made it all worth it tonight.

12:06 am
She's up again
I open my eyes, the first time of ten.

FIG PIE

ANNE J. HILL

BOYER..." AN ICY voice cut through the wind. Boots thudded against the wooden dock, getting closer with each step.

Sand blew from the desert across the rocky terrain all the way to Jorn's Port, a strip of land in Raldon caught between the desert and the sea—the merchant capital. Boyer shivered in the cold night and sunk deeper into the shadows of the surrounding shops.

All this trouble for fig pie.

"Come on out, lad," the feminine voice said, followed by a cackle that, to Boyer's shame, sent fear scraping down his spine. If he'd been bigger and braver like his papa, he wouldn't be so scared of the old baker chasing him down the docks.

A tied-up merchant boat creaked in the salt water to his right. If he made a run for it, he might be able to skid through the sand, jump on the boat, and escape down the channel.

Boyer looked at his shaking hands and mumbled, "Blasted cod," cursing himself for being so small. His papa said the same swear earlier that day when he was angry, so Boyer thought it was fitting. And he imagined his papa yelling it with a brutal beating if Boyer stole a boat and got lost at sea *just* because he was scared of an old woman—future Guards weren't scared of anything, his papa always said. Not of the sea, or sand storms, or pirates, or ghouls, or even death itself.

But Boyer was only five.

His cloak flapped in the ocean breeze, sandy wind hitting his face. He pulled his kerchief over his mouth and nose, wrapped his arms around himself, and swallowed back tears. If his mama was still around, he wouldn't be in this position.

"I'll tell your papa you've been stealing my pies again if you don't come out." Her footsteps paused, and Boyer could feel her gaze crawling closer to his hiding spot. He covered his mouth so she couldn't hear him breathing, a trick he'd learned to do when his papa drank too much of his gross vinegar—especially on nights like *this.*

I didn't steal any pie! His lip quivered. He had certainly tried to, but the old lady had caught him.

He knew he could outrun her, but he'd run out of dock, so he stayed between the shop shadows and prayed to the dragon-god Belok above to turn her into a pile of ash.

Boyer pinched his waist and cursed himself for thinking such horrible thoughts. *Forgive me, Belok.* He swallowed. If Papa knew he'd wished an old woman dead, he'd slap him and make him apologize for a harmless thought she hadn't even heard.

Her footsteps creaked closer along the dock again. "I know you're here, you little brat. If I find you making trouble again, you'll lose every shot at the Raldonian Guard when they hear about you stealing."

Boyer balled his hands into fists. She was lying. He would sail the seas with his papa and then grow up and be the best Raldonian Guard ever.

His eyes watered, and he pushed away his tears. His papa said to be brave, but he also said bad words and threw things.

Boyer took a deep breath and stepped out from the shadows, fists at his sides.

"There you are, brat." The lady smiled, her grey hair dancing in the breeze.

Boyer stomped his foot. "I'm not a brat! You're a mean old sea bass!" His papa liked to call people a bass, but sometimes he dropped the B if he was extra angry.

The baker blinked, then frowned. "Your papa is going to whip you for that."

When Papa yelled, people listened. Why hadn't the baker listened to Boyer? He noticed a small shell minding its own business a few feet away and grabbed it. His papa yelled *and* threw things...

"Go away!" Boyer threw the shell with all his might, and it landed at her feet.

The old lady laughed. "What wannabe Guard can't even throw?"

Boyer *almost* understood her not wanting him to steal, and he had *almost* felt bad for her old legs chasing him, but now he did *not* feel bad about wanting her to be a pile of ash.

To treat him so poorly today of all days.

Boyer puffed up his chest. *Don't be afraid. Guards aren't afraid.* He marched over to her, looked up into her dark eyes, and said, "Belok'll send you to the fiery seas. I'll be the biggest and bestest Guard ever!"

Wrinkled knuckles slapped against his cheek, but Boyer only smiled.

"What old lady can't even slap?" he taunted.

Her face flushed. "Someday, you'll get yourself in trouble with that tongue."

Heart racing, Boyer mustered up all his courage and forced a careless smile, shrugged, and walked past her. She may be right, but he realized something—his papa especially liked to throw things at people who hit Boyer.

His papa said he beat Boyer to keep him safe, and his mama had loved his papa. And that was why Boyer had to steal pie. His papa couldn't celebrate his birthday on just vinegar alone.

Boyer circled back to the bakery, snatched up the fig pie while the old baker screamed curses Boyer knew far too well, and headed home.

He slipped in through the front door, lowering the bar to lock it. Faint snoring echoed throughout the house. He sniffed in the stinging vinegar smell and tiptoed to his papa's room. The door was ajar, and Boyer edged it open with his foot. His papa was lying on his back, arm dangling off the edge of his bed with a brown bottle lying just beneath it.

Boyer snuck in with no more sound than a mouse, set the stolen pie beside his bed, and quietly wished him a happy birthday.

He wanted to wake him and tell him about the mean baker slapping him and accusing him of stealing the pie for himself. About how brave he had been and *not* about wanting her to be ash.

But instead, Boyer shifted on his feet and imagined his mama, who he couldn't see anymore but whose voice he still heard singing a birthday song to his papa. She'd told Boyer to never forget fig pie on his papa's birthday. And he'd fight every old sea bass in Raldon if it meant keeping that promise.

Boyer will return in Anne J. Hill's debut novel, Thorn Tower

STILL HERE

DENICA MCCALL

Promises and mountain air
Still here
If these lungs could release memories
Still here
When chaos walks among dreams
And imagination has misplaced investigation
Eyes don't see those mountains anymore
The ocean's only a sound, distant like the cry of
My newborn lips
Years ago, yet
Aren't moments captured and frozen
In hearts?
Still here
Though feet meander through thorns and this mind
Forgets what it's all for
The birds overhead don't speak like they used to
The bob of a boat doesn't sing
But this longing stings, so

This heart beats but without melody
Because the song brings pain
Still here
This body holds recollections
But knowledge evades
The key's gone missing, yet
Not the breeze
So let sweetness invade, let these
Tears bust through
Let these hands unclench and
Fear be loosed
Memory doesn't lie, at least
The version narrated by truth
Still here
In the air, in hearts, in skin, in birth
You're still here
In me
Stillness at the water's edge
Magic in flight
Mystery in moonlight and
Dancing grass on rolling hills
Your whisper weaves
Through it all
Still
And always

A LIFE FOR A LIFE

LARA E. MADDEN

FIVE YEARS.

Mikey sits down on the park bench. Cars pass by on the street in front of him. Behind him, people mill around. He stretches his legs and breathes out a long, heavy sigh. It's been five years since the last time he saw this place. Almost nothing about the location itself has changed, but everything about Mikey's life has.

He can't help but feel unnerved here. He doesn't like to sit without his back to a wall. Everything feels too...open. It's funny how confinement can do that to you. Make you afraid of being free.

Mikey spits on the ground. A mother passing in front of him grabs her child's hand and walks a little faster. He winces. People used to trust him with their lives. He knows what they see now. Dark, shifty eyes. A hard-set jaw. Bitterness etched in the lines of his face. He has scars he didn't have a few years ago. Mikey's toughness used to instill confidence in people during his paramedic days. Then it kept him safe in prison. Now it scares ladies on the street.

He isn't entirely certain why he's here. His feet lead him to this spot. But really, sitting on this park bench today might be the only thing that makes sense. His mind hasn't left this street since the night of the accident. He's been in a sort of limbo. A fog. Nothing has felt real since then, as if he's been living someone else's life all this time.

Mikey folds himself in half and leans his elbows on his knees, puts his face in his hands, and rubs his eyes. He's so tired. He hasn't slept since he got out three months ago, and he wonders if he's ever going to again. Mikey looks up and stares hard at the little white cross on the side of the road, directly across the street.

The roadside marker is all that's left now. It's small. The area around the cross is filled in with white pebbles. It's clean and well-kept, just a little memorial across the street from a park, in a nice neighborhood where people drive slowly. He wonders how many drivers and pedestrians pass it every day, and whether they notice it at all. They don't see what he sees.

He sees the front half of a car crumpled like an aluminum can. Ambulance lights reflecting off pooling blood. A body contorted out of shape in the driver's seat.

Mikey and his partner were the first ones on the scene that night. They were hardly able to get to her. The driver. She was the only person in the car, as far as they could tell. It was obvious before they even pried the door off the car, that, if she wasn't dead yet, she would be by the time the firemen got to the scene to cut her out.

Back then, Mikey was the guy who made the hard decisions. Risky, psycho, brilliant, genius: he was called them all. Everyone knew that his paramedic career was a stepping stone. He was in school to become an emergency surgeon, and he would have been a damn good one.

Among other EMS workers, he was a legend. He read textbooks for fun. He studied surgery techniques before going to bed every night and visualized performing them in detail as he fell asleep. Every steak in his freezer had stab marks and sutures in it. He used to like to hunt. But instead of killing what he shot, he would drop a medical bag beside the wounded animal, sedate it, and operate on it to save its life.

Psycho. Genius. But no one could deny he would have been a damn good doctor—he was obsessed enough.

He was the first to discover that night, when he reached into the wrecked car to find the driver's pulse point, that she wasn't dead yet. Her pulse was faint and breathing undetectable, and he couldn't find any sign of consciousness. To make matters worse, her body had been thrown around in the crash, and the top half of her was pinned to the seat, but the bottom of her bulging torso was partly exposed. She was pregnant, Mikey realized. Very pregnant. He would never forget pressing his stethoscope to her belly and hearing that fluttering heartbeat, the strong, panicking child fighting beneath his hand to stay alive. There were only seconds to make a decision.

"Karkov? What are you seeing there?" Command sputtered over the radio.

He shouted fast, "I have a pregnant patient here, unconscious, weak pulse; she won't live long enough for us to get her out of here. I can get to her abdomen, and I've confirmed the baby is still alive. We have three minutes, *maybe,* but the patient is no longer breathing, and this kid is going to run out of oxygen real quick!"

"Protocol is to do CPR to keep the baby alive until you can get her to the hospital."

The tiny, fluttering heartbeat dimmed slightly, and he adjusted the stethoscope, desperately trying to find it again.

"There's a steering wheel in this woman's chest; CPR isn't an option. Listen! I can do a c-section right now, but it needs to be *now*. Do I have your permission or not?"

The line went silent for a moment that felt like eternity.

"Karkov, you're in hot water as it is; we can't afford the liability."

"Screw your liability! I have a mostly-dead patient who is completely unresponsive and a still-alive patient inside her. The answer is simple. I can have this kid out in two minutes!"

"Karkov, I'm going to make this very clear: You do *not* have permission to perform a perimortem c-section."

"But—"

"NO!"

He felt around for the heartbeat again but couldn't find it. Either the baby had shifted, or...

There was a thump on the other side of the woman's abdomen. Mikey stopped breathing, pressed his stethoscope harder against the round belly. A foot kicked forcefully against the pressure. That was it. There was no more decision to be made. No turning back.

In a minute and a half, the dying woman's abdomen was splayed open, and a cold, bloody, mucousy newborn was screaming in Mikey's arms. He threw his coat off and wrapped the baby in it. The radio screamed curses at him from the place on the ground where he'd tossed it.

When the cavalry arrived, there was a dead woman in one vehicle, a dead drunk in the other, and a newborn in desperate need of oxygen and a heat lamp. The only other detail Mikey remembers from that night is the look on the husband's face when he arrived on the scene. He'd been on his way home late that night, had seen the flashing lights and the remains of his wife's car. The man barely managed to struggle out of his vehicle before he collapsed in the street. Mikey's partner helped the husband to the side of the road, and when the man could breathe again, Mikey put his baby son in his arms and drove them both to the hospital.

The following details are fuzzy: he knows that he lost his job, that papers with a court date showed up on his doorstep, and that four months after that he was sentenced to six years in prison on charges of criminal negligence and performing surgery without a license. It was a rare sentence for a paramedic to receive, but it wasn't the first time something like this had happened, and the judge wanted to make an example of him. His first day in prison, his cellmate asked what he was in for.

"I saved someone's life," he told the man. "I did my job." Since then, he found himself with an excruciating amount of time to analyze every decision he ever made in his career as a medic. And to think about all he could have accomplished as a doctor.

He got out early. Good behavior. But the thing that broke him wasn't the months in court, the years in a cell, or even the struggle now to get his feet under him. The worst thing was the future he'd watched burn to ash. Everything he'd built, everything he would have been—gone. He would never get a job in medicine again, the only thing he'd ever been good at. He'd surely never be a surgeon. One crazy stunt, one moment where he thought he knew the right thing to do. It had cost him everything. A whole life.

He never stopped reliving it. And for at least three of those years, he'd asked himself every day if it was worth it. If breaking the law to save one life could possibly outweigh the hundreds of lives he could have saved as a surgeon.

Five years. An eternity, and yet, an impossibly short time for everything to implode.

One thousand eight hundred and twenty-five days.

One hundred fifty-seven million, six hundred eighty thousand seconds.

Mikey chuckles sourly as pressure builds behind his eyes. He rubs at his face again and shuffles between wanting to erase the memories and needing to pick at his wounds.

"Why are you laughing like that?"

Mikey jumps and shifts away from the squeaky voice beside him. A small boy is trying to climb up the back of the bench by pushing his feet against the wood and hanging onto the top rung. His floppy blond hair and big eyes are disproportionate to his pouting mouth, and the thick coat he's wrapped in makes him look a bit like a penguin.

"Your face is sad," the boy says, partly distracted by his climb. "But you laughed."

"What's it to you?" Mikey asks.

The kid shrugs and drops to the ground. He walks around to the front of the bench and hops up next to Mikey. The boy waits for an answer until finally, Mikey grumbles and rolls his eyes.

"It was an ironic laugh."

"What's *ironic*?" The boy's round face scrunches.

"Ironic means...you expect one thing, but then life gives you the opposite thing."

"Why?"

"Because. Sometimes life is just fu—" Mikey halts. "Sometimes life is kinda messed up like that. Okay?"

"Why?"

Mikey sighs so deeply his whole body rises and deflates with the breath. "I don't know, kid."

The boy sighs heavily too, and Mikey can't help but grin a little.

"Hey, are you supposed to be somewhere right now? Where are your parents? Or babysitter?"

"My dad's over there." The boy stands on the bench and points to the playground. Mikey turns his head and sees the man trudging toward them.

"You ready, Michael?" the man calls. The boy hops down off the bench.

"Bye!" The kid waves and runs to join his father. They trudge together across the street, the man's left hand wrapped tightly around the boy's much smaller hand, and his right holding a bundle of flowers. They sit on the grass together in front of the memorial, the father pulling his boy into his lap and letting him place the new flowers on the white stones. Mikey watches them for a long time as realization floods over him.

The boy must be five years old. The last time Mikey saw the father, the man was sobbing and shaking, clinging for dear life to a tiny bundle wrapped in a medic's jacket, bathed in red and blue flashing lights. From across the street, Mikey stares at the man, trying to tell for sure whether they are the same father and child he's seen in his memories every day since the accident. He barely notices himself rising from the bench, taking steps forward until he is on the street curb. He stops himself.

The man sitting beside the memorial turns his head. His eyes grow wide the moment he recognizes Mikey. The two men hold eye contact across the street for a long time. The father's expression wavers. He leans down and kisses his son's head, and when he looks up again, there are tears in his eyes. He locks eyes with Mikey and mouths, "Thank you."

Five years, a career, and a whole future sacrificed. In this moment, watching a five-year-old boy who was once a baby in a dying woman's womb, Mikey knows, with the same absolute assurance he'd had when he felt that kid kick his stethoscope:

Worth it.

LOVE IS, LOVE ISN'T

EMILY BARNETT

Love isn't always what it seems.

It's tears and time outs.
Reprimands turning
attitudes inside out.
We bleed for these small humans,
then tend to their preventable wounds.

Love is kind,
and then,
it's the kind of love
that bares souls.
Bearing up
the sins of our children.

Love is patient.
And not-so-patiently

waiting for change.
But returning
day in and day out
just the same.

Love is perfection we can't attain,
but look what it contains.
A perfect opportunity to
let all perfections die.

Love is, "I'm sorry."
"I made a mistake."
"I shouldn't have yelled,
or made you feel less
than you are."

Love is our children
bearing our sins
like cattle brands.
We hold the rod too tightly,
its burning end
near innocent flesh.

Love isn't *being* right.
It's setting things right.

Love.
It isn't always
what it seems.

THORN TOWER EXCERPT

BOYER & KATOLLIA

ANNE J. HILL

BOYER COULDN'T WAIT to save enough money to someday move out of the mountainside, enjoy the sun in all its glory, and marry Katollia. And probably shove Waldren into a spare room.

He pulled his mare up to the main communal building, dismounted, and hitched her to the fence. The front door swung open. "Papa!" Katollia's son darted out. As much as Boyer thought of the boy as his son, his heart ached to have his own with Katollia.

Boyer laughed and scooped him up and squeezed him to his chest. "What are you doing awake so late, Floppy?" Boyer ruffled the boy's floppy bright blonde hair.

"Mama said I can!"

Katollia leaned in the doorway, her arms folded over her chest. "He's been fighting sleep every night since you left."

Boyer chuckled, walked over to Katollia, and gave her a quick kiss. The moment they were settled and the boy was asleep, he'd sweep her off to bed behind closed doors.

"Really? You can kiss her better than that!" Waldren dismounted his horse.

Not with you around, Wally.

Katollia chuckled. "Jikal and the boys are eating soup if you want any."

Boyer smiled, stroking her cheek. "That sounds lovely. Do the girls have jobs?"

"Yes. They're out."

Boyer nodded and stepped into the house.

Waldren followed but paused at Katollia. "Where's my kiss?"

Katollia pushed his face away with a laugh. "Not in many lifetimes." She looped her hand around Boyer's and followed him in.

Boyer shook his head at Waldren. "Find your own lady."

"Oh, I have plenty all over Nathal." Waldren grinned.

Boyer rolled his eyes. Waldren was hopeless.

Thorn Tower *will publish soon*

ACKNOWLEDGMENTS

Thank you to all the authors who poured their hearts and souls into this project. Without you, there would be no book.

Thank you to all the beta readers and editors that jumped on board. You saved us from completely falling apart.

Thank you to *coffee* for the same thing.

Thank you to God, also for the same thing, and for choosing to love us unconditionally.

And thank you, reader, for going on these adventures with us.

—Anne J. Hill and Lara E. Madden

ABOUT THE AUTHORS

ANNE J. HILL

Anne J. Hill is an author who enjoys writing fantasy for all ages. Her love of words has led to her career as an editor and content writer. She runs Twenty Hills Publishing with the help of her circus-performing best friend, Lara E. Madden. She spends her days dreaming up fantastical realms, researching ways to get away with murder…for writing, arguing over commas at the kitchen table, talking out loud to the characters in her head, promising her housemate that she isn't, in fact, crazy, and rearranging her personal library—affectionately dubbed the "Book Dungeon."

Instagram @anne.j.hill.editing
Twitter @AnneJHillAuthor
www.annejhill.com

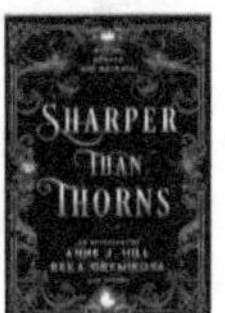

LARA E. MADDEN

She might be crazy—the jury's still out—but Lara E. Madden would consider herself to be widely fascinated, with an affinity for wonder. She is madly in love with Jesus, with storytelling, and with the tribe of colorful characters that is her family and friends. When her feet are on the ground, she lives in Lancaster, PA with her housemate, Anne J. Hill, without whom she would likely never finish any project she starts. She is a novelist at heart but is currently focused on creating short fiction as she hones her writing craft.

Instagram @lara.e.madden
Facebook @Lara Madden
LaraTheWanderer.blogspot.com

KATIE FITZGERALD

Katie Fitzgerald is a trained children's librarian turned stay-at-home, homeschooling mom. Originally from the Hudson Valley in New York State, she now lives in Maryland with her librarian husband, four daughters, and one son. She has published two textbooks for librarians and is a monthly contributor to CatholicMom.com. Her flash fiction has appeared online at Spark Flash Fiction and Havok Publishing. When she's not writing sweet short story romances, she's usually listening to an audiobook at triple speed or buying used paperbacks to add to her to-be-read pile.

Instagram @read.at.home.mom
Twitter @mrskatiefitz
katiefitzgeraldwrites.blogspot.com

MASEEHA SEEDAT

Born and raised in sunny South Africa, Maseeha takes inspiration from the most memorable moments of her life, from road trips to the beach to the greatest family meals. She made her publishing debut in *What Darkness Fears*, and a year later released her first novel: *The Littlest Voices*. When she's not writing, Maseeha can be found dreaming about dragons and werewolves, drowning under a pile of textbooks or binging old animated movies as the sun rises.

AJ SKELLY

AJ Skelly is an author, blogger, and lover of all things fantasy, medieval, and fairy-tale-romance. And werewolves. An avid reader and a former high school English teacher, she lives with her husband, children, and many imaginary friends who often find their way into her stories. They all drink copious amounts of tea together and stay up reading far later than they should.

Instagram @a.j.skelly
www.ajskelly.com

LINDSI MCINTYRE

Lindsi McIntyre is a linguaphile from Texas who hopes to use her words, both written and spoken, to bring glory to the Lord Most High. When not writing she can be found within the pages of a good book, or watching the latest episode of her favorite TV shows, and drinking way too much tea while doing both. You can check out more of her work on Havok, grab a copy of *Moonlight and Claws* and/or *Tales from the Tower* anthologies from Ye Olde Dragon books, and look for her award-winning novella *Broken Pieces* on Amazon.

CRYSTAL BAILEY

When not writing or homeschooling her son, Crystal enjoys reading, watching old television shows (*The Golden Girls* and *I Love Lucy* are her all-time favorites), satisfying her relentless sweet tooth, and spending time outdoors with her family. She also has an obsession with all things dystopian. Though she's called both Idaho and California home in the past, she now lives with her husband and son in the beautiful state of Texas.

BEKA GREMIKOVA

Beka Gremikova writes folkloric fantasy from her little nook in the Ottawa Valley, Ontario, Canada. When she's not trekking across the globe, she plays video games, dabbles in art, or curls up in a cozy corner with a mystery novel. Her work can be found in various anthologies, and her indie debut, *The Other Cinderella*, is now available in ebook and paperback from Amazon. Her first full-length book, codenamed *Project Dragon*, will release with SnowRidge Press in Fall 2023. To keep up with all her writing mayhem, you can sign up for her newsletter or join her reader group, "Beka's Books," on Facebook.

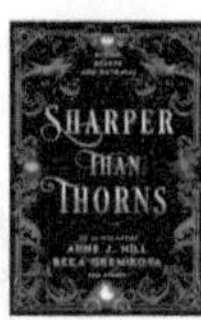

Instagram @beka.gremikova
www.bekagremikova.com

KATHLEEN BIRD

Kathleen Bird is the author of the *Adven Trilogy*, a Christian fantasy series, and the *Isles of Miadhra*, a series of steampunk fairytale retellings. You can also find her writings included in the following anthologies: *Tales from the Tower & Finding God in Anime: Volume 2*. She loves traveling and seeing new places, which give her inspiration for her writing; but when she and her husband are not traveling the world, they live in Des Moines, IA.

Instagram @birdsthewords
www.adventrilogy.wordpress.com

BETHANY KOHLER

Bethany Kohler is a writer and poet with a penchant for witty banter, a weakness for verbose descriptions of scenery, and a passion for weaving truth into fiction. She carries a deep regard for nineteenth-century literature, and counts many dead authors among her mentors. When she is not reading or writing, Bethany might be found baking delectable pastries, sewing historically inspired dresses, or singing anything from folk songs to Broadway tunes.

Instagram @bethany_kohler_author
www.bethanykohler.com

MARY E. DIPPLE

A lover of all things magical, Mary uses her talent of spinning stories, to shine a light into the darkness that so easily entangles our lives. She is currently writing her epic-fantasy series *The Lotus Chronicles*, due out between 2025-2027. When Mary isn't slaying the darkness with story, she enjoys spending her days tending her ever growing rose garden, playing with her lovable furry assistants, and writing flash fiction.

Instagram @mary.e.dipple_author
www.marydipple.com

KRISTEN BAZEN

Kristen Bazen discovered the magic of the written word in elementary school, and she completed her first novella in fifth grade. Now, she mainly writes speculative fiction with a Middle Eastern flavor and strong Christian themes. Every so often, she writes poetry both to process life's difficult seasons and capture the wonder of life. Her poetry is featured in the anthologies *The Heights We'll Fly To* and *Masquerade*, and she has a short story published in *The Willow Tree Swing*. When she's not working or writing, Kristen dabbles in languages, trains in martial arts, and raises awareness on how ordinary people can fight human trafficking.

Instagram @kristen_thewriteending
www.kristenbazen.com

HANNAH CARTER

Hannah Carter is just a girl who loves to dream and write and still wakes up every day hoping to figure out she's secretly a mermaid. Hannah's debut YA fantasy novel released from SnowRidge press in November 2022. In her spare time, she's probably either cuddling her cats, drinking tea, reading, or practicing for her imaginary Broadway debut.

Instagram @mermaidhannahwrites

MEGAN DILL

Megan Dill was born and raised in a rural part of Maryland, which is really just a nice way of saying that she grew up in the middle of nowhere. As a Christian, her faith is a huge part of her life and is incorporated into her writing. She spent her childhood lost in the pages of books, dreaming of fantastical worlds and crazy adventures. Her stories are clean and are typically fiction. She has a bachelor's degree in Business Administration: Marketing Analytics. When she's not reading or writing, you can find her watching anime, listening to k-pop, or spending time with her family and cat.

Instagram @the_bookish_raven

MIRIAM WADE

Miriam Wade is a Minnesota native who writes young adult fantasy, adventure, and urban fantasy driven by resilient young women, filled with twisty plots, and garnished with a hint of romance. She loves coffee, playing video games, and riding her bicycle. When she is not writing, she enjoys spending time with her husband, their two young daughters, and their cat. Wade is the author of the award-winning steampunk Arthurian inspired series, *One Sword Saga*, and a featured poet in *The Heights We'll Fly To* anthology.

Instagram @miriam.wade.author
Twitter @wade_author
Facebook @miriam.wade.author
www.miriam-wade.com

HAILEY HUNTINGTON

Hailey Huntington loves adventures, and she's always ready for another one—whether it's discovering Narnia, traveling across Middle Earth, hiking a mountain in Iceland, or simply going on a walk with her family. Aside from adventures, Hailey also loves board games, music, ice cream, laughter, witty characters, fantasy, emojis, and Jesus—though not in that order.

Instagram @haileyhuntingtonauthor
Facebook @haileyhuntingtonauthor
haileyhuntington.com

CASSANDRA HAMM

Cassandra Hamm is a psychology nerd, cat mom, jigsaw puzzler, and art collector who spends most of her time lost in another realm. Her award-winning work appears in various anthologies, including Havok Publishing's collections, *Warriors Against the Storm, Fantasea, Sharper Than Thorns,* and *Exquisite Poison.* A mental health advocate with a passion for social justice, she writes about shattered girls finding their way in the world.

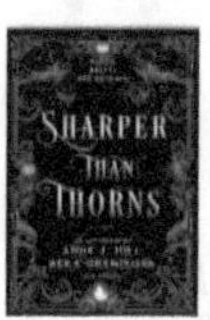

EMILY BARNETT

Emily Barnett resides in Colorado with her husband and two sons dreaming up magical worlds that feel a bit like home. She has contributed to several anthologies such as *What Darkness Fears* and *Fool's Honor,* and was the two-time Editor's Choice winner for Havok's *Casting Call* and *Animal Kingdom* anthologies. Her debut novel, *Thread of Dreams,* will be published in 2024 with Owl's Nest Publishers.

DENICA MCCALL

Denica McCall is a young adult fantasy writer, poet, dreamer, and deep thinker who grew up in the Pacific Northwest and now resides in Kansas City where she enjoys working as a nanny, attending dance classes, drinking coffee, and planning her next travel adventure. She is currently working on her third YA novel which features fairies, a pegasus, and cave-stars. Find out more and sign up for her newsletter to receive a free short story at http://denicamccall.com/.

Instagram @denicamcauthor
denicamccall.com

CRYSTAL D. GRANT

Crystal D. Grant grew up loving stories and sometimes spent more time in her imaginary worlds than the real one. She's had multiple short stories published through Havok Publishing. She also works as a copy/line editor for Twenty Hills. During the day, Crystal shares her love of books and writing with her kindergarten and first-grade students. She spends her spare time doing jigsaw puzzles, watching old movies and TV shows, or reading books that sweep her away to another time and place.

Instagram @crystalgrantauthor
www.crystalgrantauthor.com

S. M. JAKE

Sarah is a sinner saved by the mercy of Jesus Christ. Her writing is an amalgamation of truth and fantasy, exploring truths from Scripture such as real love, forgiveness, or gentle strength, through characters dealing with the less relatable, be it magic swords, floating islands, pegasus ranching, or the occasional Prairie Dragon. Besides God and writing, her other loves include an adventurous husband and two boys, their mid-century modern home, chaotic sewing projects, rainy days, dad jokes, and semicolons. And guac. Always guac.

MARY AGNES RATELLE

Museum professional by day and writer by night, Mary Agnes Ratelle is a lover of all things old, dusty, and antique. With a master's degree in art history and museum studies, Mary Agnes has a particular interest in historical fiction, immersing the reader in the aesthetics, culture, and complex issues of the past. When writing, Mary Agnes enjoys intersecting themes of faith, womanhood, family, and healing, hoping to come to a deeper understanding of the human person's greater purpose of love.

L.A. THORNHILL

L.A. Thornhill is an epic fantasy and steampunk writer who deeply loves her Savior, and has a severe addiction to caffeine. She currently has one novella *The Lost Descendants* in her fantasy series "The King and Prophet Chronicles" which is available in ebook, print, and also in audiobook in the near future.

Facebook @l.a.thornhillauthor
Instagram @l.a.thornhill

KAITLYN EMERY

Kaitlyn Emery was obsessed with dragons and fantasy at a young age. When she grew up, she learned reality was darker than anything she read in a book. Through writing, she learned to cope with the world around her and find a voice in fiction. Kaitlyn has written short stories for various magazines, Flash Fiction for Havok Publishing, and been published in several anthologies including *Rebirth, Sensational, Prismatic, When Your Beauty is the Beast, Moonlight and Claws, Tales From The Tower, The Depths We'll Go To,* and *Aphotic Love*.

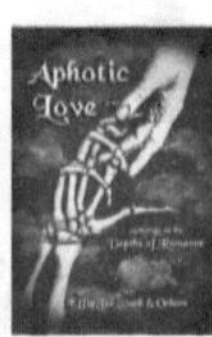

Instagram @kaitlyn_scribbling
Kaitlyn-Emery.com

DAVID LASLEY

David Lasley is an aspiring poet who resides in Illinois with his wife and kids. He writes to process through everyday experiences of life and faith. He enjoys reading, watching sports, eating tacos and floating muddy Illinois creeks in his kayak. His poetry can currently be found in *The Depths We'll Go To, The Heights We'll Fly To, Fools Honor, Exquisite Poison* and on Instagram.

Instagram @dlasleyramblings

RACHEL LAWRENCE

Rachel Lawrence writes from South Carolina, where she lives with her husband, four children, and no pets (despite the kids' constant campaign for one). She processes the world spinning around her and the thoughts swirling within her through stories and poetry. Her favorite poets range from King David to Elizabeth Barrett Browning to Taylor Swift. Her favorite Story is still being written.

NOBEL SHUT CHAN

My name is Nobel Chan and I'm a student at Boston University, majoring in English and minoring in Deaf Studies. Hailing from Hong Kong, I love reading, writing, and musical theatre. My poetry has been published in various school and nation-wide magazines. In the future, I hope to continue honing my craft and writing more poetry and short stories.

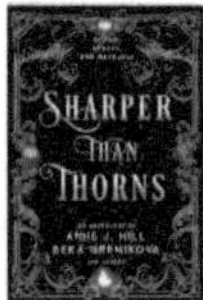

ELAINE WELLS

Elaine Wells is a 17-year-old crazy cat lady, and an aspiring author with a poet's heart. Her poetry portrays her truth-seeking attitude. Some of her favorite poets include Edgar Allen Poe and Emily Dickinson, while drawing inspiration from Olivia Gatwood. She has a passion for writing about mental health, and she also loves photography, good books, deep conversations, and soft blankets.

Instagram @elaine.wells.poetry

AUDRAKATE GONZALEZ

AudraKate Gonzalez started writing horror stories when she ran out of Goosebumps books to read as a child. While she will always love horror, she decided to branch out and write something lighter for this anthology. She has a BA in Creative Writing and is working on her MFA. AudraKate's other published works are her first novel, *Tomato Juice*, and a short story called *Imagination*. She lives in Ohio with her handsome husband, and her adorable furry bad boys, Zero and Scrappy Doo. When AudraKate isn't writing, you can find her reading, watching scary movies or sleeping.

AMBER KIRKPATRICK

Amber gleefully genre-hops from fantasy to sci-fi, from her own brand of wacky humor to the occasional foray into dark poetry. But most of all she loves exploring character-driven stories that seek light and hope, even in the midst of darkness. Amber lives in the Texas Hill Country. When not writing, she is busy homeschooling her three wildlings, and pretends to do housework.

KAYLA E. GREEN

Kayla E. Green is a school librarian and speculative fiction author living in eastern North Carolina with her husband and their furbabies. When she isn't writing, reading, or taking photos for her bookstagram, she loves singing loudly and off-key to KLove Radio, napping, and pretending she's a unicorn. Her debut YA fantasy novella, *Aivan: The One Truth*, is now available through book retailers. Kayla also has stories and poems featured in various anthologies.

Theunicornwriter.com